Order your autographed copy of any of Jihad's books at a 30% discount at www.jihadwrites.com And family, please post a review on www.amazon.com and e-mail Jihad at jihadwrites@bellsouth.net

AUTOGRAPH PAGE

To be used exclusively to recognize that special King or Queen for their support.

I0658512

This is a work of fiction. Any references or similarities to actual events, locales, real people, living or dead are intended to give the novel a sense of reality. Any similarity in other names, characters, places and incidents is entirely coincidental.

Envisions Publishing, LLC
P.O. Box 83008
Conyers, GA 30013

BE: The Re-Awakening: copyright © 2017 Jihad

ISBN: 978-0-9990412-1-5

First Printing October 2017
Printed in the United States of America

10 9 8 7 6 5 4 3 2

Submit Wholesale Orders to: Envisions Publishing, LLC Envisions2007@gmail.com P.O. Box 83008
Attn: Shipping Department, Conyers, GA. 30013

BE: *The RE Awakening*
Is dedicated to Ebony Gibson. A woman, a queen that is the definition of love in action. Unselfish, unconditional love to any and every hand that reaches out to her is what she gives. Without her none of **BE** would be.

Is dedicated to Dr. Brian Williams. A man... A strong Black man that embodies the spirit of revolution. Dr. Willima is the modern day Che Guevera that I am personally striving to BE. I celebrate you king for the spirit of DOing and BEing who and what you say you are.

Dr. Brian Williams is the director of the Alonzo A. Crim Center for Urban education at Georgia State University.

In the words of the late great Teddy P, Ebony Gibson, Dr. Williams, *you two are my latest, my greatest inspiration.*

Last but not least, **BE:** The RE Awakening is dedicated to the Freedom and unification of ALL peoples of the world and anyone working towards this end.

BE: *The RE Awakening*

APPRECIATION PAGE

First and foremost I wanna thank the Creator, without your inspiration and your spirit to guide my mind, my action, and my fingers this work would still be a culmination of thoughts and beliefs

KING Uncle Jake this is for you, for without you being who you were I wouldn't be who I am. You got me to see through your actions. QUEEN Dr. Georgene Bess Montgomery if it weren't for you injecting African centered spirituality in our class readings I would have never challenged your teaching, and yes tis is one of the times I am so happy that I was wrong, without you I wouldn't have told the truth in this book. King Rev. Dr. Mukungu Akinyele, the most valuable lesson you taught me was in South Africa, it was the lesson of controlling my anger that helped me write this book. My friend and mentor KING dr. Akinyele Umoja, your book "WE WILL SHOOT BACK" and the ancestors you revealed to me helped tell our story, Thank you Tawanna Morgan right right and left hand, the mother of our Sunday morning children. Reverend Angela Brown, and my FACDC food pantry family I love ya'l and thanks for being. Carvel, Brotha Mehib, Luscious, Dwayne, Claude Clopton, Queen Roz, Queen Afriye, Carlton, Dorthea, and all of my First Afrikan family thank you and I love me some all fo you. KING Rev. Dr. Mark Ogunwale Lomax your absolutely amazing African Centered spiritual teaching seriously helped inspire this BE series. Without your presence in my life there is no way I would have done the research, communed with the right ancestors to produce the reality that is typed on these pages. My man, the baddesssssttttttt, realessttttttt, 'Keep it 100' bout it – bout it pastor I have ever heard, Reverend Daniel Kelly you are my hero… If any do not know this man, you need to come to Lithonia Georgia to meet and hear him at First Afrikan Church, he is the UNDISPUTED TRUTH. So much of this book has come form the messages I heard on Sunday Mornings between January 2014 and June 2014. Mom, you have always supported me in my writing and of course I wanna thank you. Andre Frazier, my brother, I said my last book was going to be my last, but it was the first book you ever read and your questions and your understanding of what I wrote made me throw the notion to STOP writing out of the window, thank you. I WANNA GIVE A SPECIAL THANKS TO FIRST AFRIKAN CHURCH AND ALL THE KINGS AND QUEENS THAT HAVE SHOWN ME AND EVERY ONE ELSE THAT WALKS THROUGH ITS DOORS UNCONDITIONAL LOVE. You truly embody the mission we all recite every Sunday. For more info on this spiritual revolution of love go to firstafrikanchurch.com.

Of course I will never leave out my fans and the Captives held in America's prisons – men and women who are the sole reason that I am able to write. If half as many people in the freeworld supported my stories – our stories I truly believe that we would be so much closer to FREEDOM. I need you fam. Keep on doing what you do buying, reading, and becoming the Kings and Queens that I know we are.

I need help fam. I CAN NOT CONTINUE TO WRITE WITHOUT YOU SPREADING THE WORD. YOU READ

ME, YOU FEEL ME, PLEASE BUY DARK HORSE ASSASSIN OR WORLD WAR GANGSTER FOR A FRIEND AND GET THEM TO SEE WHAT YOU DO.

FirstAfrikanTruth.com

SUPERFANS

Queen Ann Joiner of Norfolk thank you. Queen Kariymah of Philly thank you. Queen Tazzy Fletcher thank you. Queen Iliene Butler, New York thank you. Queen Martha and the queens of IPS transportation Indianapolis, Thank you.

And again I want to give a very special thanks to the Kings and Queens living behind America's prison walls. I personally read all of your letters. And I may not respond to all letters, but just know that I read every one of them.

THEY SAY BLACK MEN DON'T READ. FOR ALL THE KINGS ON THE INSIDE AND OUTSIDE KEEP PROVING THAT MYTH WRONG.

By supporting my books, you help our young brothers and sisters realize the kings and queens that they are.

Please log onto www.firstafrikantruth.com or www.jihadwrites.com to find more about Jihad or to purchase any of his books 30% less than the store price. Purchase 3 books on www.jihadwrites.com you get the 4th book absolutely FREE.

Please tell others what you think by posting a review on www.amazon.com. Log onto www.firstafrikantruth.com or www.jihadwrites.com to sign the firstafrikantruth and Jihad's guestbook.

7

Also by Jihad/J.S. Free

Friction Fiction
STREET LIFE
BABYGIRL
RHYTHM & BLUES (PREACHERMAN BLUES PREQUAL)
MVP: **M**urder **V**engeance **P**ower
PREACHERMAN BLUES
WILD CHERRY (BOOK 2 IN PREACHERMAN BLUES SERIES)
PREACHERMAN BLUES II
MVP RELOADED
WORLD WAR GANGSTER
BE: *The Rise*
BE: *The Re-Awakening*

Self Help
THE MESSAGE: 16 Life lessons for the Hip Hop Generation

Anthologies
GIGOLOS GET LONELY TOO
THE SOUL OF A MAN

Please pick up any of Jihad's books at a 30% discount at **jihadwrites.com** and if you buy 3 books you get any one of your choice FREE only at **jihadwrites.com**. and books ordered from **jihadwrites.com** will be shipped FREE. You can also order at Amazon.com or get Jihad's books at your local bookstore. All of Jihads books are available on kindle and nook.

BE:

God is ALL and ALL is God

Peace family. Although my name is on the cover of the BE series, I assure you that I am not the only mind behind this body of work. All of humanity authored this re-telling. I am merely the hand that was used to type the words. I will take credit for one thing though, the Swahili that the chapter numbers are in.

I am Afrikan as we all are by way of the first woman and man so I decided to use chapter headings indicative of who we are. If we can use Roman numerals and Euro-American numerals I decided to use Swahili, an Afrikan language to distinguish chapters. It is my prayer that everyone that reads this series will know some Swahili numerals.

Before this re-telling I could not tell you one number in any Afrikan dialect. Why, because no one ever taught me to even think to ask the question *Why* until now.

This place, this land mass called Afrika is unquestionably the cradle of civillization. It's where hue-manity began right? So, why do we Western society begin history at the decline of great Afrikan civillizations. I mean we, hue-manity had civillizations over 9,000 years old when we began our western interpretation of history. Isn't that like learning your time time tables beginning with the number five. Impossible right? So is beginning the history of mankind two thousand years ago. Let's move on before this becomes too preachy.

BE: The RE-Awakening

Yes, I spell Afrika with a K to denote the human consciousness shared by every human being on the planet – a consciousness that inherently is ruled by love and the preservation of hue-manity. And, I spell it with a K because I can. Now, back to the jaw dropping revelation that we hue-manity are all from Afrika. Hmm, lets see... our darker hued brothers and sisters have been telling our light-close-to-white little brothers and sisters forever that hue-manity began in Afrika. Of course they didn't believe us until in the early 1970's a light-close-to-white brother named Leakey verified the origin of hue-manity in Afrika, a truth that Afrikans have been telling for centuries.

So if the first man and woman came from Afrika, that means every human being is essentially Afrikan.

This series is a retelling of what is to come for mankind if we don't come together as a family and cure or kill the evil in hue-manity. This book is written in storied parables so 21st century hue-manity can understand why humankind is perpetuating genocide. Most important is that this a re-telling - a guide to moving all humanity to that biblical Promised Land of complete freedom.

The stories are very graphic, very real. It is my hope and prayer that all who read this series will BE come: The Rise and BE come: The Re-Awakening so hue-manity can BE come: Re-Membered back together as **ONE** collective body working to make life **GOoD** for all of humanity.

It's all Love fam,
Jihad Shaheed Uhuru

O

August 25, 1955
<u>Money, Misissippi</u>

The cargo on the old pick-up's rusty bed banged and rattled around while the two men drove through dirt, mud, and wooded terrain as they headed toward the Talahatchie River.

"Fuckin' niggers." Roy spit in the old soup can before placing it on the seat between him and his brother-in-law. "Betcha bottom dolla' JW, one 'em 'on't evah as much as look at my wife let alone speak to her again."

"I'm wit' ya Roy, but the li'l nigger watn't even n'ere that day. Hell, boy can't be mo' 'en se'em ah eight," J.W. said.

"I'm sorry God for whatever I did," Emmett cried from the back of the truck. "I'm sorry God."

Roy turned his head, "God don't hear heathens boy, now shut up all that damn cryin'," Roy hollered before turning back to face the wooded terrain in front of him. "Can't hear a cotton pickin' thing with all that whinin'."

"I was saying," JW said, "what we oughtta do instead of killin' the li'l darkie, we make him watch what we do to our niggers that get out of line and then," JW pointed a dirty, pale finger in the air, "we sen' 'em back ta' tell the otha' niggers what happens when ya' disrespect our women folk."

"Me too. Me too God." Emmett's younger cousin, Treble cried. "I'll do right. I won't talk back no more. I promise."

Roy slammed on brakes.

"Help!" Help!" fourteen-year-old Emmett shouted.

"I want my momma!" Seven-year-old Treble cried.

Roy jumped out the truck, grabbed his shotgun and ran to the side of the rusty, old pick up. After throwing the shotgun onto the bed, he climbed over the side and grabbed the gun from the floor.

The two boys hands were tied to their ankles before they were stuffed into two large burlap sacks.

"Please... I'm sorry. I'm sorry. Please let us go," Emmett cried.

"Pleaseeeee," Treble cried.

Roy turned the shotgun so that the wood stock was furthest from him before lifting it above his head and bringing it down on the smaller burlap sack.

Treble screamed.

"Got dammit, Roy, The li'l 'on is jus'a pup." JW pointed.

He continued beating the boys until he was exhausted. Both bags had turned from brown to a blood colored brown.

Roy held onto the shotgun by the barell while the bloody wood stock rested on the rusty old cotton gin fan. He was bent over trying to catch his breath before he blurted out, "Nigger pups grow inta' full grown dogs. How'd ya' like it if one of 'em whistled at yo' wife, JW?"

"If ya' kill the damn pup Roy, niggers won't know fa' sho' what happens when ya' says sump'in out da way ta' one of our white women."

Moments later, Roy and JW were back in the truck.

A short while later they pulled up to a clearing.

JW turned to Roy, "I swear ta God Roy, if you killed that pup...

"Well Hell's bells and shit cocktails JW," Roy turned, "if you don't sound like a nigger lover."

"Brother-in-law or not," JW pointed a finger, "call me a nigger lover ag'in Roy, swear ta God almighty, you'll be in that river with that nigger on back'a da' truck."

While they were arguing, Treble managed to untangle himself from the knots tied around his hands and feet. "Cuz," he whispered. Treble still couldn't see, but he could feel his cousin's body after he rolled over to the burlap sack that Emmett was hog tied in.

"Cuz," Treble whispered again while rubbing up against the cotton gin fan that was cutting his back while tearing the burlap threads of the bag he was in.

JW and Roy were still sitting in the truck arguing when the burlap strings began to come apart.

Roy saw movement out of the rearview mirror right as Treble began to climb off of the truck.

"God damn it, we got a runner this time," Roy said before he and JW jumped out the truck.

Treble had only gotten about a hundred yards before Roy and JW closed in.

"Shit," JW said.

"A god damn bear," Roy pointed at the huge black bear that was circling Treble.

"Sum' bitch," Roy said realizing that he and JW's shotguns were a football field away back at the truck.

"Quiet, you fucking retard," JW said, slowly backing away. "The bear is eyeing the little nigger, probably smells the blood on the li'l fucker."

Roy turned and ran away screaming.

JW followed suit a second later.

The bear was still circling when Treble passed out on the forest ground.

****

"Sun, rise," ALL spoke to the sun that fell. "I am the God that gave birth to gods. I am ALL since all came from my imagination. Everything is imaged, animated, and created by Me, even what you see and do is part of Me, my sun.

Seven-year old Treble Lee Frazier opened his eyes and sat up. "Where am I?" he looked around the nothingness void.

It wasn't dark. It wasn't light. It just was. All Treble saw was nothing. When he looked down to see what he had been laying on, nothing was there and when he tried to feel it, he felt nothing.

"You are here my sun. What you see and touch is only as real as you imagine them to be."

"So," Treble asked, "Where exactly is here?"

"Peace."

"This place is peace?" Treble asked.

"It is."

"Peace, Mississippi?" Treble looked around at nothing thinking that ain't no where in Mississippi that look like this. "What state is Peace in?"

"Of mind."

"That was a good one. Peace of mind," Treble laughed.

"I'm serious, sun." ALL said.

"How did I get here? When can I go back home? What happened to my cousin?"

"I'm here cuz."

14

"You okay Em? I thought you were dead. Why can't I see you?" Treble turned around in a circle. "What did them white men do to you Em?"

"I'm fine cuz," Emmett said. "They sent me home."

"Home? Where's Auntie M?" Treble referred to Emmett's mother, Mamie.

"Not that home cuz," Emmett said.

"Sun," ALL explained, "what your cousin means is that he is back with Me. I am the father and the mother that gave birth to all life."

"Huh?"

"You won't understand everything that I am saying now, but you will sun. Just listen and see with your mind. Imagine and you will see all you choose to see."

"Huh?" Treble frowned.

"Sun, I'm sending you back to the wilderness."

"The bear," Treble just remembered.

"Is your animated friend," ALL said. "She will protect you while I introduce you to who you are and your mission. Most of what you will see, hear, smell, and learn you will not remember when you return, but you will be able to use all seven of your senses fully. You will also understand your physical strengths and weaknesses."

"What mission?" The seven-year old asked.

"To protect and prepare Zion and Miracle to defeat the source of all evil," ALL said.

"Zion and Miracle?"

"A sun will be born, you will name him Zion, for he is, as you are, a descendant of Heru, Shango, David, Jesus."

"Shango?"

"Yes sun, Shango. The great Afrikan warrior king and god of thunder and storms. You are also sun of Oba, Shango's first wife, a warrior and great fighter herself, she is water, symmetry, balance. Miracle and Zion will be the last redeemers descended to hue-mankind. Together Miracle and Zion are the essence, the masculine and feminine energy of Me. They are the Messiah.

"Like Jesus coming back to save the world?" Emmett asked.

"Yes sun," ALL said. "But Jesus, as you were taught to call him, is the embodiment of goodness. A pure heart. One that embodiment is represented by male and female energies that work together to further the lifecycle of the One."

"The one?"

"The One is all of mankind. Each individual is like an organ and the body is all of hue-manity."

"Why I never heard of Shango and Oba?" Treble asked.

"But, you have sun, you just didn't know it. You and most have been trained to think in terms of what you can see with the two eyes sticking out of your head and not with your mind, which is what gives you thoughts to interpret what your mind is telling you that you see," ALL explained. "What I'm going to do over the next seven years is teach you who you are."

"Seven years," Treble said. "What about Emmett?"

"I'm home cuz. I don't ever wanna go back to Mississippi or anywhere in that world. It hurts too much to feel and see so much self-hate in the body of men," Emmett said.

"I can't do this alone," Treble said. "I'm only seven."

"You will never be alone sun," ALL said. "I will always be with you. I am in you. I am you. This you will come to understand before I send you back to your godmother."

"Momma? She probably already on her way to Money, Mississippi to check on me. I can't be gon' no seven years. What if them white men get her?"

"Sun, relax," ALL said. "Three days will pass on Earth before you return."

"But, you said seven years."

"You will insperience seven years of divine education in three Earthly days."

"Insperience?" Treble asked.

"Insperience is the emotions that move you from understanding, to believing, and finally to knowing."

"Huh?"

"In time my sun. In time you will know," ALL said. "Once you return you will be guided, protected, and raised by Oshun Orthine and her brother John."

"What about my godmother, Hattie Mae?"

"She is fine. She will be fine sun."

"So, I'm gon' have a son one day, and he gon' be Jesus come back to Miss'sippi. You shoulda' made him come back before slavery. That's what started all this mess," Treble said.

"Sun, this mess as you call it started way before enslavement in the America's," All explained. "Before I created the first man and woman, I chose Zion and Miracle to be the Messiah, and they both have been back several times in different physical bodies, different names, just as you have."

"If I done been here a lot, why didn't I pave the way for my son any of the other times.

"It was not time."

"So, I'm going to be like a super hero?"

"No, you are a super hero. You are Heru, descended from the first hero, Horus. Your son Zion will be *The Rise,* while the last descendant of Oba will be *The Re-awakening.* Together, they will either defeat evil and return humanity to the Garden of Eden or all life as you know it will end."

"All life?"

"All life, sun."

"I sorta understand *The Rise*, but if my son is gon' be *The Rise* then why is there need for anyone to be *The Re-Awakening.*

"Sun," ALL explained, "Every sun rises, but every sun also sets, and it is during the sunset that darkness rises, and it is up to the re-awakened to guide the sun through the darkness and vice versa.

"I don't understand."

"You will sun. You will."

"Who gon' raise Miracle? And how her and Zion gon' meet and fall in love?"

"Everyone will help raise her," ALL said. "As far as everything else, it's up to you and the twelve disciples of truth to help and protect Zion and Miracle as they are being raised and re-awakened.

BE:

The RE-Awakening

MMOJA

40 years later

7:00 AM

October 16, 1995
Decatur, Georgia

The Saturday morning Georgia sky was pink with hues of blue, yellow and red. The moon was about to hand the baton of light off to the sun. A relay race in slow motion. A thing of beauty. A thing that Stonewall Duke never took the time to notice although he often left for work and came home from his shift at the sun and moon's meeting times.

"Hmph," The thirty-four year old Atlanta, Georgia police lieutenant dragged himself out of the unmarked squad car. "Whew," he stretched. "Million Man March," he shook his head before walking around the car.

"Always marching for something or another, riling up the docile niggras for what? March from issue to issue in a god-damn circle. Shit, in the war we marched with guns straight ahead wiping out anything that stood in our way," The widowed father of one trudged up the Duke plantation stairs.

"Buzzzz," his cell phone vibrated.

20

"Yeah," he answered.

"Duke! Crow."

Two words were more than enough for the widower to recognize the police commissioner's crypt, grunting voice.

"Yes, sir."

"Tired son?" Commissioner Crow asked.

"Exhausted. Twenty-hours straight. Me and my men doing what you requested."

"Son," the commissioner barked, "Jackson, Young, Campbell, Franklin, Reed. May-ors, Hell. May-I's. Dancin' jungle monkeys. Seen come. Seen go. Same music. Same beat. Me. Still here. Thirty-four years. Done. Seen. Everything. In you son. I see me. Soon. My backing. You're next. Imagine. Stonewall Duke. New Jim Crow. Police Boss. Commissioner. Law. Then Mayor."

"I can't tell you how much I've appreciated your guidance and support all these years, Commissioner."

"Jim. On phone. In private. Call me Jim. Son. Two hours. Need you. Your men. Niggas march. They burn."

"Sir, I don't think a cop in the city has slept in a week."

"City thanks you. All overtime. Compensated. One more day. March forgotten. Guard perimeter. Do not. Do not. Let them breach. Let them burn. Let them loot each other if it comes to that," the commissioner said before disconnecting the call.

Stonewall hadn't made it in the door good before he heard the scampering of little bare feet on hardwood.

"Daddy? Daddy? Daddy?" the little blonde child ran into Stonewall's legs. "Guess what? Guess what Daddy?"

Stonewall placed his badge and keys in the tray by the door before bending down. "What are you doing up this early on a Saturday morning, boy?" He wiggled his nose against his sons.

"Daddy, you have to guess!" Luke jumped up and down.

The elder Duke put a finger to his temple and frowned. "Hmmm, you gettin' married?"

Luke crossed his arms, "Daddy... I'm only seven."

"Okay, okay. I got it! I got it! You hit the lottery. We're rich."

"Daaaaaadddddddy?"

"Okay," the elder Duke sighed, "I give up."

Little Luke jumped up and down. "Me and Tamir are going to do the Million Man March in the backyard. He said we gotta show support for our brotha's and sista's."

Worry lines appeared on Stonewalls rugged pale face. Anger was building as he thought about the words, "brotha" and "sista." And then his face began to turn red as he imagined black and white people holding han...

"Oh no," he shook his head. Sleep had to wait, his son's mortal soul was at stake he surmised as he carried his son out to the backyard and down the quarter mile winding trail through the woods. Stonewall stopped and put his son down in front of the old poplar tree.

"What happened to the grass daddy?" The child referred to the ground around the huge tree.

Stonewall sat down on the red dirt in front of the old tree before patting the ground.

"Right there," he pointed. "On the dirt?"

"Yes, son."

Luke looked up at the huge tree. "Is it dead?"

"Is what dead son?"

A little pale finger pointed. "The tree."

"Of course not, son. It's still standing ain't it?"

"Why ain't no green on the tree daddy? And why it ain't no grass on the ground around it?"

"I don't know son. Never really gave it much thought. Matter of fact, even before the rust...

"The rust?"

"The rust I'm talkin' bout son is a disease that causes the leaves to die and fall off.
Come to think of it, I can't recall ever seeing anything grow from that old tree.

"Bout twenty-five, twenty-six years ago, I was knee high to a grasshopper 'bout like you," Stonewall pointed. "Tree caught the Rust. Bark fell off the trunk and limbs." He waved an arm around the barren land surrounding the tree. "Killed everything it touched and ain't nothing grown on the dirt since."

"Why didn't you just cut it down?" Luke looked up at his dad.

"This old thing is more than just a tree. It's a symbol of justice son. The Dukes have been the law for over three hundred years and over three hundred bad Niggras have hung and rotted from those limbs," Stonewall pointed at the thick bare limbs above, "limbs of justice that strangled the strange fruit that didn't grow from its limbs. Do you know what justice is son?"

"Uh-huh," he nodded as the sun peaked through the forest area of the Duke property. "Like what me and Tamir…"

"No!" he shouted.

Luke frowned.

Realizing that he had scared his boy, Stonewall took a deep breath and exhaled. "Son, you see, Tamir's kind, Black people are like us when they're children, but they grow up to be savages unless we," he pointed to himself and then to Luke, "good white men train them to be respectable. Even then many of them still go out and hurt others."

"Why?"

"Well son, the niggra comes from the dark continent, Africa. A big old jungle with snakes, lions, tigers, every wild and dangerous animal on God's green Earth. Good Christian white men rescued the savage niggra from the harsh jungles, disease, and from his cannibal brothers and sisters. So, son ya see we brought them over to America to train them, teach them how to be more," he searched his mind for the word he was looking for, "human."

"Why?"

"Well son, it's what God wanted. Matter of fact the niggra is like a dog. If you don't breed fear in them they will attack you and attack themselves. In Africa, they eat each other."

"Eyooouuuu, that's gross dad."

"It is. But it's the way of the savage," Stonewall said. "It's in their blood."

"Who put 'it' there?"

"Huh," the elder Duke looked confused.

"In their blood daddy. You said it was in their blood."

"Well," the elder Duke looked at the old tree, "the good Lord did son, and if he put it in their blood, he must have wanted it there."

"Well, if God put it in they blood, and He wanted 'it' in they blood then why we trynna' take it out?"

"We're not son. We just tryin' to teach them to be more human, like us."

"Well, if God wanted them to be like us, why didn't He just make 'em like us?"

"You see son, the bible tells us that we the 'White race' are the chosen people meant to lead and keep the world in order."

"Why?"

"It just is son." The elder Duke picked up a dirt rock. "Now, I'm not saying all niggras are bad." He pitched the ball of dirt forward, "but, every really bad person," the ball exploded upon impact with the tree, "is a niggra. Now grant it, thanks to us son, there are a few half decent Christian niggras out there that follow and embrace our teachings in the good book and the schoolbooks. But they are still inferior."

"Infer-or?"

24

"Inferior." he corrected his son. "Means less than, not as good. Let me put it to you anotha' way son. 'Member what happened to ole Cash last week?"

"Uhm-hm," he nodded.

"Now Cash done had that dog near all his life. Wherever you seen Cash, you saw Rock," the elder Duke stated as fact.

"Yep," Luke nodded. "And daddy, Rock ain't never lost a fight until he bit Cash."

"That's right son. Cash fed and trained that dog from day one. Made that dog a fighting machine. Look what happened. Damn dog turned on his master nearly killed Cash." The elder Duke paused for effect. "That's what Tamir will do to you one day boy."

Luke cringed.

Stonewall pointed an accusing finger at the boy. "If you play with Tamir long enough, you will begin to act like them. Killing your own, robbing your own, beating your own, and I dare not think of how you will treat good white women."

The little boy's eyes were wide with fear.

"No matter how bad I want to help even I can't once you begin showing signs of niggraopathy," The elder Duke closed his eyes and shook his head. "I've know men to get niggraitis by just touching a niggra." Stonewall shook his head while whistling. "Baddest case of witch warts I ever did see."

Luke's face wrinkled into a mask of sadness.

"But, son, the witch warts, and the niggraopathy are nothing compared to the fiery furnaces of Hell that awaits the niggra and the niggra lover."

"Who says?"

"The good Lord says," Stonewall raised a finger to the sky, "and it is written in scripture."

MBILI

Subjective Realm

"Scripture! We all know that the '*Word*' is certified USDA man made bull-doo doo. Hell, me and ole King James rewrote and revised so much of it." Constance Greenspan, the chairman of the United States Federal Reserve Bank, laughed.

"Yes." The chairman shot a victory fist in the air as he swiveled around in his leather high back office chair. "Evil ole Stonewall, A true soldier of hate. A general. A man after my own heart made in my image," The chairman continued basking in negativity. "The irony. Old Stony showing so much love to one part of him self and so much hate to another part of the body." The chairman's head dropped back. "Praised your name at home, church, at work and even after taking the physical lives of all those Black hue-men. I still remember the first Black life ole Stony took." The manifestation of evil took a deep breath. "The first is always the sweetest," the media and bank mogul closed his eyes and exhaled. "What was that good ole dung monkey's name?"

TATU

10:00 PM

October 16, 1995
Buckhead, Georgia,

"Matthieu," Jon Love, the NBA ALL-Star, belched after draining the bottle of Corona. "He put his arm around the groom before slurring, "You a better man than me dog."

"Hell, if he is," Marc slurred.

The three childhood best friends stood at the entrance of Jon's basement indoor full basketball court admiring the scene created for Matthieu's bachelor party.

"I mean this shit here," Marc held his arm out, "Egyptian baths, booty-butt naked Cleopatra white broads dancing and serving all the homies."

Matthieu still couldn't believe all the trouble Jon went through, the truckloads of sand, the black curtains that covered the thirty-foot walls. The ten-foot palm trees. The Egyptian baths.

Marc continued, "The chickenheads at Magic City ain't got shit on these white broads," Marc looked up at both of us his friends. "Now tell me I'm lying."

"You lyin'," Matthieu said.

Marc looked at Matthieu. "Name one."

"Look, I'm blown away by all this fellas," Matt pointed to the naked white women dancing. "I don't wanna sound unappreciative, but all the black queens dancing up in Magic City are badder than these pink toes."

"Jon," Marc playfully slapped the six foot nine Atlanta Hawks power forward on the back, "Sound like Matt hangin' out at the strip clubs again."

"Nah, baby boy," Matthieu smiled. "I ain't been on that since I found Ebony."

"I admit," Jon slurred, "Ebony is cool as a fan, fine too, but she ain't God."

The look on Matthieu's face said differently. "Look," Matthieu put a hand over his heart. I love both of you, and I know all 'dis," he looked off at the six strippers entertaining the others, "was done out of love, despite the fact that I told you two knuckleheads that it was too late for a bachelor's party. Shoulda' done that before me and my baby's eyes touched."

A moment passed.

Marc snapped his fingers in front of Matthieu's face. "Okay dog come back to Earth."

"Yeah, dog, come back, but when you get here no eye touching. We don't do that on Earth," Jon laughed.

Marc got down on one knee and looked up at Matt. "Oh my dearest darling Matthieu," he did his best to sound like a female, "where art thou eyeball to toucheth mine in the sunshine on the frontline next to the stop sign."

Matthieu slapped at his boy's hand. "Oh, the hate that hate produced. That's okay," tomorrow's groom said, "I understand you fools are still trying to catch up to yesterday, and I'm off to forever."

"Forrrrrrrr-ever-evah?" Jon asked.

"Ever, ever." Marc followed up.

28

"It's called love," Matthieu said, "You know that thing you fall in and never want to fall out of."

"What's love got to do. Gotta do with it." Jon sang before Marc joined in.

"What's love, but a second hand emotion," Marc and Jon sang the Tina Turner classic while Jon waved an arm around the basketball court.

Marc pointed at the strippers. "Six top choice prime pale, white tenderloins cooked and ready," Marc said, "Now that's a whole lotta love my nigga."

"Yeah," Jon chimed in, "A man should at the least have a last meal before he go on lockdown," the all-star NBA forward said.

"Says a man that has never experienced Heaven." Mathieus's face lit up.

Marc looked at Jon, "So is Ebony God or is she Heaven?" Marc asked.

"I promise you I'm confused," Marc and Jon said in unison before balling up their fists and giving each other a pound.

"Let me ease some of your confusion mini Mouse and Super size," Matthieu said before looking off into space, "Her name is Ebony Oshun Mapenzi," Matthieu closed his eyes and smiled.

****

Fifteen minutes later, Matthieu was driving home. He loved Marc and Jon too much to ruin their night. They were still searching for satisfaction between a woman's legs. He tried to tell them...

Flashing blue lights in his rearview interrupted his thoughts.

"Damn."

This was the third time he had been pulled over in the six months since he and Ebony moved to the affluent Atlanta Chastain Park area.

You would think 'they' were used to seeing a non-drug dealing black man driving a Porsche through Buckhead by now, Matthieu thought while reaching into his back pocket. "Where is my wallet?" He asked himself before remembering that he had never taken it out of the glovebox after he and Ebony came from the gym this morning.

"Hands on the wheel now," The cop shouted as he approached the white Panamera Porsche that Jon had bought him as a wedding gift.

Matthieu turned. A fist of fear grabbed hold of his heart upon looking into the three eyes that stared back. Despite the fact that Matthieu had never done anything to end up in the back of a police car, this wasn't the first, second, or third time in his twenty-two years that he looked into the blue eyed, black barrel trinity of hate.

Although his eyes were paralyzed, his mouth wasn't and couldn't afford to be. In his best smiling Harvard graduate voice he asked, "What seems to be the problem Officer, sir?"

****

It was as if someone had flipped a colored light switch inside Stonewall Duke's head. His whole face reddened as he envisioned Little Luke and Tamir. Holding hands? Skipping down a prairie on a Sunny day. Birds singing. Laughing. Laughing at him. Even the Darkie holding on to the steering wheel in front of him was smiling.

"Officer, I'm getting married tomorrow, and I..."

His biceps threatened to break out of the police blue shirt. Veins swam down his hand as he strangled his service revolver. He didn't realize he had spoke out loud before he'd uttered, "Goddamn niggras.

"Excuse me?"
POW!!!!!

NNE

Subjective Realm

"Pow!" Chairman Greenspan blew on the finger that he had aimed in the air. "First kill." He looked off into the nothingness that surrounded him. "Like that first hit of crack cocaine," the chairman inhaled. "Always chasing that first high. The adrenaline." He squeezed his fists together and hurled his arms up in the grey space. "The power," he closed his eyes, "of taking a hue-man life." He opened his eyes and jabbed a finger into space.

"That last look of '*Why*' before the bullet separates the spirit from the body." The chairman chuckled.

"And then there's the aftermath which I like to refer to as the Afterparty fire and Afterparty hell. See, afterparty fire is the delectable delightful feeling of chaos that I feel in my gut as I comfort the killer's conscious with reasons why it was his or her duty to extinguish the light out of his same-father-same-mother-brotha of another color. And then there is Afterparty hell. It's only a moment. But it's my "ah hell" I'm coming moment. The moment that I absorb all the anguish and pain from the victim's loved ones. Mothers, fathers, wives, husbands, and my absolute favorite, little fucking children." He looked up, "Old Ancient One, me and You would be alright if you just admit that you fucked all the way up when you gave hue to man. Breathing hue into man was by far the dumbest idea you ever had. They fuck everything on the planet up. Give 'em free will, and they'll find a way to kill," he sang. "You say you made them in your own image and I'm dumb." He threw his arms in the air as he whirled around in his high back leather chair."

The sound of thunder exploded in the nothingness.

The chairman fell over backwards in his chair. He held a hand over his heart, "You gotta quit doin' that."

"Scary self. You talk real big when you don't think I'm there," ALL said. I usually let you, but when you voice extraterrestrial-beyond-this-realm-Donald   Chump-times-ten ignorance I have to respond my pale, dark sun." A bolt of lightning lit up the void.

The chairman put his arms up over his face. "Always gotta be the brightest light in space. If you would just turn it down about a gajillion watts. Damn."

"Punk ass..." ALL grumbled. "Numb nuts, without 'free will' you would not be. Like I told you the last nine-hundred, ninety-seven trillion, eight-hundred, seventy-six, billion, five-hundred, forty-two million, three-hundred twenty-thousand, nine-hundred, ninety-nine times that every hue-man being has just as much power in them as you dumb, dumb."

"Dumb-dumb?" The spinning chair came to an abrupt halt. The chairman jumped to his feet. "You call me dumb when in 1783, seven years after I led my troops to victory over England old Horace Mann, the Massachusetts Secretary of Education in 1783, he and I created the public school curriculum – one that has divided, controlled and still ensures that your yellow and brown children would never rise up from that slave mentality that I created way before I ame up with Chatel Slavery. But I'm dumb. I mean, me and ole Horace just put a lot of bullshit together; the country was only a seven years old at the time. Wasn't any history worth writing about. So we had to be creative with our fiction. As long as the stories made my white hued bretheren look good, they would become true. Horace still owes me a penny. Didn't believe that I could take the word savage, make it a noun, and use it to describe the peace loving indigenous fucks that inhabited the land before my followers took it." The chairman shook his head. "I'm going to be the better, bigger god this time Old Ancient One. I'm not even going to be all anal and give you a count. I mean, you got way too much time on your hands to keep count of how many times you told me that backward ass equality bullshit. You drinkin' some of my Kool-Aid if you think that any one or all six billion hue-mans are my equal. The retards still send their children to public school. Really? That's like a mother hen sending her chicks to the weasel to be educated in the fox house. See," the chairman shook his head in exasperation. "You done sidetracked my happy hate with all that equality craziness. Now where was I," the chairman sat back in his chair and began spinning. "Pain, I was talkin' about pain. How terribly good it feels to cause it. I been stickin' it in the Dukes and the Chumps for generations. Raping their minds, impregnating them with hate. Generations and generations of hate, hate, hate, hate, hate," the chairman said as he sped up.

"What do you have to say about that, Ancient One who created the created, however flawed your creation may be?"

The Creator answered, "Sadness. Our creation fighting against itself. We did not create a black man or a pale man. We did not create an Asian or a European. We created hue-mankind.

The chairman laughed while spinning around in his chair. "Ain't worked out so well for ya huh, Boss?"

TANO

Twenty one years *later*

3:33 AM

April 4, 2016
Decatur, Georgia

Thunder exploded right before an invisible streak of lightning lit up the early morning blue-black Decatur, Georgia night sky.

"Shit," Early jumped, sending the grey and green buds from the cigar paper to the black floor of the pink sports car. "Damn."

"Miracle chuckled. "Scared of a little thunder?"

"Hell nah," he looked up. "Zion, see when the next time I put money on your books." The young man went back to feeling around the floor for his marijuana. "Made me drop all my bud. Damn. Been waiting to smoke all night," he said.

Miracle turned her head. "How you know it's Zion and not Shango, ALL even?"

"Come on Shawty," Early looked at his childhood bestfriend. "Really?"

"Coincidence," she said.

"Three times," he held up three fingers, "The last three times I pulled out a bag in your car, sheeeeiiiiiittt. It's a wonder we ain't weavin' in the road, as much of my bud your car done ate."

"Thunder is natural Early."

"Naturally Zion trying to steal my thunder. Why you gotta spray perfume on the carpet anyway." He dropped the perfumed buds out of the window as he picked them from the floor. "'Sides, look how clear it is outside." He rolled down the window as they continued speeding down the I-20 expressway. "Every star in the sky is as bright as Beyonce's smile."

"Boy, if you don't stick your head back in this window. Drunk self. Beyonce ain't no more thinking 'bout you than she is the man on the moon."

"Glad I ain't on the moon then," Early chucked. "I'm just biding my time until Jay Z mess up."

"You still haven't answered my question?"

"What question? Hell I'm still trying to figure out why you spray perfume all over your carpet? You see how it ruins my bud, Mira."

"That's exactly why you should stop bringing weed in my car, you think?"

"No, I don't think."

"That's the problem right there..."

"You see Mira, I stopped smoking weed years ago when I was around 18." He waved a slender arm across the black carpet under him in the passenger's seat. "This is Dro, fresh and naturally hydroponically grown on some senator's farm right here in the good old U.S. of B.S. And for your information all of my brain cells are intact. My memory is rock solid like a diamond."

"Well, search your diamond memory and figure out the question I just asked."

"Oh my coal colored six-foot Nubian sister, I believe you want me to tell you how I know that it is Zion, the incarnation of Horus, Jesus by another name, last descendant of

Shango who caused the thunder to thun and the lightning to light."

Miracle shook her head laughing. "That's the liquor talkin', fool. Boy, you drunk."

"Nah, but real talk Mira, I may be a little drunk, but drunk or sober I know my dude's footprints by now, just don't know why he ain't been done stepped up outta that penitentiary. It's been dang near seven years he done did for killing two CIA niggas that he ain't even kill."

"NSA agents," Miracle corrected.

"Same thang," Early said, "Just different letters."

"Why you think yo know Zion so well?"

"Back when your moms… You know… Uhm."

Miracle interrupted, "was killed by the man who I helped free; the man who I thought was my dad."

"Yeah, you know when all that went down, you checked out for over two years Mira. I mean, I saw you evey day but you was comatose. Me, Zion, and you lived together the whole time in a small backwoods cabin and I got to know him like I know myself. How he works, how he moves, I got his swag all the way down. That's how I know it's him."

The pink convertible was on the road alone as the two friends took the Wesley Chapel exit off the I-20 interstate.

"Something about to go down," Miracle let the driver's window down and took a deep breath. "Trouble."

"Only trouble I see is my Dro that your car done ruined. Damn, I been wantin' to smoke all night."

"I heard you the first five times, Early."

"What are you –

"Shhh," Miracle brought her head back inside the window before turning to her childhood best friend. "I feel it."

"Feel what. I don't see nothing but an empty street and the lights from a Quik Trip gas station," Early quipped as he looked down the dark street. "What you feeling Mira is them hot wings and that con-yakity-yak we had at the club."

"Shhh," she repeated, decreasing her speed.

"Yakity-Yak don't talk back," Early slurred his words. "Why ALL gotta make life so difficult? I mean he got his kid down here rotting in the Pen for some shit he ain't even do." Early shook his head. "Don't make sense. ALL need to holler at your man," Early patted his chest, "real talk."

"Shhh!"

Early's rambling became rumbling, "Give me the gun. I'd get the world real right, real quick," he slurred. " I mean real talk, before I took out Chump, Greenspan, or any of them white niggas, I'd take out them miseducated, misinformed, misguided, ass-backward black boot lickin' negroes. Clarence "Uncle" Thomas, Dr. Benjamin "no vaseline" Dover, Karl "the wiener" Webber, Death. Babygirl, I wouldn't even make 'em suffer."

"Shhh!" Mira said.

He took his finger and slid it across his neck before whispering. "Then I would invent the 'stupid police.' Police officers that just arrested and locked dumb ass people up for doing dumb ass shit. Hell, Chump already got a life sentence and a life after death sentence waiting for his ultra nutty butty ass and all his followers, 'specially the Blacks, Latinos, and women that follow him. Oh, and we can't forget the new fools. The Constance Greenspan dummies."

The siren came on before the bright blue lights lit up the night.

"Shit," Early said. "Give me some light Mira."

"Use the light on your phone boy. I ain't turning on the interior lights."

"Pull over!" a voice boomed from the police loudspeaker.

"Hurry!" Miracle said as Early chewed and swallowed what little reefer buds he could feel on the floor and his seat.

Miracle slowed down and put on her blinkers.

"Whachu' doin' Mira?" Early aked.

"What do you think I'm doing? I'm pulling over fool."

"Oh Hell no," Early said, "You'll be the fool if you pull over while I'll very likely end up dead. Have you not watched the news over the past forever. Five-oh killing Black folks like they getting paid to do so," the young black man began to panic.

"Calm down, boy. All cops ain't killers."

"I ain't talking about all cops. Just the ones that wear blue and carry guns." The young black man cuffed his hands in a prayer motion and closed his eyes tight. "Zion, Shango, Ogun, Oya, Yahweh, Oludamare, ALL, please don't let anything happen to Mira and please, please Lord, save me."

SITA

Subjective Realm

"Ignorance and hate have rattled what little sense you have." Thunder exploded. "Don't you ever forget that I am Somebody, Any body, Every body, No body, Some thing, Any thing, Every thing, and No thing. I am All," ALL said.

Constance Greenspan relished in all the chaos surrounding the upcoming Presidential election. He sat in his chair slowly spinning around in the grey space of no-where as the voice of ALL continued speaking.

"I spoke you into being and I can speak you into not being."

The chairman put a long pale finger in the air, "But you will not. You know that without me there can be no them. They exist because I exist. You tell them that it is you that give them free will. A lie. It is I that give them free will and you are angry that your loves always choose my reality of gluttonous individuality."

"My sun. My unenlightened, evil, ignorant, discombobulated sun. You confuse anger with love my pale dark child. Furthermore, you know there is no always, only today and yesterday exist."

"And tomorrow?" The chairman asked while takin' a bite from a juicy apple.

"Tomorrow is but a memory yet to be remembered but, you know this. You just won't accept this."

The chairman smiled, "I don't have to, and you can't make me do otherwise."

"Silly devil. I breathed Me into being and I'm the only breath, but out of My breath hued you. I breathed life into you and your brothers and sisters and with that breath came responsibility. Responsibility to shepherd over all of our creation. Creation is but a dance floor. I am the music. My messengers are the record spinners. The DJ plays different types of music so we can dance in harmony with all cultivated souls. We want everyone dancing. It won't be to the same beat, but everyone still needs to dance."

"Ladi-dadi, we like to party," the chairman sang, "yada, yada, I'm really not interested in hearing those same old musings. You sound like a two million year old broken record. Maybe you need to step down and let me take over. Hell, I'm already running your show and have been running it for a couple thousand years and some change. Your hue-mens love me."

"No they do not. They lust for the dream you imagined for them."

"Which one?" The chairman said. "There are so, so many."

Thunder exploded.

The chairman jumped. "Will you stop that? I know who you are."

"You keep forgetting. I have to remind you."

"Anyway, which ingenious dream were you referring to old unloved One?" The chairman asked while still spinning around in his chair.

"The idea that money is the key to happiness and joy."

"Oh, that imagination," Greenspan said. "Are you angry because I imagined every monetary unit used to exchange goods and services, or are you angry that I have perfected the idea so well that your children as you call them choose my imagined reality of you."

"Anger is the inability to be Me. I wouldn't be Me if I carried anger."

The chairman interrupted, "You did not get a little angry anytime during the two-hundred forty six years my children raped, murdered, experimented, maimed, and beat your children during Chattel slavery?"

"Your children," All said, "All of them are descended from me. Even your spirit belongs to me. And no, I did not get angry. Those two hundred forty six years with you made them stronger. It prepared them for now. It prepared the chosen few to re-member all of hue-mankind back to Me."

The chairman laughed. "Now it is you that is dreaming, old timeless One. I have less than three percent of the world controlling the ideas and ideals of the other ninety-seven. They come to hear about you on Friday, or Saturday, or Sunday for two-three hours tops and then they praise and worship me for the next six days of the week. Your name is only at the tip of their tongues when they want you to give them some of me. Ironic right," Greenspan laughed. "They pray to You to get to me. They pray, 'Lawd please let me hit the number. Lord please let me get this good job so I can buy a new car a new house, Lawd, I promise if this house got at least twenty thousand dollars in valuables I won't rob another one. Lord, please give me the strength to blow my baby daddy's head off for the insurance policy so I can provide for me and mine."

Thunder exploded.

"The chairman jumped. "I told you…"

Lightning lit up the grey space. "You don't tell me anything child. I am the Light. My loves understand not what they do, so when they do pray to you, they do not have a clue but remember child, all of my children have my hue and that's all they need to end you. Furthermore, you know that they pray for me to deliver them from you. Even when their words don't talk, their hearts do."

"Now you confused old ancient One. Like you, I see everyday as they plan, plot, and try to kill you."

"What was the first thing that came out of your mouth when they began to pray? Do you even remember Constance. I can't hear you," ALL said. "It's Lord."

Thunder exploded.

The chairman jumped again. "Fuck."

"Just reminding you that I am ALL."

"That's the thing. No one really cares anymore," the chairman said. "It's really gon' take a miracle to change that."

"She's coming," ALL said, "I promise you that. Miracle is coming."

SABA

3:36 AM

April 4, 2016
Decatur, Georgia

"I do not care what you have to say. Do not talk! Do not move! Stay in the vehicle." One of Dekalb County's finest shouted over his police loudspeaker before getting out of the grey Dodge Charger.

Miracle looked over at her best friend. "Early, do not open your mouth under any circumstances. Please," Miracle pleaded, "I got this."

Before Early could respond, the officer shined his flashlight inside the car before knocking on the driver's window.

Miracle pressed the down button.

"License," the cop flashed his light inside the two-seater Mercedes.

"Can you please tell me why you pulled us over Officer," Miracle read the officer's nametag, "Duke?"

"License," Officer Duke spoke in a much louder stern tone.

Miracle reached into her purse.

Duke took a defensive stance and pulled his gun. "Hands on the steering wheel now!"

"All that ain't necessary man, she was just reaching for her..."

"Shut up boy!"

"Boy," Early said. "Nigga I'm a grown ass... Ever hear of Black Lives Matter..."

"Click-click!" the cop chambered a bullet. "Ever hear of White Man's Justice," the cop said before making long strides around the car.

"Fuck that nigga. Pull off Mira! Pull off!"

"Relax boy, he aint' gon' do nothin'. Besides another patrol car is pulling up now."

"Relax," he threw his arms up. "This white nigga in blue on steroids carrying a big ass gun bout to get at me and you talkin' bout re-motha' fuckin-lax."

She was about to tell Early that the officer pulling up was a brotha before the passenger's side door flew open and Early's five foot eleven hundred sixty pound frame was dragged from the small hard top convertible.

"Hey, you can't do that?" Miracle said before doing something to her phone and jumping out of the driver's seat and running around to the passenger's side.

By the time Miracle made it around the car, the left side of Early's face was kissing the pavement.

"Ahhhhhhh!" Early shouted. "Mira this nigga got his knee in my back."

"Do I fucking look black?" The six-foot, two hundred thirty-pound officer pressed his knee further into Early's spine. "Do I look like a nigger? "

"I can't breathe," Early shouted.

Although the officer stared right at Early's face, he didn't see him. He saw what his daddy, Stonewall Duke trained him to see, a savage penguin strutting, pants sagging animal that raped white women, robbed the poor, and often killed each other over a dollar. The officer's gun arm rose.

"Early!" Miracle shouted right before she lunged head first, bowling the officer over. They tumbled from the pavement onto the Wesley Chapel Public Library grass.

The cop punched Miracle in the face like she was a punching bag. That still did not deter her teeth from making contact with his left ear. She didn't let go until...

"POW!"

A searing pain that exploded in her head from the gun shot only made her angrier.

"Fuck," the officer said as he gingerly touched what was left of his bleeding ear. He raised the gun again, right as Miracle lunged.

"POW!"

"Mira!" Early shouted.

She crumpled into the grass.

Officer Duke turned from the fallen woman.

The hate in that white cop's eyes paralyzed Early's vocal cords. Before now, Early had never looked down the barrel of a gun.

"POW!"

The will to go to his best friend was greater than the pain of the bullet. Fear was replaced with need. The need to save Miracle. Early stood up tall. "Miracle!" he shouted as he reached out. The geyser of blood gushing from his midsection didn't slow his determined gait as he marched forward.

"Stop!" Officer Duke commanded.

Early continued. "You better pray that you kill me before I make you swallow that gun, big boy."

"POW!"

The next bullet went through the back of Early's foot, shattering bone and cartilage.

"Shit!" Early shouted. The first bullet didn't hurt. But this one. He wanted to scream but that wasn't an option. Early refused to give the eyes of hate that stared back at him the satisfaction. The slender young black man bit part of his tongue off to prevent from screaming out.

"POW! POW!"

The nine-millimeter bullets tore through the flesh, shattering the bone in his other ankle while the other entered Early's leg right above the ankle, finally dropping the young black man to his knees.

Early's midnight brown eyes never wavered from the dark blue eyes of hate. Despite his broken and shattered bones, Early rose to his knees and began crawling. He was determined to get his hands on the cop. He had to get to him before he killed Miracle if he already had not.

Fear gripped the officer's heart. Duke looked down at his gun and then at the bleeding corpse that was still breathing, crawling, rising.

"POW! POW! POW!" Bullets riddled the young black man's back and side.

"As I crawl through the valley of death," Early began.

The officer looked at the police issue nine-millimeter that was trembling in his hands.

Early balled up his bloody fists and began to rise up. "I'll rise up a mighty…"

"POW!" The bullet entered the flesh right above Early's nose.

"Nooooooooooooo!" Miracle shouted as she came to. She rose from behind the grassy knoll where Duke had left her for dead.

"Make them remember me Mira," Early said before falling in the street. Make them remember me."

The black officer that had pulled up after Duke was now standing at Duke's side. Both had their guns raised. But only one of them was smoking.

"What did you do?" She demanded of the white cop holding the smoking gun.

All love and compassion was gone when she turned back to the officer. "What did you do?"

The white officer pointed his gun at Miracle. "Give me that phone!"

She looked down at her hand. She didn't even realize that she was still holding the iPhone.

"You heard him," the second officer blended into the night so well that Miracle almost forgot he was there.

"Seriously. I mean really brotha?" Miracle pointed her phone at the white cop holding the smoking gun. "Arrest him for murdering an unarmed black male."

"First, his name is not him. It's Officer Duke and second I am not your brother."

She looked at the phone, then at the two men. One white. One Black. Same blue outfit. Why didn't I listen? Why didn't I just keep driving? She asked herself before Early's words popped into her conscious. *Make them remember me.*

"We will make them remember. All of them Early, I promise."

Thunder crackled through the calm grey-blue, black, night sky.

Both officers jumped.

"Last time I'm telling you," the white officer warned, "Now, drop the fucking phone bitch.

"Yo want it?" she asked. Before either cop could respond Miracle threw a fastball breaking the racist officers nose with her Iphone 7.

"POW! POW! POW! POW!POW!POW!" the black cop unloaded half a clip into Miracle's flesh.

Miracle fell into the grass. Like Early, she rose up until her six-foot frame was an arrow.

Officer Duke and the black cop's guns locked up as they attempted to discharge their weapon once again.

Head held high, standing straight up with her harms lifted to the sky, she whispered, "Wind."

What started out as a barely audible whistle of wind morphed into a nine hundred foot funnel cloud with three-hundred and thirty-three mph swirling winds that swooped the officer's and Mira in the air.

"POW! POW! POW! POW! POW!"

The staccato sound of gunshot fire exploded in the wind as the three beings were tossed around in God's blender.

Seconds later, the officer's lifeless bodies were strewn across the street from Early's. All three bodies were riddled with bullet wounds.

NANE

Subjective Realm

"Homerun," The chairman swung an imaginary bat, "Knocked that bitch right out the park." He dropped his imaginary bat and smiled. "How many times do I have to show You. Every time you send a Miracle, what do I do?"

"You run your mouth until I shut you up," ALL said.

"Not for long," the chairman sat back down in his chair. "Your love can't defeat temptation. Just admit Old Ancient One, your little hue-man creation just didn't work. "I'da' wiped out all of 'em a long time ago." Greenspan resumed whirling around in circles. "You soft as Charmin, weak as puppy piss. Way too cushy to rule if you ask me. Hue-mans are your creation. You birthed, fed, and nurtured them, yet they keep stabbing you in the back to obtain more of my essence." He threw a handful of hundred dollar bills in the air. "Whores. All of 'em. They dance, screw and do who and what I pay them to.

"In the words of a black rapper, them ho's don't love you. And you shouldn't love them whores either, old ancient One. I'll take a dog over a hue-man in a New York minute. Hell, I'll take a dung beetle over a hue-man. Dumber than dirt. All of 'em, the whole damned race. You keep sending these broke bastards to show love to hue-manity, but they never hear them. If I was all of You, I wouldn't have stopped at Sodom and Gomorrah. I wouldn't have stopped at Babylon. I would have called upon Yemeja to rise up her waters and Bam! Tsunami the world! You wanna get rid of me old timeless One. You want them to remember you, then dammit, be the parent. Do it! Do it! Do it! Dammit, do it! Drown every last one of the sons of bitches. If I was all of You, I would have drowned Noah in his mother's womb."

Thunder exploded. "No you would not have. The Me in you would not allow you too."

"Sheeee - ittttt, hell if I wouldn't. Furthermore, I run the you in me OG, have to, you don't know what the Hell you doing."

Thunder exploded. "You don't run anything but your mouth, chair-man. You know who I am. You've seen my work and you know I can crush you with a thought."

"Yada, yada, yah," the chairman waved. "Same ole song. I mean we been at odds ever since you created me all those eons ago. Since then I have never agreed with the way you run your shop, and I've proven time and time again that I'm the best of you, but after seeing the Donald, the finished product of my re-creation," the chairman shook his head, "for the first time in my existence I almost agree with you. The Donald has more of me in him than all of my kids. But the waste that spews from his lips." The chairman shook his head from side to side. "I'm negative, evil, you could even say that I'm a fool at times, but you can not say that I'm a damn fool." The chairman waved a pale hand in the air, " I mean, I'm a fool damned, but not a damn fool, there is a difference, old ancient One."

"No there is not," ALL said, "damn fool be damned."

"Whatever," the chairman waved a hand thru the grey void. "I'm saying that Chump is far dumber than I could ever conceive. If you got designs on him taking my place," the chairman shook his head, "ain't gon' happen. Chump is ignorance on steroids."

Thunder exploded. "We told you this before you breathed the word enslavement into the Caesar's. We told you this before you led Columbus to the shores of what is now North America. We told you this before you influenced the Pope to allow King James to flip the script on scripture. We told you this before you manipulated the fifty-three that drafted the document that Constitutes chaos."

"You mean the fifty-three rapists, child molesters, murders, and slave holders you created, great wonderful divine One."

"No, I am talking about the fifty three hue-men I created Divine but got lost in your pale darkness." Thunder exploded. "It was you that influenced them to rape, to kill, to enslave and to draft that decisive United States Constitution of injustice.

The chairman stopped spinning and shot a finger in the air. "Don't forget, 'to steal'. You have to admit old ancient One, The United States Constitution is probably my greatest –

"Con," ALL interrupted.

"I was going to say work. My greatest work," the chairman emphasized. "Legal enslavement. The protector of my greatest Ameri-con, I mean American creation. Race. You have to admit. The way I constructed ideas around superiority and inferiority to rationalize, nationalize and internationalize the enslavment hue-man beings." He whistled while spinning around in his chair. "I mean, they even go to church and proclaim to love you while thinking of ways to enslave their hue-man brothers and sisters. Ungrateful fucks." The chairman stopped spinning for a moment and looked up. "You do know that you look pretty retarded allowing things to exist that are trying to hurt You."

"Satan, why must you always try and bait me? I'm at peace. I created all of this for a reason. One single reason that encompasses everything."

"I'm just telling truth," The chairman said.

"Although there is one truth, there are different angles of that truth. Context, context, context and then there is you, chaos, confusion, and un-truth. No matter how much you try you will never dismember mine. I am ALL and even you are mine. I am love and love willed all manifestations into being."

"Why do I even try? Esoteric self-righteous know it all." The chairman quipped. "Your knowing is always the greatest knowing. No aspect of You can contextualize a better conceptialization than the other." Visibly frustrated, Greenspan threw his hands in the air. "You do know that you are a narcissistic hypocrite right?"

"You know better than to compartmentalize Me my dark sun. I am those and all. I am every thought and idea. I am. And all I do I do for love because that I am."

"There you go again. Broken record. Damn, sing another tune. Always that I am we, I, you, love garbage."

The grey space lit up before horns began to blow.

"I guess you wonder where I've been. I searched to find the love within... Came back to let you know."

ALL reached out to the chairman.

"Got a thing for you and I can't let go."

The chairman shouted. "I hate music. I hate love. I hate everything. I hate."

"What you Won't Do For love," ALL sang. "Now that's my sun Bobby Caldwell shining bright as can be."

The chairman smiled, "Oh, I think I'll just pay a li'l visit to old Bobby Scaldwell."

"Go head and try. You know were he lives."

"I ain't scared of him," the chairman said.

"You should be. Don't listen to me though."

"I never do," the chairman said.

"Well, take your never-do, evil, negative soul on over there, see if Bobby don't put My 'Word' on you. You a bad so and so. You've pitted fathers, sons, and nations against each other. You influence others every day to rape, kill, maim, and enslave. After saying all that, I dare you. I double pinky dare you to take your evil behind on over there. My sun sang, I came back to let you know," and then he sang, "I got a thing for you and I can't let go." "Do you feel the vibrations of Me coming out of my sun's mouth?"

"I am –

"No, I am," ALL cut him off, "and you are only because I am."

TISA

3:36 AM

April 4, 2016
<u>New York, New York</u>

When people think of the wealthiest people of the world, The Waltons, Gates, Rockefellers, Turners, even Chump comes to mind, but no one but the heads of the seven wealthiest families of the world knew that one man controlled it all.

"Mr. Chairman sir," The chauffeur curtsied while her eyes followed the little ant that ran across the world's wealthiest man's grey and black cowboy boots.

"I know you," The doorman said. "Oh my god."

If you only knew, the chairman of the United States' Central Banking System, thought to himself as he approached the Chump Towers hotel glass double doors that were almost completely hidden by the wide, heavily breathing doorman.

The huge man stood in front of the chairman and in a low scratchy southern drawl he said, "Want some mustard on 'em biscuits."

The chairman wanted to take off his mirrored Ray Ban shades so bad. The irritating-heart attack-waiting to happen just needed to look into my grey orbs - orbs that would draw him into pain and hurt that the fat doorman can't imagine.

The chairman had a long pale finger on his plastic Ray Ban frames when he realized that the idiot, like most, thought he was...

"Carl," the doorman said, "your movie, '*Sling Blade*,' me and my wife's favorite line. Did you really eat those biscuits with mustard on 'em?"

The chairman removed his hand from the rim of his glasses and extended his arm. "Bill."

"That's it." The doorman snapped his fingers. "Billy Bob Thornton. I knew it. Sir, welcome to Chump Towers," The doorman stepped aside.

"I know it's late or early."

"3:36 A.M." the chairman said.

I could get fired for this, but I swear to God, Mary, Joseph, and baby Jesus," the doorman made the sign of the cross with his fingers, "My wife would die right now and go straight to heaven if I sent her a picture of me and you... Together..."

"Sure," The chairman smiled.

The doorman stepped over and put an arm around the chairman. The two men looked like best buddies after a night of heavy drinking. They both held their Samsung Galaxy 4's away from their bodies before snapping a few pictures.

"Thank you! Thank you! Billy, I mean Mr. Thornton, sir. God bless you," the doorman slightly bowed, dropping his phone.

Before the big man reached to pick it up, the chairman was already coming up with the Samsung Galaxy in his hands.

"Here you are friend," the chairman smiled before switching phones.

"We need more kind folks like you in this world. I really appreciate you Mr. Thornton."

"It's nothing," The chairman waved.

"It's something to me," The doorman's voice broke. "You are Billy Bob Thornton, and I ain't nothing but an old, overweight, diabetic redneck with high blood pressure. Married forty-years, thirty-five of 'em hell for my Lilly-Beth. She put up with the women, the ass whippings, and all the broken bones. Took me to get sick to see her for the angel that she is. Now, I just spends every moment of every day that I'm not working trying to make her happy and you's her favorite actor in the whole entire world," he teared up. "I just wanna thank you sir."

The chairman hugged the big man, "Don't thank me. Thank God. I am just a vessel that the Almighty navigates."

Most fans like the one he'd just passed didn't even question his burnt fire colored hair, which was a far cry from Bill Bob Thornton's black and grey.

A few minutes later, the chairman stood at the penthouse elevator. He looked at his watch.

The elevator doors opened.

Right as he got on he heard people screaming.

A smile appeared on his face. "Exploding phone kills them every time," he said to himself. "Wish I could see the carnage, but duty calls."

A slight bell rang as the golden elevator doors opened on the fifty-first floor.

As usual the Chump campaign headquarters was at the center of controversy because that's where Chump spent most of his time these days. Four months ago in January, the frontrunner for the republican presidential nomination turned his penthouse apartment and the rest of the fifty-first floor into his primary campaign headquarters.

Even at quarter til four in the morning Chump's campaign headquarters was alive and tweeting. People were moving from suite to suite in all different directions as the chairman exited the elevator. Just doing damage control for the insanity that Chump tweeted daily was a twenty-four hour job.

No one seemed to be paying attention to the man who regulated every bank in America and over a hundred banks abroad. Greenspan casually strolled past folks shouting and bumping into one another. He stopped at Suite 510, closed his eyes and inhaled. *Fear. Insecurity. Self-hate. Greed. Envy. Selflessness.* His favorite scents rolled into one. The scent of Chump. Intoxicating, the chairman thought as he became lightheaded. So high off all the chaos he was inhaling, the chairman's body began to shut down. That's when he realized that he had forgotten to exhale.

Pheeeewwwww. He took off his shades after entering Chump's private apartment. The six thousand square foot paradise in the sky was beyond extravagant. Every room on both levels was a different shade of grey. The chairman's gait remained steady, his eyes forward. He seemed unimpressed. Not even the hexagon shaped indoor pool could espouse the slightest facial tick from the chairman's stone mask.

Not even the escalator inside the penthouse fazed him. After reaching the second floor of the suite he stepped off the escalator and took a deep breath. The only fragrances more tantalizing than chaos were hate and ignorance, and Chump had enough of both to keep the chairman in a drunken stupor for eternity.

Chump's scent led the chairman to a fifteen-foot painting. Chump's head was painted on Adonis' naked body. He was lying in a garden with his mouth open while Aphrodite, the Greek goddess of love, fed him a three-dimensional brown grape.

A cluster of the strange fruit dangling from a grey stem hung from Aphrodite's free hand. A semblance of a smile appeared on the chairman's face as he reached forward and wrapped his hand around the three-dimensional brown grape and turned it. The painting opened up into a bedroom.

KUMI

3:39 AM

April 4, 2016
Decatur, Georgia

Power would be restored to Southwest Dekalb County before most of its residents awoke. But for now, the forty thousand residents of the affluent African American suburb was without power. Fallen trees and downed power lines littered the long dark road.

The freakish tornado only lasted nine seconds, but that was six seconds longer than needed. Now everything was still. The living, the dead, the animals, the trees, the leaves, even the wind. It was as if time had taken a break.

And then a hole the size of a mustard seed opened up in the night sky illuminating a golden eye of light. The small beam traveled millions of miles from the sun all the way through pine needle leaves, tree branches, and what was left of the twenty-square foot area that was paved seconds ago. The light did not stop until it found its mark.

Three attributes of ALL; Compassion, Wisdom, Justice. Mother godesses, queens, triplets sashaying through the light. They moved as if the world were at their feet. Each

60

step. Harmony, grace, oneness. Each movement fluid. Heads held high. Divine royalty.

With each step, the godesses got smaller. They were barely the size of a baby ant when they entered the portal that the bullet opened in the middle of Miracle's forehead.

The wounds in her hands, feet, heart and head closed as soon as the last triplet stepped inside.

The pink light that surrounded the mother godesses wrapped itself around the fallen young black woman. The way Miracle's body ascended through the pink light. It was like something off of Star Trek. Miracle was half way to the Sun when a green light from the same source was illuminated on twenty-five year old Early's lifeless body. The light disappeared inside the young man's forehead for a moment before reappearing and rising up into a grey fog floating over and into Officer Luke Duke's twenty-eight year old lifeless body.

KUMI NA MOJA

Subjective Realm

"Early!" Miracle reached out. She was awake before she opened her eyes. "I can't see anything." She turned her head from left to right before looking up, "Hey, where's the sky?" She looked down. "What happened to the ground?

"Shhh." A calming voice entered Miracle's conscious. "Be still child."

Peace and calm engulfed her entire being. She had never felt more relaxed. Pressure? There was none. It was like she was standing in space without wind, without air, without anything. There was no thing to see, no thing to do, yet Miracle was content. She wasn't scared. Nothing mattered and yet everything mattered. She felt a presence, but it wasn't something that she could see. "Who are you?" Miracle turned to her left and then to her right.

"I am ALL."

"Where are you?" Miracle looked to see where the Voice was coming from.

"I am here."

"Where, I don't see anything?" she turned in a circle.

"I am no thing."

"I don't see you." She looked around. It was like she was suspended in outer space with no stars, no light, nothing. "I don't see anything."

"I am not anything. I am no thing and I am every thing, but never any thing. I am formless, yet I can transition into any form that the imagination can imagine. Call me by any name and that I am. I am Allah, I am Jehovah. I am Yeshua. I am Elohim. I am God. I am Malcolm, Marcus, and Martin. I am Zion. I am Truth. I am Septima, Harriet, Ida B. And I am Free. I am ALL."

"Why can't I see you?

"But you can my child. You just have to close your eyes. Relax. Will your mind to manifest Me in anyway you want to imagine.

KUMI NA MBILI

Subjective Realm

"Yum-Yum," Miracle called out using her bestfriend's nickname. "Why Early?"

"Why not, Early?" ALL asked.

"He's a good brotha, a good man. He's my best friend. He don't deserve to die. I need him," she pleaded.

"My love, no one deserves to die, and no one ever will. Every being transitions into another state of being, but no one ever dies. Early, Zion, Sunny, they are with you. They can never leave you. They are inside you. They are a part of you."

"No," she shook her head. "I need them. I need to see them. Feel them. Touch them."

"You can and you do. You see, feel, and touch them every day with your mind."

"I want to see them with my eyes, feel them with my hands like I used to."

My daughter-sun. My light, hear me with your heart and not your ears," All said. "Every thought and imagination I

64

or you breathe into being is of Me. You, Early, every hue-man beings essence are but a breath of Me. I am and so you are and everyone and everything else is."

"What about Raynelle? What about all the racist police officers murdering our black children? What about the racist cop that killed Early?"

"What about them?"

"Are you saying that you are them as well?"

"I am the best of them."

"What best? How can there be a best behind all that bad?"

"The bad brings out the best of the good. The bad unites the good in an effort to defeat the bad. Behind, between, under, and or inside bad is good. Your mother's rapist, Raynelle, the racist police that are killing the bodies of our brown children, they have taken on falsehood as their god and their guide. But, I am in them. Buried deep inside them. But, it is because of my essence and your essence that you and Zion must educe our essence out of them. Reach through the ignorance, anger, hate, and pull love from the deep recesses of the their subconscious. From the three year old child to the one hundred and three year old child, the good, the bad, and the terrible. Fight with love to save them all."

"Fight to save evil?"

"Fight to save hue-mankind. Evil may be in hue-mankind, but evil is not hue-man kind. You, Miracle are hue-man kind," ALL said. "You are them and they are you, daughter-sun."

She started crying. "I don't know what to do." She put her head in her hands. "I don't even know where I am. I'm scared, confused. You let Raynelle torture and kill my mother. You tell me in order to save mankind Zion's soul and mine have to unite, but he's in the penitentiary for," she threw her hands in the air, "God knows how long. And you let them kill Early."

"First, daughter-sun, you do know where you are. You just said it."

She looked up.

"No where. Nowhere is a place daughter-sun. It's any place you imagine. Second, you don't need to fear anything because you helped create everything. The same way you helped create everything, you can destroy any creation that hue-mankind created. You are the god of your fears Miracle. Third, you will be confused until you become one with all life. Put your trust in My heart. When you do this you will realize that I don't exist outside of you. We exist. I am the formless that can and does become any form you imagine.

"I hear your words, but I don't understand half of them. This is too much. I'm only twenty-four. I'm a woman. A black woman with nothing, and no one, and you expect me to defeat something I can't even see?"

"No, I expect you to defeat evil, something you can see with your eyes open and closed."

"I'm scared."

"I know you are. You fear the unknown. You fear what you cannot see, what you can not hear, what you can not taste. You fear the objective reality, which is mankind's own creation. But, what you should fear is the subjective reality, which is the unchanging reality that guides mankind's conceptualization of the objective. Muslims describe this fear as *Taqwa*."

"I don't know."

"But you do know my Miracle child. You share a conscious that created and destroyed the world as you know it ten times over. Mankind is merely an infant when it comes to destruction and creating. Mankind can do no thing without Us. So right now, this moment, Miracle Joy Brown, close your eyes. Exercise the god within. Concentrate. See the bad. Remember Emmett Till. Remember the day he was taken. Remember the brutality. Remember Trayvon. Remember

Rakia. Remember Nicholas. Remember Sandra. Remember Early."

Miracle's head began moving in a circle as she went into a humming trance.

Are you remembering?"

She nodded. "Yes, I see them all."

What do you want for them?"

"Justice. That's what I want. Justice. Too many Black Lives lost. Hmmmmmmmmmmmmmmmmmmmmmm-hmmmmmmmmmmmmmmmmmmmmmmm.

"Can you envision what justice looks like?"

"Yes. Hmmmmmmmmmmmmmmmmmmmmmmmmmmmmmmmmmmmmmmm mmmm."

"Are you envisioning all of them getting justice. Are you envisioning the faces of those after you get justice for them?"

"Yes," she lied.

"Now that we know what you want. What are you going to do?"

"I'll go from police precinct to police precinct. I don't know."

"Relax my child. Breathe. Think. Now begin again."

"Wisdom. Hmmmmmmmmmmmmmmmmmmmmmmm. That's what I need to stay ahead of injustice. Hmmmmmmmmmmmmmm. Compassion to keep me from annihaliting all racist police. Hmmmmmmmmmmmmmm. Father ALL, I beg you to allow me to be the hand that rocks the cradle of injustice to eternal sleep."

Thunder and lightning struck as she prayed.

"Free me from indecisiveness." She balled and unballed her fists, her anger rising. "Allow me to definitively leave no doubt in any ones mind as to the question of the value of Black Lives," she prayed. "Zion, if you can hear me Baby, I love you, and I'm coming for you."

KUMI NA TATU

Subjective Realm

"You don't have to come far," Zion said as he walked into the nothing.

"Zion!" Miracle jumped into his arms.

The momentum sent them falling through space. Miracle felt like she was floating on air in slow motion. Zion's smile took away any fear she might have had of falling through the unknown. Just his presence made her feel safe, made her feel that everything was going to be all right. "I love."

Zion put a finger to her lips. "Shh."

She looked into his smiling brown eyes. Like a leaf floating through an autumn breeze, arm in arm they drifted through the unknown.

Zion pointed down.

"OMG," Miracle stared at the indigenous African flowers, "Are those? Are those African Lilies, Agapanthus Africanus. My favorite."

As far as the eye could see, the ground was covered with all different hues of the indigenous South African flower.

"Beautiful," she said looking into Zion's eyes.

Zion smiled.

She put a hand over her mouth, "I'm sorry, that's right." She zipped her lips.

Moments later nine million flower petals rose as the two of them landed softly on the universe's largest flowerbed. Yellow, gold, pink, brown, red and purple petals danced in harmony with the wind. Even the pitter-patter of purple raindrops bouncing off of the reddish, pink elephant ear leaves on the great tree were in rhythm.

"Heaven," Miracle sighed. She turned to face Zion with her eyes closed.

While she ran a finger down the side of his face, he took a golden brown petal and drew the words *"I'll Always be here for you. Always"* over her body.

The touch of the petals skin on her nipples unlocked feelings of pleasure that were more intense then any orgasm she'd had or imagined. She felt her body becoming drenched and not a drop of the purple rain had even touched her flesh. She was almost afraid to open her eyes. Afraid that this moment would end. Afraid that this was not real.

And then Miracle did the thinkable.

She opened her eyes.

****

The floating flower petals, the purple rain, the great tree, gone. Nothing. Just him and her holding each other as they floated through the void that he called space.

Zion gestured for her to look down.

A football stadium sized igloo with a swimming pool sized jacuzzi in the middle of it was below.

"Oh so long this night I prayed."

"Is that?" She put a hand over her mouth.

"That a star would guide you my way."

"Stevie Wonder," she mouthed as they floated though an opening in the ice dome and into the Jacuzzi that bubbled in tune with the Stevie Wonder classic.

"To share with me this special day."

Zion pointed up.

Seven thousand red and pink ribbons did a *two-step* in the air.

"There are ribbons in the sky for our love."

She'd just realized that she wasn't cold. It had to be freezing, yet her naked body had never felt more comfortable. Her gaze descended to the hot water that danced on and around her and Zion.

"This is not a coincidence."

She put her arms around him.

"And far more than a lucky chance."

She took a deep breath, wanting so bad for what she was seeing to be true.

For the second time she did the thinkable and opened her eyes.

****

Again her world changed. This time there was no falling through the grey space.

She was on top. Zion was on the bottom.

She didn't think anything abnormal about the pink sun, or the purple sky, except that they were her favorite colors.

Not even the sky being down and the ground being up surprised her. She knew who her man was. The blonde brown sand actually felt good on her back as she straddled Zion who was pent down on the air still gazing into Miracle's eyes.

The purple ocean behind them sang, "I've been so many places."

Ocean waved.

"I've seen so many things."

The air became thin as Miracle and Zion's bodies drew near. Their eyes danced as Ocean sang the Teddy Pendergrass classic.

"But none quite as lovely… as you."

Zion looked deep into Miracle's eyes.

"You're my latest."

He lightly ran a finger down the side of her face.

"My greatest."

He took a deep breath.

"My latest, greatest inspiration."

Zion exhaled.

"Things never looked clearer."

Zion traced the laugh lines on her face with his pinky finger.

"Peace within never felt nearer."

He squeezed her body tight.

"My burden's gone."

She had to have him now, inside her, really inside. And then she did the thinkable. She opened her eyes.

****

"Damn!" she put her hand over her mouth. Just as she thought, her and Zion were floating into yet another reality.

Zion smiled.

Again she was in his arms as they fell up from space instead of down. This time she kept her eyes open.

The world was right side up when Miracle and Zion emerged hand in hand from the deep. They found themselves waste deep in a river of chocolate. It was as if they were in Willy Wonka's world.

Zion held Miracle from behind. Ever so slightly, his lips grazed the back of her earlobe as his minty cool breath tickled the hair behind her left ear. In a perfect Peabo Bryson tone, Zion sang, "Close your Eyes."

That's when miracle saw it. Reality. Any reality the mind could imagine the mind could create. It's the mind that makes reality real. It's feelings that drive every reality. That's what ALL was trying to get her to see.

KUMI NA NNE

3:42 AM

April 4, 2016
Manhattan, New York

Neither woman saw or paid attention to the chairman stepping into Chump's bedroom suite.

"Jesus Christ!" one of the interns moaned. The source of her pleasure was hidden between the dancing battleship grey silk sheets.

Slithering from up under the grey was a golden leg that straightened into a ballerina stance. The air served as the ground between the intern's leg and the chairman's face. Two golden smiles popped from under the grey sheets, "Wanna play poppy?" they chorused.

He wouldn't entertain verbal barb. They didn't even know him, yet they were so willing, he surmised. He needed release. He needed to feel the pleasure of their pain. He lifted the Ray Ban's form his face.

"Wow," both girls said upon first glance into the darkest eyes they'd ever seen. It only took a few seconds for the women to see and feel what Hell felt like. The skin on their faces wrinkled into masks of pain.

The barely legal young women jerked back and forth a few times until they began crying blood. A moment later they hardened into mannequins, frozen in the Hell that the chairman imagined for them.

"It just pained me so much to see you two so happy." He put his glasses back on. He pointed a finger at the Hispanic looking intern that had stuck her leg out a minute ago.

"Pain! Horror! Fear! Much better look on you virus breeders." The chairman smiled. "Don't worry, I'll snap my fingers when I finish here. You bottom feeders will return to some semblance of normality. You won't remember much, but it is imperative that you remember this." He held a finger in the air. "I will always be in your lives to slay every smile you two ever have."

He lifted his baseball cap. "Now you two sperm toilets have a most terrible day."

The chairman turned from the women and walked a few steps before turning and twisting another brown grape. He felt so good causing so much pain. The phone bomb that he detonated in the fat-fuck doorman's face, the intern whores, and now the Donald.

Chump never turned from the mirror when the bathroom double doors opened. "Damn it Con." The new toupee he was trying on slid down into the 18 carat gold bathroom sink. "How did you get in here anyway?"

The chairman shot Chump a *'did- you-really-ask-that'* look.

"Dumb question," the frontrunner for the highest office in the land acknowledged. "Con, you can not and I mean can not be here ever. Do you have any idea of the political shitstorm I'll face if anyone suspected us of colluding?"

The chairman took a seat on the edge of the pool sized Jacuzzi tub in the middle of the extravagant bathroom. After crossing one leg over the other the chairman said, "Make that the last time you address me as Con."

Chump smirked. "Ah, come on buddy, I was…"

"You will address me as Mr. Chairman or Mr. Greenspan." Absentmindedly, the chairman's arm rose up. A long index finger tapped the *Ray Ban* insignia on his mirrored frames. "I think you may have mistaken our relationship as one of a friendly nature. I assure you that it is not. Your existence means absolutely nothing to me Donald."

The real-estate mogul wagged an angry finger in the Chairmen's direction, "Only reason I call you Con is because I just can not address a grown man as Connie. Do you have any idea how many whores named Connie I have screwed over the last fifty-years? No you do not," Chump huffed. "If my extinctness means absolutely nothing to you, then you wouldn't have risked exposure wearing grey-black cowboy boots, with white FUBU jeans, those stupid shades, and a dumb baseball cap. A Yankees cap at that. Everyone knows that the Yanks don't have enough taco, goat, and fried chicken shitters on the roster to even compete."

"Are you finished Donald?"

"Mr. Chump. If I can't call you what I want, then you can't call me Donald. If you want to keep our relationship professional, then we should keep it all the way superfluous of any misconceptional bias…"

Greenspan lifted the shades from his head. Chump glimpsed into Greenspans dark orbs for only a millisecond. But that was more than enough to render the presidential nominee mute.

The chairman stood from the Jacuzzi's ledge. He used his long pale fingers to smooth out his white jeans. "Donald, if I could give you back to ALL I swear I would." The chairman looked up, "And you call me the author of confusion."

"I have called you no such name," Chump mouthed. Mute, and his lips still didn't stop moving. "Who said I did? I bet it was. Hell, what's his name?" Chump nodded before he continued his silent rambling, "That crippled nigga. Shoeshine boy in the lobby, What's-his-name.

"Donald?" The chairman shouted over Trump's lip moving.

"See what happens when you try and take one of them off the street and let them work. Old one-legged ape too old to sell drugs, too blind to steal, too weak to kill, and sure can't have pups, so now he resorts to defaming my good name. After all I've done for the boy. You would think at eighty-one, he would be a tad smarter than a fucking door knob."

"Donald!!!!!!!" The chairman shouted louder this time. "I was talking to ALL, I mean God."

"Why would you talk to yourself? You say you're God. You should already know the answer. Never could make sense of people talking to themselves."

The chairman closed his eyes and slowly inhaled until his human lungs could take in no more. The chairman knew that getting high off Chumps ignorance was the only thing preventing him from burning Chump alive. "Bar-b-qued fool."

White meat had been the chairman's favorite since the first leper. The whiter the berry the more sour the juice he always said.

"Donald... I am ALL and God is ALL. We are part of the same consciousness, but I am the greater part. You have chosen me just as the lower part of me, the God you read in Bible, Quran, and Torah has chosen you to prove a point."

"What point would that be?" Chump asked.

"That the intuitive nature of Western humanity would overpower objective desire."

"Yeah, I would like to see that other God do that."

The chairman closed his eyes and inhaled before explaining, "Job. The biblical story,"

"What about a job. You need me to hire...."

"Job, like J-O-B-E. The man that ALL, I mean God made go through all types of hardship to prove that no matter

76

how lost mankind is, they always find their way, and they always use love as a compass to do so.

"Anyway, I told ALL back then that Job was only one soul. I told ALL that I was No one to prove any thing to. But ALL is so arrogant and insecure that It just had to keep trying to show me that if given a choice, no matter what calamity, confusion, or misdirection Western hue-mankind befalls, their loving nature would cause them to ultimately choose the preservation of the subjective over the objective realm."

Chump looked completely lost.

"Humanity over money," the chairman said.

Chump's body rumbled into silent laughter. "That's about the dumbest thing I ever heard," he mouthed. "I have never shared air with a White, kike, Nigga, chili shitter, slant eye, or piece of ass that I could not buy.

The chairman smiled. Chump's thoughts were music to his ears. He basked in delight when mankind lifted him up over ALL.

"Before you, Con, I didn't even believe in God. The concept just didn't make sense. I mean if God s'pposed to be about all this love bullshit, then why in the hell is there so many poor people. If I loved somebody, I'm not going to allow them to go hungry or be poor. I mean if God loves everyone the same and everyone is supposed to be His children, then why does He treat everyone different. I'm rich. Always been rich, and four hundred years after I'm dead the future Chumps will still be living off the wealth I built. What kind of father makes his children suffer? What kind of god allows a Nigger to run the U.S. or any damn country for that matter?"

"Exactly," the chairman said, "so, do you really wanna worship a God that loves the imbecile just as much as the anointed?"

Chump looked as if he wasn't sure what the word imbecile or the word anointed meant.

"Even after Job, the ALL written about in the Holy Bible chose Lot. I was never allowed to choose anyone for the game. I still won. Just because the people of Sodom chose my way over ALL's way. He destroyed them. ALL is the big kid in the sandbox that knocks all the other kid's construction's down when they are not constructed they way ALL wants."

"Sounds like all my whores." Chumps silent laughter continued. "God forbid God is a woman. Every thirty days the bitch would destroy the world."

The chairman pointed a finger. "Comments like that reveal how ignorant you truly are. Now I'm not saying that your words do not ring truth, but do you really think that the abuser will instantly love the abused?"

Chump had a questioning look on his face.

"In other words, you have to lie. Women vote, idiot. Did you forget that we have an election to win?"

"If I am such an idiot," Chump mouthed, "how have I managed to be so popular and so rich? I don't have to lie. Women, men, the people love me because I tell the truth. America needs me. America doesn't need another politician to run this country. What America needs is me. And, Mr. Chairman you are the idiot if you think I don't know what I'm doing."

"Donald, you have no idea how hard I have worked over the last few thousands years to cultivate human kind's ignorance. Electing you and allowing you to take office will show just how much I am loved over any other God. Now I've groomed some doozies in the not so distant past Nero, Herod, Caesar, King James, Washington, Wilson, Hitler, Baby Doc, Mbuto. But you Donald," the chairman pointed, "you are the greatest ignorance that I have ever raised. You have the potential to do what Charlie, Jimmy, Ses, and Adolph only dreamed about, but you have to lie. And lie with the appearance of calm and dignity."

Chump mouthed. "I am the calmest..."

The chairman ignored Chumps' mouthing. "Every time you speak in a public forum I have to pay a personal visit to the unconscious consciousness of the over three hundred and twelve million souls that live in this land. Three-hundred and twelve million, Donald. All because you take ignorance and hate to new levels. Now, I'm not saying all that hate does not feel so, so good, oh so very good." The chairman closed his eyes. Guttural sexual sounds came out of his mouth.

"Uhhhhh.Uhhhhhhhhh.Uhhhhhh, " Greenspan grunted.

Chump's eyes widened in horror.

The chairman reached over and grabbed the face towel that Chump washed his face with moments ago. Next, he hawked and spat a glob of saliva in the middle of the face towel before putting it down the front of his jeans.

"Ahhhh, your hate and ignorance feel so, luxuriating," he looked up, "Donald, you have to quit compartmentalizing the hate. Embrace it. Internalize it. I'll teach you to manifest it under the cloak of love. Disguise love as money. Do that, then the people won't care what you say, how you say it, or when you say it, hell they won't even care what you do. The voters will be hooked on the way the words you say make them feel."

Chump could'nt believe his eyes.

Greenspan pulled his hand and the soiled rag from his pants and put it to his nose and inhaled. "Just look at my recent body of work. Racism! Chattel Slavery! Jim Crow! Capitalism! Clarence Thomas!"

"You just... You used my." Chump pointed. "In front of me. My face towel that you saw me wash my face with. What are you?" Chump frowned. "Some kind of."

"Put your finger down. And close your mouth before I rip your toenails off and use them to peel every inch of skin from your wrinkled up body," The chairman said. "Now I listened to every idiotic thought that has ever come out of your head, and I have loved them all but like now, you are so focused on what you see today that you can not see tomorrow."

Chump pointed at his face towel.

"Despite what you saw me do before and after I took your washrag, you are still going to do what I say, when I say, and how I say."

The chairman sat back down on the ledge of the Jacuzzi tub before crossing one leg over the other. He rested his hands on his knee and looked up at Chump. "Why? Because you worship me, and you believe that you cannot exist without me. But, you won't grow your hate unless you shut up so you can hear me guide you."

"What did I do now?" Chump mouthed.

Just last month you told an audience, and I quote, 'I think the only difference between me and the other dipshits running for my rightful office is that I'm more honest and my women are more beautiful.' You even followed that up when you were being interviewed by a female journalist with. 'You know, it doesn't really matter what assholes write about me, as long as I got a young tender piece of ass worshipping me, who gives a flying fuck."

Chump smiled as he reflected upon words he had spoken just weeks ago.

"You have no earthly, spiritual or universal idea of how much heaven I went through to convince the American people that what they heard was not hate but tough love. Just the thought of people loving each other is torture," Greenspan shivered.

"I'm winning and that's all that matters. So you better consider yourself lucky Mr. Chairman that I'm on board with your One World Order."

"That mission could be delayed if you don't start lying with a smile."

"Why do I have to lie? It's not like anyone can stop me. Please, don't give me that Miracle Brown stuff. How dangerous can a twenty-four year old cunt be?"

KUMI NA TANO

3:45 AM

April 4, 2016
Decatur, Georgia

Between Snapfinger and Kelly Chapel, Wesley Chapel Road, the main thoroughfare, was impassible. Dekalb County police officers taped off the area and were preparing to reroute any early morning traffic. Four paramedics were on the scene and more were in route.

"Never seen nothin' like this in my life. " the chief said. "Tornadoes don't touch down in one spot with this type of veracity and just stop. This is an act of God."

How can you attribute three dead bodies and all this destruction to being an act of God?" a junior EMT asked?

"Call it," the chief EMT said referring to the black officer lying dead in the library grass. "What you see as destruction little lady, God may see as reconstruction." He looked up and around the area at the fallen trees, downed power lines, debris in the street and at the other two bodies lying in the street. "Look at this. Now you tell me what natural force could have done this type of damage."

"Who cares," The lead detective on the scene said, "Let's move people. Bag 'em and tag 'em. It'll be light in a coupla' hours, I want the streets clear by then. Chop, chop," he clapped.

Two paramedics were covering the body with a white sheet. The black officer's mid section was ridddled with bullets.

Sandra, the only female and youngest of the four EMT's, rushed over to Early's body with paddles in her hand.

"Too late for that little lady," The chief said.

"Why?" Is it because he's black, the junior EMT wanted to ask her boss. Before she could decide whether to voice her thoughts and risk her job, her boss explained.

"Look at his face," the chief pointed. "So peaceful. Now the body looks like hell, but that's the peace of God on that youngn's face.   Done seen it more times than not. But didn't know what it was until 'bout three years ago. That's when the Cancer took my RuthAnn." A tear ran down the chiefs face. "That's when I realized that man can't put that look on someone's face. And shouldn't no man try to disturb that kind of peace."

He smiled down at Early. "Take me to a place where people don't have to live with the pain."

Behind the chief and junior EMT's, a spiritual world of turmoil was on the rise.

****

"No. Hell no. Double Hell no!" Early said while his soul floated up from his body. "Not today, tomorrow, or the day after never! No! No! No!"

"We need you Early," ALL said. "Your brothers and sisters need you sun."

"They got along just fine when I was among them."

"No they did not."

"Nah Pop, I see what you doin'," Early pointed out. "You ain't slick."

"What am I doing, sun?"

"You trying to make me like Zion. First, I don't wanna be holier than a donut. I like my weed, women, and my will. You know that thing you gave all of us Pop? Will."

"I know it well. I also breathed compassion and love in all of you. And love and compassion is why you need to want to go back."

"Oh, I love alright. I loved my black skin. I loved my black mother. I loved my black friends. I loved my Black Jesus when he was Yeshua, and I loved my Black Jesus when he came back as Zion. I even loved John Brown once I read through his pink-grey skin and was able to see that he was a pale-pink Afrikan. I loved Michael Moorer, another pale-pink Afrikan."

ALL laughed.

"But Pop's real talk and I'm just gon' keep it one-hunnerd times infinity real," Early said. "I know you been doing this creation and this loving thing a lot longer then me, but ain't enough love in creation for me to willingly jump in this redneck peckerwood's body, especially the fact that he the cracka nigga that shot me."

"Sun, you have forgotten that I hued everything as far as the mind could search and the eye could see with a single thought: it's because we said be. Now go back and remember so all can be free.

October 30, 2007*

"Mira!" A wave of grief washed over him. "Mira? is she... Is she... Did she make it, Pops?"

"You see her."

No." He shook his head. I'm mean in the present. She was shot."

"The past is the present. You seen two Mira's, one looking at her past and the other, living her past. The past and future are one and the same, Sun. Tomorrow is merely a reinterpretation of yesterday."

"Come on Pop, you see her," Early said. "She's in pain. Why you making her live this again?"

Early saw Ray-Ray, a man Miracle once thought was her father. A man she trusted. Loved. Raynelle James Tolliver was forcing himself on Miracle's birth mother while punching her in the face.

"Stop!" Early shouted. "Please?"

Time stopped. Everything was still. Suspended in motion. Even Miracle's spirit was still.

"You see the pain she's in and the evil causing it? ALL asked.

"Yes."

"Mulitply that pain by a thousand," ALL said. "That's the caliber of evil coming Miracle's way. Evil will love nothing more than to inflict a world of hurt on her and everyone you and her love and hold dear."

"You tricked me, Pop."

"No sun, I breathed love into your being. And it is the love in your heart that wills you to fight. Sun, with you fighting for and with Miracle she might make it but without you fighting she won't stand a chance."

KUMI NA SITA

Subjective Realm

"Foul!" The chairman bounced out of his chair and pointed. "Foul! Foul! Foul! You can't just make Miracle disappear. Hell no. She was dead. She is dead. You can't do that?"

"Do what?" ALL asked.

"Change history. That's not the way it happened. Miracle Joy Brown was dead. They were dead. All of them. Dead! Dead! Dead!" The chairman jumped up and down. "Crash and burn, stick a fork in 'em," He kicked the air. "Dead! Dead! D-E-A- dead!"

Space brightened as ALL spoke. "Love. Love. L-O-V-E love. That's what everything and nothing is all about, my negative spawn," ALL beamed. "Whether you accept it or not, there is no his or mys-story. I was never broken. I don't need a pre fix. I am the story. I am every story, every imagination."

The chairman poked the air with his index finger. "That still doesn't give you the right to resurrect the dead in real life. You can't just change yesterday. It's just not right."

"Right," ALL said. "I am the right."

"I ain't trying to hear that non-sense."

"You will hear what I want you to hear. You don't have to listen, but you will hear. Now understand this child. I am and you are because I allow you to be."

"But, your promise?"

"I have broken no promise. My words may change, but my message will always be the same. Love. This is the Word. Love is my promise. Love is the right. Every story I have ever told was done out of love. That's why no matter how you skew my words evil one, the message of love cannot be removed from the story. Why do you think I allowed you to fool My creation into manipulating My bibles?"

The chairman spinned. "I don't give an ant's eyelid why you do anything."

"Yes you do." ALL said. "No matter how much confusion, chaos and hate I allow you to breathe into my suns, they are still suns that I hued my word into. It's all love. Historical, imaginative, and spiritual bibles are maps to lead hue-mankind back to loving ALL."

A still image of Miracle and Zion materialized. The two were embodied as one being. The black woman and man re-awakened. Warriors standing in front of the rising sun.

"My sun. My light. My I am."

"I ain't trying to hear all that Romeo and Juliet crap." Spinning around, the chairman swatted the air with his arm. "How many times are you going to send a human Miracle?" He asked. "How many times do I have to send them back to you. I'm steady breaking every limb you send from Your tree." The chairman karate chopped the air before continuing. "Old Ancient One, maybe you do need a pre-fix, a little his-story," the chairman stopped spinning before pressing a finger to his temple, "Let's see hmmm, I ran up in Horus, no Vaseline. There was Shango, Akhenaton, Buddah, Jesus."

"Yeshua." ALL said.

The chairman waved his arm in the air. "Tomato, tamotto, Jesus, Muhammad, Harriett, Septima, Malcolm, Martin, and now Miracle, Zion, oh well." he shrugged his shoulders before he went back to spinning around. "Another nut to bust."

Thunder exploded. "You have never sent anyone anywhere. I called my suns home. They had done their part. Now they're basking in the paradise of being the gods of their own imaginings. If you weren't always high on hate or drunk on ignorance you would have seen that you can't do anything to my creation that I don't allow you to."

The chairman stopped spinning. "Your creation?" he looked up. "Now you smoking too much of that love. Did you forget that I'm the author of chaos, the author of everything opposite of you, ain't no other me unless I make them be, and as you see, I have taken your form and made them me."

"Fool, you wouldn't be a me if I didn't say be."

"Yeah whatever. Like all the rest, I'm just going to wave some of this mess," an instant stack of hundred dollar bills materialized in his hands, "And your creation will forget all about you... faster than they do after church and Sunday school.

KUMI NA SABA

3:48 AM

April 4, 2016
Decatur, Georgia

Back at the scene where the freak tornado hit, the police, the paramedics, everyone was too busy trying to sort out what happened to pay attention to the fog rising from Early's nose.

The junior EMT's eyes travelled from the sheet that covered the black cop to Early Morning and finally to the deceased white officer, Luke Duke whose body was on the other side of the street.

The fog that came from inside Early floated over to Office Duke before going up his nose.

"Chief," the junior EMT called out.

The Chief was talking to a detective, when he looked up just in time to see the white sheet fly off Officer Dukes' bloody corpse.

"What in God's name," The chief said as he and the others witnessed the man that they pronounced dead minutes ago rise from the ground. "Officer Duke," the chief called out as he and the others timidly approached.

"Officer who?" Early's voice came out of the rising white officer's mouth. Officer Duke began walking backwards in a circle.

"Officer Duke," Luke said. "You heard the good white lady, yard boy."

"*Who you callin' a yard boy, peckerwood?*" Again Early's words came out of the white officer's mouth.

"Who responded?"

"*You must be referring to your momma. Call me yard boy to my face? Stop hidin' white boy.*

"We're right here Officer," The young blonde EMT held her hand out."

Officer Duke responded to Early, "I'm referring to a dumb nigger that says anything when he doesn't have anything to say."

As more red and blue lights approached, the young EMT had a moment of clarity. She realized that reading about and studying mental instability did not begin to prepare her to deal with a raging police officer with a split personality disorder.

"*You sound real good bitch ass peckerwood. All this air and opportunity between us and all you doin' is making sounds. Take your white sheet off or hell keep the damn thing on, but come out and face me like a man cracka'.*"

"Like a man. That is an oxymoron you moron. I am a man while, on the other hand, you're a black ass nigger!"

The others stood around not knowing exactly what to do. They all knew that the dead man talking was the polic commissioner's son, and Stonewall Duke had proven time and again that he wasn't someone you wanted to get on the bad side of.

An officer opened the back door to the black government Suburban that had pulled up into the Wesley Chapel Public Library yard.

Officer Duke looked up.

Georgia Police Commissioner Stonewall Duke got out of the back of the Suburban.

Luke put his hands up in front of his face. *"Hell nah."* He broke the zipper trying to get his pants undone. All at once he dropped gunbelt, pants and boxers. Sweat began to pour off the officer as he and Early's thoughts, feelings, and realities bagan to integrate.

They looked down at their shriveled up pink manhood before fainting.

KUMI NA NANE

5:33 AM

April 4, 2016
Decatur, Georgia

Officer Luke Duke had been comatose since passing out in the street over an hour ago. Since then, the medical staff at Dekalb General had cleaned and stitched his wounds. All four bullets went through and came out clean without damaging any major arteries. The doctors assured Stonewall that his son was a living miracle and would have full mobility in his hands and feet were the bullets came out.

The injury he sustained when passing out and hitting his head in the street was the medical team's only concern.

Stonewall and his much younger fiancé had just been granted permission to see Luke.

"Stoneyyyyy!" The Miley Cyrus look-alike crossed her arms. "Everything is always getting in the way of me doing what I wanna do." The Georgia Police Commissioner's fiance stuck her bottom lip out, "How much longer Daddy?"

Stonewall looked at his watch. "We've only been in here six minutes, honey bunny."

The twenty-something looking nymph licked her lips. "Really Stoney-poo-poo-poo. It seems like we've been here forever."

"I know honey bunny," he tapped her on the behind. "If this weren't an election year, we would've been out of here five minutes ago." The elder Duke turned towards his comatose son. "After all he is my boy." The elder Duke nodded before sitting down between the life support machine and the son he reared.

"I thought I was your little boy," she pouted.

"You are honey bunny, but remember what we say about what happens at home," he nodded.

"Stays at home," she said before a devilish grin appeared on her face. She moved like a dancing cobra as she sat down in the metal grey chair at the end of Luke's bed. She put one leg on the wall and one on the bed rail before rearing back.

Not taking her eyes off her broad-shouldered, tall, Tommy Lee Jones fiancé, she spread her tanned pinkish grey ballerina legs exposing her waxed womanhood. "Naughty, naughty boy," she waved a finger. You wanna come under mommy's curtain and give Miss Kitty your confession."

"*Mother may I?*" Early's voice came out of Luke's mouth.

She turned her head. Her mouth flew open but nothing came out. Her eyes were motionless blue marbles staring at the ghost that had just risen from the bed.

"Honey," Stonewall pointed to her legs.

She blushed before closing her legs and putting her feet on the floor.

Stonewall stood. "Uh, uh, how do you feel, son?"

Luke opened his mouth but the words and tone that came out was Early's. "*You gon' stand there with your big mouth open and act like you and Daisy wasn't about to get freaky while your son in here fighting for his motha fuckin' life.*"

Stonewall never played poker because his face always betrayed his feelings. This time was no different. The commissioner's face went from blue to red without stopping at any other shades. His eyes were screaming. It was like he was having a heart attack in slow motion. His mouth opened. Not even a breath emerged. His arm rose and when it was aimed at his son's smiling face he shot out an accusing finger.

When no words came forth, Luke turned his attention back to Stonewall's fiancé. "*Look here babygirl,*" the black and blue, heavily bandaged younger Duke smiled, "*go play. But don't go too far. I got twenty dollars for you to let Miss Kitty here my confession.*"

After she had made a hasty exit, Stonewall exploded, "Got dammit boy, what has gotten into you. And why in Sam hell are you talking like one of them pants on the ground black baboons?"

Luke balled and unballed his fists. Don't do it. Not yet. Let me show you how to handle a Stonewall, Luke thought to Early.

"Father, please accept my apologies," Luke said. "Maybe it was the trauma from being shot in my hands and feet. I don't know why I was talking like a niggra."

Stonewall took a deep breath and exhaled. "Forget about it boy, probably the head injury. You bumped your head real good on that pavement."

Luke looked up from the hospital bed and smiled at his father.

The elder Duke put a hand on his son's shoulder. "In a few days, you'll be just like new. I need you back on the force. And don't worry about that niggra you killed. Matter of fact, I'm damn proud that you finally picked up your balls and fired your damn weapon."

"Dad, it was a bad shoot." Luke said. "He wasn't armed."

The Elder Duke nodded. "He's a niggra, son." He shrugged his shoulders. "Who cares?"

"Dad, can you please come closer," Luke whispered.

"Son," The elder Luke looked concerned. "Is something wrong?"

"Closer," he signaled his father with his hand.

Luke gently placed his bandaged hand over his father's grey head and pulled him to his chest.

"Listen father. Listen to my heart."

Stonewall did as his son asked. For the first time in years Stonewall felt what he thought was genuine love from his son.

"Do you feel it father."

"Yes," The elder Duke acknowledged. "Strong heart beat son."

"The Duke heart, right father."

"It is son." Stonewall nodded. "It is."

Luke reached up from the hospital bed and took his father's head and lifted. "Father look at me."

The greying Duke gazed upon his son.

"I am in love father. What you heard, what you felt was love. The unconditional undying love that I have for my fiancé."

Stonewall's eyes widened.

"Dad, every night before I lay down with Tamir," Luke paused, "You remember Tamir, Momma Fluffy's grandson that you forbid me to play with because he was a niggra. We hooked up after he got out of prison three months ago."

Stonewall tried to pull his head from his son's grasp.

"I knew he was the one after the first kiss."

Stonewall broke away from his sons hold and pointed. "You!"

"Don't worry, we're waiting until he gets off parole next year before we walk down the aisle."

The elder Duke placed his hand over his heart before he collapsed to the floor.

You are doin' too much, way, wayyyy too much. Overkill, Early thought to Luke.

"Kill over, over kill it's all the same, Early. Don't be jealous because I killed him." Luke pointed to where his father was lying on the hospital floor next to the bed.

Why couldn't you have fallen in love with a black girl? Why it had to be a gay Black con?

"My dad, my whole family hates almost everyone that's not white. Blacks and gays are at the top of the list. I had hoped my false confession would have killed him."

Come on Luke, twelve hours ago you were just like him, Early thought.

"Only because all my life I was taught these ridiculous things about black people?"

"What type of things?"

"Read my mind, I don't even want to voice some of the things my daddy told me," Luke said, "What about you. What's the dumbest thing you were told about white people?"

"Most of the dumb things are true, but hmm, let me think a minute. Okay, Jesus and God. Growing up, I worshipped white Jesus. Black grandmothers all over the south had John F. Kennedy and or Jesus hanging on their wall somewhere."

"What's crazy about that?" Luke asked.

"There was no one hanging on the walls that looked like us unless they were family photos. And we all know that Jesus wasn't white and that God could not be white because of mere evolution," Early thought. *"What about you Luke?"*

"Savagery. My dad use to say, it was in all black people's blood."

"What?"

"Savagery. He said robbing, killing, raping, and maiming was in black people's natures. He said that the white race had the responsibility of keeping black people and all other races in line."

And you believed that bullshit Luke?

"Did you believe what you were taught?"

KUMI NA TISA

5:33 PM

April 4, 2016
Terre Haute, Indiana

Blending into a world of societal outcasts, state labeled miscreants, murderers, rapists, and thieves would be impossible unless you were one of them. Gladiator School was what the residents called the maximum-security federal penitentiary in Terre Haute, Indiana. This is where the U.S. government sent some of the hardest core criminals in the country.

Five foot eleven, bright skinned, no tats, no piercings, clean-shaven, short cropped hair, Zion Uhuru Jones looked like anything but one of the most dangerous criminals in America. USP Terre Haute was the seventh prison he'd been transferred to over the last six plus years.

Zion sat up front in the television room. His attention was focused on CNN. He wasn't paying attention to the inmates whispering about him in the back.

BE: The RE-Awakening

****

The Chicago-born Black Peace Stone Rangers, the Gangsta disciples, The Latin Kings, the Indianapolis-born 30th Street Maddogs, and the Naptown Riders had all been united by one man, Owen "Nap" Cowherd back in '09. Nap was sittng in the back of the small room sizing Zion up.

"Nigga don't look so tough," Nap said.

Nap was an urban griot, a gifted storyteller who was so passionate about rhythmic story telling that he'd sold, stole, and cajoled any and everything to finance his dream. Nap was hood born, hood raised, but he wasn't a hood. He just pretended to be, a survival technique that had worked well until a Chicago grand jury refused to indict two white cops.

The same two cops that had watched him take the red Nike book bag into his grandmother's house nine years ago. The same two white cops that had watched him come out of the house without it.

Less than an hour after he had left his grandmother's she was dead. The Epsom salt he'd brought so she could soak her feet spilled out of the hole where one of the policeman's bullets pierced the red Nike book bag. When the paramedics arrived, the seventy-seven year old grandmother cradled an old rusty unloaded shotgun.

The community had been outraged, while Nap had been transformed. Not by the act but by the reaction of a greater society that refused to condemn men who used self-defense as a reason for firing thirty four bullets into a closed front door. Twenty-five of those shells left dark marks around the grey leather where they entered the back of the chair his grandmother was sitting in while soaking her feet and watching *Days of Our Lives*.

Nap had always been a fun-loving, happy person just glad to be alive until that day. The Medical Examiner's report stated that sixteen bullets had entered his grandmother's head neck and back.

What happened to his grandmother sparked him to start writing and performing songs about resisting police. The song "*A life for a life*" went viral the week after the grand jury refused to indict. His song, "*They goin' in, they goin' out*" began uniting several Midwestern gangs until they came together as the Noon Crew. Like Nap's song says, "*Light 'em Up, Take 'em Out*," that's exactly what the Noon Crew was planning to do until Nap got popped with a kilo of heroin and an AK-47.

Nap had been in the Pen now for close to seven years, just like Zion had.

The prison television room was near standing capacity. Everyone was trying to see the suburban Atlanta street that was demolished by a freak storm early this morning.

"Let me get at him Nap, I'll pull his card and check the nigga's gangsta real thorough," one of his enforcers barked.

"Nah Big Rod," Nap said, "that goes against the code. "Dude ain't crossed no boundaries yet. I was just speaking."

"I thought Lieutenant Quisling was getting you the 411 on dude," another rider said.

"He did. Pretty mufucka s'pposed to be Black Jesus or some such non-sense," Nap said. "Came in with two life sentences for offing a coupla NSA cats and done picked up another for offing a convict at the Atlanta pen."

"Damn, triple life!" Black said.

"Oh, you've added math to your repertoire," Big Rod said.

"I added your mother before that," Black whispered.

"Dude seem so calm and shit sitting over there watching CNN," another rider remarked.

"Anyone watching this bullshit?" Charlie White came in and slammed the TV room door. Everyone but the C.O.'s called White by his prison moniker, Psycho.

"Funky mu' fucka' ain't sent me no damn money in two months." The big man barked. "And then how 'bout the bitch gon' hang up on me knowin' a nigga gotta get back in the phone line. What the fuck?"

"My woman pulled the same shit last year, amigo," a Hispanic brother said.

"Nigga," White sucked his bottom lip in and breathed through his cheeks. "Fuck you and your woman. I'm talkin about my momma, fool, not my motha' fuckin' tramp. Further fucking more did a nigga ask you any damn thing?"

"Shhh. I'm trying to hear this next segment Mr. Charlie," Zion said. "Can you please bring it down?"

The loudest phoniest laugh spewed from the huge man's mouth before his voice went up several octaves. "Nigga! Who dis bitch nigga callin' Mr. Mu' fuckin' Charlie?"

Zion got up and walked up to the huge black man. "Shhh!" he put a hand on one of Psycho's huge shoulders.

The prison mob enforcer looked down at the much smaller hand on his shoulder before returning his attention to Zion's face.

Barely above a whisper Zion said, "You will leave this room now and you will not come back when I am in here. Do we have an understanding?"

The three-hundred pound Goliath swung.

With catlike agility, Zion ducked while stabbing a finger into the pit of the enforcer's huge armpit dropping the man to his knees.

ISHIRINI

3 days later

3:03 PM

April 7, 2016
Atlanta, Georgia

Dekalb County, Georgia was the wealthiest African-American county in the country, but you couldn't tell by the lack of respect the police there had for black life and themselves.

"It's huntin' season boys," Officer Mason said, "You know everytime we exterminate one of them a whole bunch more seem to come out like roaches to march or loot.

Officer Mason stood in the middle of the officer's break room with his hands on his hips. He looked at both cops he stood between before looking at the other three that had stopped laughing, "The man's a friggin hero. Like daddy like son, Luke stomped on a young roach with his gun and you fucks are up here niggerizing a great America hero just for fun."

"Yo, G, my name be Early, and I'm tired of you Johnny come lately's," Officer Dixon turned his blue hat to the back before grabbing his crotch, "hatin' on my swag," the white officer threw his hands in the air. "Is you mad?"

Sergeant Line stood up from the break room table and undid his belt, letting his pants drop to his knees.

"Nooo." The officer next to him laughed. "You guys are killing me."

"My nigga, pit bull, big dog, bitch ass ho, I know you ain't talkin' to the poh-poh," Sergeant Line said before throwing his hands up in an exaggerated motion.

Officer Mason pointed both arms at his fellow officers before shooting them with his fingers.

Both dropped to the floor.

Officer Mason walked over to the fallen Officer Dixon and lifted his foot, "Somebody go get the RAID. I don't wanna get my shoes dirty."

****

Luke didn't know if he was more disgusted at the officers on the live feed they were watching or at the brown faces in blue that watched Luke's cellphone screen.

Detective Ben Brown slapped the phone out of Luke's hand.

"Don't kill the messenger, I'm just trying to show ya'll how them white boys feel about you," Luke said.

Detective Brown stood face to face with Luke.

"A week ago you was Kool and the Gang with them. So now what? You kill a little nigga, and your conscious won't let you rest, soooo you come back to work walking and talking black. And now after you've obviously planted a hidden camera in the break room, you get us in the restroom where you show us a friggin' live feed of our brothers having a good time celebrating the fact that the grand jury refused to indict your white ungrateful ass."

"Dude," Luke began before Early took over. *"Motha fucka, these crackas making fun of black life. They ain't celebrating me. They laughing at black life. They calling us roaches."*

"Us," Officer Ward Back interrupted, "If you haven't noticed your skin is the same color as most of them in your little feed. Besides Sergeant Line is the ranking officer in your little video, so do not make everything about race. The brothers are just having a little clean fun imitating the stomping out of crime. "

"Just because Sergeant Line black, you sayin' it can't be about race. I know you ain't sayin' that black can't hate black," Luke said.

Officer Ward countered, "Black can hate. White can hate. Yellow can hate. But all of us in here are blue. Plain and simple. Inside the Fraternal Order of Police we are all Blue. I wouldn't be surprised if every police department in the state is celebrating you Duke. Tensions were already high when you took at that trash. Only hours before, did you forget that Atlanta police officer, Sergeant Che' Zapata was gunned down after pulling a car over for not having a license tag. Killing that boy was like raparations for what happened to Zapata."

"One has nothing to do with the other. Beisdes I heard Zapata was fine."

"No one is fine, if we let anyoe get away with trying to kill one of our brothers. A lot more assholes are going to die for what they tried to do to our Atlanta Police officer brotha."

Luke stood back and crossed his arms, *"Were all you niggas dropped on your heads at birth?"* Luke's bright blue eyes stared into the six dull brown orbs of the men in the bathroom. "You talkin' about killing innocent brotha's for what others did." Luke shook his head. "Ya'll ain't got a problem with them laughing and joking, throwing the word nigga around like it's okay. Dumb question," Luke shook his head no. "If you don't care about cops taking out black life, of course you don't care what they call us."

Detective Brown's dull browns stared into Luke's bright blues. "If we did, you'd be in a coma brotha."

"Real talk," Luke shook his head, *"Ya'll already in one."*

ISHIRINI NA MOJA

Six Weeks Later

3:13 PM

May 19, 2016
Stone Mountain, Georgia

Exhale Luke, Early thought. *Now relax. Don't ruin this.* He turned on the cold water before bending down and splashing some on his face.

"Ruin what?" Luke asked. "We moved back in for one thing you said."

We did big homie. Relax. Don't look like Stonewall is going to be getting out of that wheelchair anytime soon if ever. The stroke did a number on him. We got time.

"I thought Miracle and Zion meant everything to you." Luke said.

Luke put his hands over his ears and closed his eyes.

What the fuck man. Early thought. *Can a nigga get a little Heaven in peace. I mean damn. I'm stuck in this body with your dumb question asking ass when a half naked, half drunk, pink toe is outside this door*, Early thought. *Besides your old man is gone and ain't coming back. We can go through all his stuff, I mean all of it, ain't like he can do anything about it.*

105

"I don't know. Nah, this isn't right. She was almost about to be my stepmother. I can't do it," Luke stood in the east wing bathroom mirror shaking his head.

What. Luke. You shot me. Pow!!! Dead as dirt. The least you can do is let me live a little. Damn, you killed my body.

"It's not right, Early. It's just plain wrong."

What was wrong was you pulling me out Mira's car and shootin' me. What was wrong was you deleting that video instead of uploading it to facebook for all to see how racist the police department is.

"What good would that have served, Early? We both know that black people wouldn't do anything but march or boycott gas for a day," Luke said.

Why we even having this discussion? You shot me. You owe me. I'm collectin' and my first payment is outside that bathroom door, Early thought. *Besides, I'm doing this for you too.*

"You are doing this for you," Luke said.

Fool, I am you. And I know your ass ain't worried about that brick dumb Becky out there. You trippin' cause you ain't never even smelled none let alone had none. I don't understand how you got to be damn near thirty and ain't never had no Heaven.

"You forgot I'm new at this. Besides it's not right to take someone else's Heaven."

We ain't taking anything. We are singing the right tune that will bring Heaven to us.

"We are still talking about sex, right?" Luke said.

Man, I'm talking about resting inside and between the thighs of vanilla cream.

"Why do you call the vagina Heaven?"

Fool, read my mind better. Context baby. I'm talking about the feeling. The feeling that you get when you are inside a black woman's warm wet thighs. When you travel up and down her wetness painting her walls with your brown. Luke closed his eyes. *Heaven. The black woman.*

"But, she isn't black?"

Uh, yes she is, just a much lighter hue.

"Knock Knock. It's Daisy," Stonewall's fiance giggled from outside the bathroom door.

Really? Her name is Daisy for real? Wowwwww. Early thought. *If you have an uncle named Jesse and a cousin named Bo, I'm outta here.*

"What are you thinking about?" Luke asked.

The redneck 80's television show Dukes of...

"Hazzard," Luke laughed.

Why you laughing fool?

"I'm the fool?" Luke laughed. "I'm white, and I didn't watch Tarzan because it was a little too far fetched for me as a child, but you.... Your, *we-shall-overcome-kill whitey* persona is a façade. You love my pale white ass and all my good ol' boy southern pale white ancestors."

Ha ha motha fucka, you got jokes now. Why you all up in my mind anyway?

"What's the saying?" Luke asked. "Ain't no fun when whitey got the gun."

Look fool, a prime piece of Heaven is on the other side of that door half ass drunk naked and you up here.

"Ahhhhhhh!!!!" Luke hollered. "I can see you now. Ten year old, Malcolm Early X, a bow tie and suit sitting in front of the TV watching a young Uncle Sam being daddy to all of Black Africa. Or how about this. How about this. You are ten. Dark glasses. Black tam, Black tight fitting leather jacket, jeans, black boots sitting in that high back wicker chair. We can't forget the AK you're holding while watching me and my brother Bo run moonshine in Ku Klux Kentucky."

A'ight man, chill. I didn't know. I was just a kid.

"Oh, your parents didn't know either, Early? What about your grandparents?

"Knock! Knock!"

I ain't trying to hear all that. Reparations are right outside this toilet, and I'm bout to get me some of that 'we-shall-overcome'.

Ten minutes later, Early was admiring the Roman columns leading into the library/office. Stonewall's fiancé sat behind the sixteen-century Kingsman's desk.

She giggled. "Stoney told me that he raised you out here." She swirled the brown liquor around in the Mason jar.

"He did. I was." Luke smiled. *"Speaking of, how is the old man? I mean father. How is father?"*

I don't sound like that, Luke thought to Early.

"The same," she said. "Sleeping most of the time. It's like he's trying to will himself to die. It's like he died weeks ago, back when you were shot."

"Has his prognosis changed at all since the stroke?"

Too much rhythm in your voice. Take the soul out Early. You sound too black, Luke thought to Early.

She turned her glass up and downed the brown liquor like a professional. "Doctors," she coughed, "say still that," she giggled. "Did I say still say? Weeee." She pushed back from the desk. "I meant," she turned her head sideways. "What did you just ask me Lukey, poo-poo-poo." She put here thumb in her mouth.

"What are the doctors saying?"

Way too black. Enunciate. Talk like a robot.

"Damn, will you please shut the fuuuu," Early realized he was speaking his thoughts. *Rrrrnace down.* *"It's a song I had been trying to recall for some time. So, what have the doctor's said."*

She threw a finger in the air. "Oh yeah, his muscle functions are repaired, Oops I mean peraired but his mind is functioning at full pacacity."

"Capacity?"

"Yep." She nodded.

"*Still not talking?*"

"Nope." She belched.

"Does he still point and shout out the word '*you?*'" Luke asked.

"Yep," She said before grabbing the bottle of Grey Goose by the neck. "Don't worry Stoney's tucked away in bed and his wheelchair is all the way by the door." She turned the bottle up.

She belched before throwing the empty bottle into the Greystone library fireplace. She smiled at Luke before taking her arms and whooshing everything off the large desk.

Her four-inch heels clanked against the dark hardwood floor as she stepped around the desk.

Luke looked up. He held his hands in a prayer motion before Early prayed. *Pops, first I wanna thank you and second, send me a sign. If I ain't supposed to tap that then say something.*

Daisy pulled off the white tennis skirt and matching white top before sitting atop the 16th Century desk and spreading her legs. "You want this daddy," she slurred.

I'm good Pops, I'm gon' use my free will on this one.

"I hope you have protection," she giggled. "I take little white pills but not the little blue ones."

After several rounds of unprotected rug burning, back scratching, tongue biting, wolf-howling passion, they fell into a deep slumber side by side on the bear rug in front of the fireplace.

Some time later, a teardrop landed on Luke's eyelid. He blinked.

Stonewall's finger was the first thing he saw when the world came into focus.

"You!" the fragile old man pointed a shaky finger at Luke before falling back into his black electric wheel chair. His cheeks trembled into a nervous smile.

ISHIRINI NA MBILI

Subjective Realm

"Wipe that evil ass smile out of your minds," ALL said before thunder crackled in the nothingness void. "I mean right damn now."

That same nervous smile was on both Luke's and Early's faces as they stood in space, standing at attention.

Pops? Early thought before looking down and seeing his feet. He looked at his hands before wiggling his fingers.

A bolt of lightning lit up the grey space. "Did I ask for your thoughts?"

Nah, but...

Thunder exploded. "Don't make me jack you both up. Early, you better think to me with some damn sense instead of thinking about running around like a four legged animal in heat."

"Please forgive me, us," Luke said.

Pops, I messed up, this ain't on Luke. But, I'm gon' change. Already have, at least as far as race is concerned. He turned to Luke. *He's actually helped me.* Early pondered a moment before continuing with his thoughts, *I mean I used to say I didn't see all crackas as crackas but deep down inside I really did. But, this brotha,* he put an arm around Luke's shoulders, *he got a good heart. He a little lame, a little slow, but Luke's an Afrikan.*

"You do know I'm hearing all your thoughts," Luke said.

I know bruh. And, real talk Luke, I'm sorry for making you feel guilty about shooting me. It was selfish. I just wanted to drive Ms. Daisy. Early looked up. *Pops, I meant...*

"Sun, I know what the hell you meant. You took advantage of my child. My daughter. What you two did was despicable, immoral, and disgusting."

"Pops, we didn't force Daisy to do anything. She was drunk."

Space began to rumble and quake. "Exactly. She was out of her mind and you two knew it and you expoited that fact. That little drunken white girl is my child. My creation!" Thunder exploded. "Let me give you two a little taste of what your selfishness and disregard for hue-man decency feels like. "

"*AHhhhhhhhhhhhhhhhhhhhhhhhhhhhhhhhhhhhhhhh!*"
Early's thoughts turned into screams of agony as a pain and hurt beyond anything he'd ever felt entered his being.

"Welcome to the feeling of Hell that you two have caused others throughout your lives."

ALL turned its attention to Early, "Sun do you just go to First Afrikan to make yourself feel good?"

"No, I... Ahhhhhhhh. Ahhhhhhhhhhhhh.

Tears began to drench the space as ALL cried. "You've walked with my eyes and you do this. Sun, I love you but I'm so disappointed."

"I feel so bad, ohh-ohhh, ahhhhhhh!" Early cried.

"Not as bad as you are about to feel," ALL said before a bright bolt of lightning struck Early and the pain and hurt intensified.

111

"AHhhhhhhhhhhhhhhhhhhhhhhhhhhhhhhhhhhhhhhhhhhhh hhhhhhh!" Early screamed.

"You, Luke. All your young Earthly life you've been poisoned with hate, anger, and fear. And now you have had the unique opportunity to see the ignorance and idiocy of hating someone for the characteristics and hue that I gave them. Look what you do."

"I tried to..."

"I'm not finished," ALL said. "You allow the same evil to rise up and cloud your brothers judgement. You are Early's keeper, yet you allowed him to use your flesh to hurt one of mine." Lightning lit up the space as a bolt surged through Luke.

"Ahhhhhhhhhhhhhhhhhhhhhhhhhhhhh," Luke cried out.

"Two thousand years after Constantine stepped on My *Word*, five hundred years after King James stomped on It, it still hasn't changed. My *Word* is and has always been *love*. Love is the reason, not the story. My *Word* is not a bunch of stories about a sun I brought to light in a manger. My *Word* is the message, the reason for Me bringing My light to life through My suns. The action, the story is just a guide for all of my earthly children to understand what love is and what love does. Love is the message. It's the weapon that I send through all of My messengers to deliver."

Luke and Early writhed and cried.

"Now listen to me you two. When I say fear Me and Me alone, I mean it dammit. Chump, Greenspan, no one can do anything to you that you do not allow them to if you exercise the Me in you. It is you that they will fear. Love is all the power you need to defeat evil and his seeds. Feel the pain."

Early and Luke were feeling all the pain and hurt of the people they had thus far deceived, all because they had planned and coerced Stonewall's fiancé into sex.

"Joy." ALL said. The pain was immediately replaced with a few seconds of extreme joy and ecstasy. "Feel the joy, suns."

"Whew! Whew! Whew! Whew-Whew-whew!"

"My sentiments exactly," ALL felt their feelings. "Before, you never experienced or imagined such pain. And although it was only for a moment you two felt joy – joy like you have never fathomed. Now, you feel and have felt firsthand why you have no thing to fear. I am the only One that can cause pain or joy. You two will be wise to keep that in mind next time the thought to plot on one of My innocents enters your mind."

"Pops, I'm confused" Early said. "Yesterday you sounded like the James Earl Jones's God voice in the movies and today you sound like...

"I sound like nobody. But every voice you hear is my voice and every face you see is my face. The point I'm making is that I'm a part of every thought and every action. I'm love unlimited sun, and I will communicate with you in the language and tone that will move you to understanding.

Now, you two are reborn in the light of Love. Let love be your motivation, for without it wholly, you will only hurt the quest to save humanity. Get back to Earth, put in work. Use your minds and your white privilege to infiltrate the system."

ISHIRINI NA TATU

Three weeks later

3:16 PM

June 9, 2016
Atlanta, Georgia

"Son of a bear? Son of a big, fat, black, flippin,' freakin,'grizzly, durn bear." Captain Lackey kicked the metal trashcan sending it flying across the precinct office.

Luke ducked just in time.

"I told you to let it go," the police captain pointed at Luke. "Other than the car, there is no evidence that anyone else was there that night.

"Captain, I was there. I pulled her over. I don't know what happened or why her body was never recovered, but I'm telling you Miracle Brown was there. If there is even a remote possibility that she was on the scene that April morning, we have to inverstigate it."

"No, *'we'* don't have to do a cotton pickin' thang but keep our streets safe," the captain spat.

"So, you're telling me…

"That you've ostracized yourself." Lackey pointed to the office window, "from your family, brothers and sisters that would take a bullet for you without a moment's thought.

They've ostracized you because ever since you were shot a couple months back, you've undermined me, this department, and that badge by stirring up mess and disobeying my orders to stop investigating the disappearance of this mystery person, Miracle Brown."

"Respectfully Captain Lackey, may I speak freely?"

"Gul Durn it," the Captain stomped. "Why do you ask now? You didn't ask before you ran off at the mouth to the press about that missing girl…"

"Miracle."

"I don't care. There was no trace or sign of her other than that car. And you know better than to speak into a mike without the department's legal counsel."

"I'm telling you Captain – "

"Telling me. You don't tell me anything. In two months you've managed to divide my kingdom," the captain said. "My men are questioning each other's loyalties now that you have started all this race crap."

"Captain, you saw the video." Luke pleaded. "You're black." Luke shook his head, "You're just going to allow…

"No son," The police captain pulled a black crayon out of his pocket and put it up to his face. "See, not even close. I'm an American son. That's the race I belong to."

"But Captain, sir?"

"The video was just a few guys having fun, no one got hurt," the captain said.

"So, you don't have a problem with white men reenacting the beating and shooting of a young black man?"

"Look son this is the last advice I'm ever going to give you," the captain sat on the edge of his desk. "I've been an American all my life. Not a black American or a white American." He banged a fist against his uniformed chest. I'm a red, white, and blue blooded, Ooorahhh! die hard, four-tour decorated Marine, American."

Ameri-conned into being all they wanted you to be, Uncle Tom house negro, Early thought.

"On the battlefield the only color is life and death and that could look like anything and could come at anytime. Americans fought for me beside me and behind me."

Dr. Logun would say that this clown has been crackerized.

"I've seen ten times more people that look like me kill others that looked like me. I've heard seven million more niggas and bitches come from the mouths of people that look like me than the one who do not. So, if all things were equal son, and they are not, if I identified as a white man then I swear to Christmas that I'd be a racist too." The chief sucked in his stomach and pushed out his wide chest before smiling. "I like to call myself an e-racist. I e-race race by not acknowledging it and being above it."

Luke regurgitated Early's thoughts without thinking, "Dog, you got life all fucked up."

"And that," The captain pointed a finger at Luke before backing up behind his desk and taking a seat. "It's like you're two people, Duke. One minute you're talking the queens English, and the next you sound like, like."

"A black man," Luke said.

"No. A nigga." Captain Lackey looked down at something that he was signing, "Your transfer will be in effect in a few days." The captain looked up. "Take the next three weeks to get you some rest. On June 30, at three PM sharp, you will report to USP Terre Haute."

"You're transferring me to a maximum-security federal prison in Indiana. Me," Luke patted his chest. "A white man that just killed a young black male a couple months ago. Everyone knows who I am."

"Son, you're yesterdays news," Captain Lackey said. "Look at the good side?"

"What good side? Sending me to USP Terre Haute... I'll be a target walking into a gun range."

"Che Zapata, the Officer with APD that got shot the day before you killed that boy just took a job as associate warden at USP Terre Haute. Look at him."

"I don't know him. Just because him and I are from here. Hell, Captain, I'm the same skin tone as the guys in the car that shot him."

"Stop trying to make everything about race, Duke. Maybe you should think of resigning, work in security or something if you are so afraid."

"I'm not afraid. I'm just concerned about my well being working inside a prison filled with black men."

"Look, son seventeen unarmed black boys have been killed by law enforcement since you shot that boy." He pointed a finger at Luke. "I'm a fair man." He crossed his arms in front of him. "Duke, I'll tell you what," he pointed a finger at Luke, "You're so concerned about the plight of black males then name five black males, unarmed black males that were killed by law enforcement from the beginning of the year until the day you shot that boy, and I'll tear the order up."

Captain Lackey tapped a foot on the grey concrete floor.

You can't name five can you, Luke thought to Early. *Wow.*

The captain tapped his feet against the concrete floor a few more times before holding up a finger, "Name three."

"I can't think..."

"You just proved my point." The captain picked up the sheet of paper he had just signed.

"What point?" Luke asked.

"That you only care about the black lives that you have a self interest in," the captain held the order out to Luke. "The directive came from your father."

"My father is..."

"Alert and talking." The Captain smiled.

"Huh?"

The Captain's expression transformed from adoration to compassion when speaking about Commissioner Duke. "The Commissioner has been thorugh so much these last coupla months. You, the stroke, and now Ms. Daisy Catterfly."

"Daisy?"

"Went missing a week ago," the captain said.

"Why am I just now finding out?"

"Because you were a – "

"Suspect?"

"A person of interest," he replied.

Luke laughed. "You thought I?"

"Your father," Lackey said.

"I should have known," Luke said before taking a deep breath.

"We found Ms. Catterfly's body this morning around oh-six hundred hours."

Luke shook his head before blowing out the air he held in his lungs.

"Body was found washed ashore on the Chattahoochee, crying shame," Captain Lackey said.

"Where?"

"Half-mile from the Georgia-Alabama line."

"Cause of death," Luke said, "I mean other than the obvious."

"Preliminary reports suggest suicide?"

"Bullshit!"

"What's that supposed to mean, Duke? Do you have anything in regards to the case to share with me Officer Duke?"

"No, but I'm tellin' you…

"Nothing," Lackey said, "You have nothing further to say to me." Lackey pointed a finger at Luke. "If it was up to me you would be on administrative leave and under psychiatric care. The department can't force you, but you really should seek help."

Luke was seething. He had no doubt that his father had killed or had Daisy murdered.

"The only help I'll need is someone stopping me from killing my father," Luke thought before storming out of the captain's office.

ISHIRINI NA NNE

3:46 PM

June 9, 2016
Stone Mountain, Georgia

     Luke was oblivious to the damage the gravel was doing to his Harley Davidson Edition F150 truck. The big brown Ford's tires screeched as he made a hard left onto the Duke Estate grounds. It left a cloud of smoke in its wake as Luke raced down and around the half-mile driveway. He slammed on brakes in front of the wrap around screened in porch.

     He didn't even bother closing the door after jumping out.

     Luke, I know you mad, and I'm fucked up too, but you have to calm down before...

     "Before what? Before I stab him in the heart with my ink pen? Or before I strangle him. Or how about before I beat him to death with my bare hands," he took the stairs two at a time before yanking open the locked screen porch door and walking across the grey wood flooring.

     You go at him like that Luke, he wins. He wants you to do some dumb shit. If he did do Daisy, then it's just as much our fault as it is his. Get it together baby-boy so we can....

120

"Our fault?"

The huge steel front door flew open.

Luke pointed, "You killed Miss Daisy!"

The accused stood in the doorway arms behind his back, a smile as big as life plastered across his face. He rocked back and forth on the balls of his feet. "Nice day son."

"You killed Miss Daisy!" Luke repeated.

"Oh, Miss Daisy is she now." Stonewall rocked back and forth on the balls of his feet.

"Did you?" Luke asked.

"Kill her?" Stonewall put a hand over his chest. "Me?" Stonewall hunched his back and bent his legs into a feeble position before slowly lifting his arm. A pale finger emerged. Trembling. "You!" He broke out in laughter.

"Your stroke?"

"Of genius." Stonewall smiled. "Pure genius. You see boy, a niggra once told me that you find out who really has your back when you're lying on your back."

"I thought you were marrying Daisy," Luke said. "She was supposed to be your first lady once you became governor."

"That's what you were supposed to think. Based on polls sponsored by your Uncle David and the Klavern, the suburb dwelling Georgia niggras that earned forty thousand and up were the voters and most of them thought I was racist. When they polled Georgia middle class white women, many of them felt that I was heartless. So, to make a long story a little shorter, the whore was hired to do two things," A finger shot up. "Show that I'm not a racist and two, show that I have a huge heart."

"How did your relationship with Ms. Daisy impact race?"

"You didn't know?" Stonewall laughed. "You really did not know?" He laughed.

"Know what?"

"The bitch was a niggra?"

"Hell nah."

121

"Her mammy was one of them French-Creole niggra whores from your Uncle David's neck of the woods.

"But she sounded so and she looked so..."

"White," Stonewall smiled. "Spoken from the mouth of a true idiot. You sound like one of them niggras."

Okay, Luke, Early thought. *Get him. Get this racist motha fucka. Get him got dam it!*

Luke ignored Early's thoughts, "So, you've been paying her for three years?"

"The Klavern has," he looked up. "I just thank God that you helped provide a way for the Duke name not to be soiled and to still win the governership if somehow Chump and that dunce Mike Dence don't get into office."

If you ain't gon' put hands on him I will, Early thought.

Not yet. Just relax. Luke thought.

"I don't care how you can twist it in the media to your benefit." Luke teared up. "I," he rested a hand over his heart, "Wanna know how you feel about sending your only son...."

"Ptou," Stonewall spit a glob of brown tobacco onto the pale grey porch floor. "My son died a couple months ago." Stonewall scowled looking Luke from head to toe. "I don't know what," he scowled, "kinda sewer waste is standing in front of me now."

Luke looked down at the wad of tobacco that landed inches from his foot.

I swear ta ALL Mighty if a drop of your daddys spit woulda' grazed the air by our pinky toe.

"Okay, I was wrong," Luke said. "I shouldn't have laid with..."

"I don't care about that whore." He waved a hand in the air. "I know it wasn't my son."

Luke shook his head.

Fuck it. Since he don't believe you exist anymore, let me just warm your hands on his neck for ten seconds. Just ten, dog.

"Chill!"

"Another bastardized niggra word. 'Chill' has everything to do with weather, moving wind, but in niggra language it means relax, stop movement," the elder Duke explained, "Only a retard would bastardize another's language. My son was a lot of things but a retarded niggra was not one of them."

I ain't even going to ask you if this man just called me a retard. I promise I'm not Luke. But I will promise you this. No, better yet I'll show you. Let your hand-crafted-bitch-made-in-America-punk-ass-cracka-nigga daddy come out his mouth wrong again. I mean one more time.

"You done really made a believer out of me boy. I mean, The Exorcist, The Omen, Carrie, none of that satanic crap ever fazed me," Stonewall said. "Wanna know why, boy? It was because I knew that demon possession and all that devil stuff was all Hollywood." He took a hand from behind his back and held a finger in the air, "Until I saw and heard you turn from being a child of God to a shit-turd-talkin' niggra heathen. I'm not talking about a white boy that acts like a niggra. I mean a real niggra." The elder Duke tapped a finger against his temple. "I went to thinkin', a man that gets shot four times, two in both feet at that, doesn't just jump up from the ground and begin arguing with themselves in two dialects. So, to test my theory I had the bitch put on that little show at the hospital."

"What theory?"

"That you're possessed by a niggra."

"What? That's insane."

"I thought so too until I tempted the niggra in you by what the niggra loves and covets most."

"What are you talking about?"

"Our white women," the elder Duke beamed. "Every half ass intelligent White man knows the animal nature of a niggra male. The niggra can't help lusting after the white woman. Why in hell you think niggra girls burn their hair, dye their skin, and starve themselves? They trynna' measure up to a white woman's beauty." He paused. "What I'm sayin' boy is no son of mine would have even looked at Daisy cross-eyed." He pointed. "Only reason you still drawing breath is because of the recent call I got from your Uncle David down in Louisiana."

"What call?"

"Once Chump and Dence takeover the White House you'll hear about it," he smiled. "That is if one of them black baboons behind the wall at Terre Haute doesn't kill you first boy."

Luke, I swear, your fake ass Tommy Lee Jones daddy got one more time to call us boy.

"If you will excuse me, I have a little ole gal coming over to do a little community service."

Luke was at the bottom of the stairs when he heard Stonewall's voice.

"Hey,"

Luke turned.

Stonewall's sadistic smile stared back at him. Stonewall had walked across the porch and was now standing at the edge of the stairs. "Something for you to remember the whore by," he tossed a magazine a few feet away from where Luke stood.

Luke stood there in shock. "Early, did my father just toss a magazine at me like I was a dog?"

Yep, that pretty much sums up what he just did.

Luke looked down at the magazine cover. She wore a red, white, and blue wonder woman outfit. The caption over a smiling Daisy Catterfly read:

BEAUTY BEYOND HIV: ONE BLACK WOMAN'S JOURNEY

ISHIRINI NA TANO

Subjective Realm

Luke and Early stood before ALL.

"HIV?" Luke said.

Pops, it was my bad. I forced Luke to bang, I mean participate in the...

"Both of you screwed my child. And now it seems as if you two may just be screwed."

Put it on me, Pops. Please don't make Luke suffer. He didn't wanna...

"Yes he did. And sun, Luke is a big boy, he could've stopped you."

But, I'm saying, Early cupped his hands and got on his knees. *I'm praying.*

"You're headed in the right direction. But, as I recall the last time you asked Me for advice sun, you said... what was it now, let me think. Oh yeah. I'm good Pops, I'm gon' use my Free will on this '*one.*' The way I see it, the HIV thing is part of the same '*one*' that you allowed your emotions to overpower the use of your *free will*.

Nah, pops. You were there. I didn't force Daisy to do anything.

Thunder exploded. "What do you think about rapists, people that force themselves on others."

Pops, you already know what I think about them.

"That's not what I asked, Early."

Lowest form of life. Rats are better than rapists. I'm the result of a rapist and although momma tried, her body language around me never let me forget what that man did to her, to me.

"By not using your *will* to overpower your animalistic desires you forced yourself onto her. Alcohol is a drug that you knew Daisy was weak for. You did to her what was done to both of your mothers."

ISHIRINI NA SITA

Three Weeks later

3:49 PM

July 3, 2016
Terre Haute, Indiana

"Whachu think," Black looked over at his man Big Rod.

Both men stared at Zion's cell door.

"It's been damn near two hours," Big Rod said. "Only reason you close yourself up with a towel over the window is when you on the toilet or when you got one of them juicy triple X magazines. Then again Z man might've gotten some bad news. Or, or, he might'a got one of dem good smellin' perfume letters from his woman, that is if she survived that freak tornado, which I doubt."

Black jumped in, "Fine mamma jamma like that is way too sexy to be in the ground. If she dead, she ain't gon' ever die in my mind. Tall glass of chocolate. I bet she freakier than a porn star. Sheee-ittt, I bet Z man got a burner phone or he buying cell time off a hack and he talking to his girl on that facetime thing where he can see her."

"You talking like you know she alive."

"Ain't nobody found no body," Black said. "All six foot of that tree bark burnt butter brown Serena Williams fine, big Betty Boop behind." He closed his eyes and smiled, "Big lipped Angela Jolie dipped in African Black. Remy, coke, my tongue down that amazon back. Beyonce hips, Sade lips, pink tongue screaming my name, Black, Black, she moan. The quiet before the storm. Lauren Hill dreads jumping and jibing, booty butt naked bucking while she ridin..."

"Nigga you stupid." Big Rod laughed at his fifty year old riding partner, "How you gon' be lusting after Z-man's woman. You know that's foul dog."

"If she dead like you think she is, ain't nothin' wrong with a little mental bump and grind." The Snoop Dogg look alike jabbed his fat buddy in the chest. "What's foul is you raining acid on my imagination."

"Imagine Zion reining fists on yo' imagination," Big Rod said. "Hell, you saw what he did to Psycho?"

"Nigga, I ain't Psycho."

"I'm just sayin," Big Rod shrugged his shoulders. "Cat ain't been right since Zion put that African Kung Fu finger on his big ass."

Black looked Big Rod up and down and then back up. "You wanna talk about what some hard leg did to anotha' when I'm trying to marinate in my fantasy."

"Marinate," Big Rod shook his head in confusion. "How the fuck you gon' marinate in a damn fantasy," the big man looked at Black, "Your old skeleton-skinny ass just say shit to say it, don't matter if it make sense or not."

Nap walked up behind the two men. "I'm confused."

Both men jumped.

"I sent you crack babies to do one simple thing and that was two hours ago."

Black held a slender long arm out toward Zion's cell. "Z-man done had the towel up over the window the whole time."

"So, you two were just camped out here rapping about my dude having his towel over the door?"

"Yeah, you know…"

"Before you even lie Black, I heard you."

"Nah man, I was just saying, you know." The thin man shrugged.

"Man up baby," Nap said as he walked past the two men, "Zee already know you got Miracle on your mind when you get under the covers with the baby oil."

Black took two hurried steps to catch up. "How he know man. I ain't told no one."

"Calm yo' scary old ass down, Black. The way you were going on about Z-man's woman, didn't take no W.E.B. Dubois to figure out you were making mental babies with her. Hell I ain't trippin'. Ever since she popped up on the news this morning looking like Cleopatra Jones 2016, I done had an unclean thought or twenty myself," Nap said. "That pic Z-man got on his cell wall don't do babygirl no justice."

"Crazy how *they* just now put out a missing persons report out after two months," Black said.

"That ain't crazy," Nap said. Donald Goines' calls that *White Man's Justice.*

Moments later Big Rod and Black saw Nap just standing outside Zion's cell.

"Who is W.B. Dubose?" Black looked up at the big man.

"That's what wrong with our people," Big Rod said. "All we know is the nigga shit. We don't know none of the superman shit our people did. Dumb niggas like you is why we so fucked up."

"Fuck you," Black said.

"You need to get hooked on black phonics like Nap, crackbaby."

"And for the second time I say fuck you. You fat grizzly whale."

"Real talk Black," the fat man began, "You ever see Nap with a book before Zion transferred in?"

The rail thin man looked up a moment. "Nah."

"Look at him now."

The thin man shook his head in disgust. "You's a fat, hatin' ass nugga," Black said. "I ain't no dick ridin' nugga, but Nap, the way he break shit down now... It's like he..."

"Don't scowl up at me crackbaby," Big Rod said, "I ain't hatin' fool, I'm celebratin' my dude. I'm tryin' to tell yo' burnt french fry dumb ass, the change is because of all them black books Zion got him readin'."

"Come to think of it," Black said. "Nap always has a book in is hand, and he always talkin' about bringing black folks together instead of making cake."

"That's what I'm saying you ignorant-no-black history knowin' fool, if you get hooked on black phonics, then you might not say and do all the dumb shit you do," the big man said.

"Your elephant ass still ain't told me who W.B. Dubose is," Black said. "I bet your fat ass don't even know."

"First, the name is W.E.B. Dubois, and the man was the first black man to put schools in the South for black kids and," The big man pointed a finger in the air, "He also created peanut butter."

"I thought Booker T. Carver..."

"Nah, he did some other shit," Rod turned around. "Nap musta finally went inside."

"Don't look at me, I was busy listenin' to yo' big ass," the thin man shrugged his shoulders. "I didn't see shit."

"Black," Big Rod raised an arm toward Zion's cell, "you was facing the damn cell. How you ain't seen nothin'? You musta been dropped on your head one too many times when you was a baby."

"Fuck you, you big fat hostess cupcake! Did your fat ass see where Nap went?"

"If I was facing the damn door I would have," Big Rod said, "Before you, I thought my baby momma was God's only mistake."

Black and Rod continued going back and forth playng the dozens while they stood guard.

Two tatted up white cons walked up. "Fellas," Grey smiled before pointing, "Your man went inside."

Black looked at the behemoth from head to toe and then his eyes stopped on Big Rod. "Do this Aryan brotherhood nigga have a death wish or what?"

Big Rod tried his best to suck up his stomach and push it to his flabby chest before addressing the big white con, "Only win you got is in them Terminator movies my nigga."

Grey put a hand in his beige prison issue sagging pants front pocket. He wasn't ashamed of the swastikas or the burning crosses on his arm. He wasn't afraid of anything other than a nation or a world ruled by primordial animals. Grey hated words like nigger, coon, dog, or any of the disparaging terms others use to describe blacks'. He believed in calling a spade a spade and in regard to black people, they were all primitive animals. With all animals you had to treat them gently, especially when they were scared like these two puppies.

"Gentlemen we did not come here looking for trouble," Grey smiled.

"Nigga, you bring your white ass over to the dog house," Black said, referring to the all Black D-Dorm unit without A/C, "where trouble live and breed. You ain't gotta come lookin'. Like Dominoes, we deliver."

Grey pulled two half full Ziploc baggies from his pocket.

"Good god almighty Jesus J. Christ, that gotta be at least what," Big Rod looked at Black.

"Do I look like a fucking scale?" Black laughed. "I know that's enough shit to keep me high until I die." Black's eyes hadn't moved from Grey's crotch where the top enforcer for the Aryan brotherhood held the two half full plastic bags of heroine.

"All you have to do is ignore us and make sure none of your brothers enters Zion's cell before we leave."

ISHIRINI NA SABA

3:55 PM

July 3, 2016
Terre Haute, Indiana

Nap sat on the bottom bunk facing Zion.

"Look into my eyes," Zion said.

As soon as his eyes locked into Zion's, Nap slid down a never ending rainbow. Every color in the crayon box was represented. The further his mind traveled through Zion's eyes the more peaceful and natural he felt.

Oceans of love washed over his soul. He'd never felt so much love. Tears were flowing as he stared into Miracle's beautiful browns through Zion's eyes.

As Miracle and Zion closed their eyes Nap felt her lips brush Zion's. Every nerve ending in Nap's body burst with joy. He felt everything that Zion did. Every feeling. Her puffy soft lips, her bumpety-bump heartbeat, and her undying love.

And then he had a thought. That one moment of realization had him rising back up the rainbow. He felt regret. Remorse. He wondered how Nap remembered all 216 black women he falsely promised a tomorrow in exchange for their dignity that day. "I'm sorry. I, I, I am so sorry."

He was in the middle of remembering when he stood up from the bunk and grabbed hold of his orange jumpsuit. He began tearing the material as if he were trying to purge himself from his past. Buttons flew across the cell. The orange material tore in two. "Twenty-five years! Twenty-five! I'm sorry. I'm so, so sorry."

Zion jumped up from the bed and grabbed his friend in a bear hug. "Let it go." Zion whispered. "Let it all out."

Racked with several lifetimes of grief, Nap cried, cried, and cried.

"I got you. On everything, king, I got you." Zion held his friend as he began to calm down.

Nap pulled back from Zion's embrace. Nap's eyes burned red with regret. Not even the river of tears that cascaded down his coal brown skin could extinguish the fiery regret that burned in his soul for the women he'd mistreated in his life.

Nap whispered, "Forgive me Davona I didn't know. I'm sorry Reeva. Tasha Please, I swear I'm sorry. Tracy, oh beautiful, kind, sweet Tracy…." He put his face back in Zion's chest while begging forgiveness from all the women he had laid with under false pretenses.

"Now that you see who and what the black woman is," Zion asked. "Do you see what and who you are?"

"I am the black woman and the black woman is me. She is the most beautiful part of me." Nap said.

"Okay." Zion nodded.

"The black woman makes me feel Heaven," Nap smiled.

"Come on now," Zion said. "Make it make sense."

"I felt Heaven in Miracle's eyes and Heaven stared back at me through your eyes, but your eyes were my eyes. I mean, straight up Zion I felt the love. It was like me, you and her were just one big ole ball of electric feel good." Nap shook his head. "It wasn't no freaky shit or nothing like that. It was pure. It a feeling. A feeling like as long as we had each other there was nothing that we could not overcome. It was a knowing. Everything mattered. I knew without a doubt and without reason that you and her had my back. It was as if we were all One being. It was like…"

"Peace. Freedom," Zion said.

"Yeah," Nap pointed. "That's it. Peace. There was only us. I mean Miracle, you, me. It was a conditionless, come as you are, do what you do, type of freedom."

"Okay," Zion nodded and smiled.

"Joy. Love. I felt you Zion as you imagined a perfect place for the queen you loved. I felt all the love you have for Miracle. I felt Stevie Wonder as he sang. Heck, I even felt the *ribbons in the sky* that Stevie was singing about. I felt all the love that everything felt. I felt the tree and all the love from its roots to the tip of its tiniest elephant ear leaf. I felt everything and everything felt me. It was like I was plugged into every life force. Every opposite was in harmony with everything."

"If you felt so much love, why the grief?" Zion asked, referring to his crying out the names of women he had at one time deceived.

Nap crossed both arms over his heart and smiled. "The grief is love. It's part of healing the soul."

Zion stepped forward and touched foreheads with Nap. "I know there is still much that has still to be pulled out of your conscious, and it will be if you will it. Do you understand?

"I do," Nap nodded.

Heads touching, Zion's arm on Nap's shoulder, he asked the former gang leader, "Who am I?"

"The arm," Nap responded without hesitation.

"Who are you?"

"The hand," Nap answered.

"Do you want Heaven?"

Nap nodded his head. "Yes."

Spittle flew out of Zion's mouth, "Are you ready for me to enter your heart, cleanse your soul?"

"I am, " Nap said. "Come into my soul. I'll do the work, just guide me. Everybody gotta feel the love I just felt. I need the world to feel it, feel you Zee."

The sound of African drums suddenly filled the small cell.

Zion placed his other hand on Nap's other shoulder before going into trance. "We are!" he looked Nap in the eyes before bouncing up and down on the balls of his feet. "What does the arm and hand do?"

Nap grabbed Zion by the shoulders before shouting, "Protect the body!"

Both men went from bouncing to jumping up and down in sync with the African drums.

"Who is the body?" Zion asked.

"Everything! Everybody!" Nap shouted.

"Now that you have accepted the truth," Zion stared deep into Nap's eyes. "Be the music. Be the beat. Be the rhythm. Be for any thing. Be for any body. Be peace. Be calm. Be harmony. Be balance. Be before thought. Be me. Finally brother, Be Truth," Zion chanted. Your testimony has been written. You are the sun. You are the light. You are the Truth. It is your job, Truth, to re-right the it. Walk the it. Talk the it. Be the it cause you the it that all come from. Testify to the glory. Not his or mys but our Story. Truth Testimony."

The drum beating stopped. Their heads were still touching when Zion took it down to a whisper, "Do you see?"

"I see." Truth whispered.

"How do we protect everything and everybody?"

"Kill."

"Kill what?" Zion asked.

"Everything that gets in the way of truth," the newly anointed messenger said.

"Nooooo!" Zion shouted right as the cell door flew open.

Grey stepped in the cell armed with a makeshift ice pick, while another had a lock in a sock tied around his wrist.

Since I didn't finish the soul transfer with Truth, I'll have to make quick work of these clowns before my body shuts down and restarts. Zion thought.

Officer Luke Duke walked in behind the Aryan assassins. "Now!" Duke gave the order.

ISHIRINI NA NANE

Subjective Realm

Miracle shook her head no, right before she sprang up from the bed, bumping her head on the metal ceiling in the process. "Noooo!"

"Well damn," the wise sister said. "We've been cooped up in this dead-body-file-cabinet-drawer for three months waiting on love to wake up and she says 'NO' before going back to sleep."

"Sister." The compassionate triplet, Oshun Yourgene placed a consoling palm on the wise sister, Oshun Orthine's back. "Before you have Sister Oya Beyond-See summon the Soul Talkers, you need to take into account how much trauma our beloved has suffered."

All three sisters looked down on Miracle. The peace on the young woman's face had been disturbed.

"A storm is coming," Sister Orthine said.

"I can feel the rumbling in our Beloveds soul," Sister Yourgene said

"Ever since that damned apple," Orthine huffed. "Love has been fighting."

"Beloved looks so tired," Yourgene ran a finger down the side of Miracle's face. "After whippin' on Herod, Goliath, Nero, Washington, Mussolini, Hitler, Crow and so many more," Yourgene said. "She should be exhausted."

"Sisters," Orthine closed her eyes. "We've been preparing love for the apocalypse since the beginning."

Oya Beyond-See drifted into trance, "Locked in this steel box, imaginings of the sly fox, wolves made up like white men, convincing black that their hue is why they can't win. Before technology it was easy to see, the Dichotomy, in a warped society. Did we prepare Miracle to defeat the man?" She paused, "or the mentality."

Yourgene squeezed sister Oya Beyond-See's hand, "The mentality is the reality."

The goddess smiled and then she hummed.

All three fell into the old school harmony. Blue, eight and sixteen notes danced out of Oya Beyond-See, that's when Harold and Teddy P took over her body.

"Wake up Everybody no more sleeping in bed," Beyond-See gently placed her hands over Miracle's eyes. "No more backward thinking, time for thinking ahead."

Orthine placed both hands over Miracle's ears. "The world's changed so very much from what it used to be."

Yourgene placed a hand in back of Miracle's head and one in front. "You're here to kill hatred, end war and poverty."

"What?" Miracle's eyelids fluttered before opening. "Where am I?"

Orthine materialized. "Love," the diety smiled, "You are inside your mind."

"Momma Orthine."

The wise sister smiled, "Ahhh, love you remember me," Oshun Orthine ran a finger through Miracle's long black locks.

Miracle turned to her left. She blinked several times as she questioned the reality before her. Beyonce Knowles was a god? No way.

"Yes way," Oya Beyond-See said as she voiced Miracle's last thought.

"But," Miracle pointed, "I just... You are...

"Oya Beyond-See Knows. But to you daughter-sun, Momma Beyond-See." The sister that represented justice said while running a finger through Miracle's locks. "Momma Beyond-See feel daughter," the sister placed a hand over Miracle's chest. "Momma Beyond-See love daughter-sun. Momma Beyond-See stand on sun 'til end of forever for daughter-sun if need be."

Miracle felt a warm, kind force squeezing her hand.

"Beloved," The compassionate sister's face lit up as she breathed in all the love that filled space before smiling down at Miracle. "We are great and grand, goddess daughters of ALL," the smile that shined on the goddess's heart shaped face sparked all seven million tiny hairs on her head to stand. "I am Oshun Yourgene Bess. Momma Yourgene to you beloved.

"Early," Miracle shouted out of nowhere.

The space began to vibrate.

The two Oshuns held Miracle as tight as they could.

Oya Beyond-See's long golden locks stood up on her head. She extended an arm in front of her as the pale darkness approached, "Stop!"

The darkness slowed, but it kept marching forward.

"Sound!" the goddess of justice summoned the Afri-Aryan, Logic's hit I am the GREATEST.

"Forrrrrr-mation!" The warrior godesss, Oya Beyond-See commanded. The Oshuns stood on both sides of the steel bed rocking to the Afri-Aryan rhythm.

Two huge blue ivy belts of hurricane bullets loaded with the seven seas danced from under the steel bed that Miracle laid on.   In harmony with everything but the approaching pale darkness, they danced their way criss-crossing Oya Beyond-See's bare chest. Twenty-four Tsunami rifles followed as they danced onto Oya Beyond-Sees back where they became wings. The wings waved, lifting the warrior goddess up into space.

The music stopped when the pale darkness stepped into the space Miracle and the sisters occupied.

His size nine white gators where the first to appear. Then the British male voice, "Hello loves," The chairman stepped into Miracle's mind. "Allow me to introduce myself," he bowed. "Constance Greenspan."

Oya Beyond-See pulled a seven-foot Tsunami gun from her back.

"All that rage," the chairman said as he walked through the gun and touched Oya Beyond See's cheek.

"Damn, damn, damn," he said pulling back his sizzling, burned and hurt finger.

"Play with fire. You get burned," the sister of Justice said.

"Beyonce, you are so beautiful that I momentarily forgot who you were," he said putting his pale burnt finger in his mouth. "Forgive me."

"Beyond-See not Beyonce."

The Billy Bob Thornton look alike placed his burnt finger in his mouth before shrugging his shoulders. "Tomato, tomorrow, it's all grey.

"See what happens when you lay an unclean finger on justice," Oshun Orthine pointed to the chairman's burnt finger.

"Embrace the rage, sweetness, all of you," The chairman said looking from Beyond-See to Miracle. "You had the power love. You could have kept driving. Early tried to tell you."

"Beloved," OshunYourgene pleaded with Miracle, "Listen to our voice and our voice only."

The chairman laughed. "Don't fall for the okey doke again, Miracle. Early is dead because of you. Dead!"

"Early, I'm so sorry," Miracle wailed.

"Cracker minded, you've been blinded, took your humanity and now you can't find it," The chairman chanted, using hip hop legend KRS-1's voice and lyrics.

"Hold up," Oya Beyond-See pulled a Tsunami rifle and took aim at the chairman. "He don't love you like I love you," she chanted in Beyonce's voice. "A meal to him, that's all he see, you are meant for one thing Miracle and that's to serve his evil reality."

Before the chairman could rebut, she pulled the trigger. A sea of blue ocean exploded into and onto him.

"Love," Oshun Orthine squeezed Miracle's hand, "It's time to go back. The chairman has grown much stronger than we had anticipated."

"Back to where Momma Orthine?"

"Ah sugar, honey, ice tea," the wise sister threw her hands up in frustration, "Love still doesn't remember."

The compassionate sister put a comforting hand on her frustrated but wise sister's back. "Our beloved will remember when it's time. Until then sister, we have to be still so we can hear ALL tell us how to guide our beloved Oba back to us."

"Beloved," Oshun Yourgene smiled, "When you open your eyes you will be blind. When you open your ears you will be deaf."

"How will I be able to see," Miracle asked. "Hear?"

"Oya Beyond-See my beloved," Oshun Yourgene explained, "you just have to open your heart. You will feel her."

"Feel her?" Miracle had a confused expression on her face.

Oya Beyond-See pointed to the pink Iphone 7 that appeared in Miracle's hand.

"Thank you Momma B-See," Miracle said. "Is your number programmed?"

Oya Beyond-See went into trance before the O'Jays took over her voice and body. Her legs started moving to the harmony of the vibrations that began before Eddie Levert's voice came out of her mouth. ""I love Music, sweet, sweet music."

"Beloved," Momma Yourgene looked into Miracles eye's. "What sister is saying is that all you have to do is click on Pandora and tune into a soul music station."

"What about my ears, how will I be able to hear the music if I'm deaf?"

"You don't hear music," Oya Beyond-See put a hand over her heart, "You feel music."

"My Beloved," Momma Yourgene placed a warm hand over Miracle's chest, that's where I'll be. And, Beloved?"

"Yes, Momma."

"Like Sister Justice say, we will allways be as long as you believe..."

"I'm backkkkkk," the chairman emerged. He morphed into a foggy gas that flooded space.

Miracle reached right through it, "Momma Orthine, Momma Yourgene, Momma Beyond-See," she called out. When the fog began to clear she saw a motionless Zion layed out on a gre cement floor covered in blood.

ISHIRINI NA TISA

3:58 PM

July 3, 2016
Terre Haute, Indiana

Miracle didn't know how she had become a butterfly and didn't have time to care. Zion was in trouble. She flew through the maximunm security federal prison. She had no idea where she was flying, but she knew she'd land where ever Zion was.

Moments later she flew through a crack in a door and landed on a ceiling. The world was downside up and seven thousand times bigger as she searched the space below.

"Zion!" she screamed.

Four men covered in blood, two white, two black. They were layed out in unnatural positions on the blood grey cell floor.

She timidly flapped her wings and flew down to the bottom bunk to get a closer look.

She felt heavy footsteps moving quickly in the cells direction so she flew under the bed just as a prison guard came into the cell.

She couldn't believe her eyes. Was this a nightmare? No way. No way. No way could she be staring at the same cop that killed Early. He was dead. She saw his dead body as she ascended through the light. She had no doubt in her mind that Officer Luke Duke had also killed Zion, just like she had no doubt that she would make him and all like him pay.

THELATHINI

11:33 PM

July 3, 2016
Decatur, Georgia

     Miracle threw off the ash grey sheet that covered her before stepping out of one of the many refrigerated dead body file drawers at the Dekalb County morgue.
     She walked out into the corridor before opening her eyes. Nothing. Blind as a bone. She saw better with her eyes closed.

THELATHINI NA MOJA

thirty-three days later

3:33 PM

August 6, 2016
Terre Haute, Indiana

Zion and Truth had been in Terre Haute penitientarie's death row, one-man cell segregation unit for over a month without being charged. Both men knew that the murder charges would come as soon as the powers that be found a way to make them stick.

In the meantime, the prison kept Zion doped up on the powerful anti-psychotic depressant Thorazine.

"Open up seven!"

"Opening up seven."

The steel grey cell door slid open.

"Jesus Christ?" The Alabama Junior Senator placed his liver spotted hand over his nose.

"Lights on in seven," Lieutenant Quisling barked.

"Lighting up seven."

"46222-019." Quisling stepped inside the small grey cell.

The black male sitting cross-legged on the bunk looked like Owen 'Nap' Cowherd but that's where the resemblance ended. The man meditating on top of the grey wool blanket was just as Zion had renamed him. Truth.

"Boy, this one here smells worst than a team of dead dogs," the silver haired man standing behind the officer said in a heavy southern drawl.

"Lieutenant Quisling, sir."

The Alabama State Junior Senator removed his hand from his nose while turning to the Lieutenant. "What'd you just say to me boy?"

"Respectfully sir, you addressed me as boy and I just reminded you that," the large black man pointed to the gold bars on his white shirt, "I carry the rank of Lieutenant." He smiled. "Lieutenant Wolf Quisling."

The southern politician frowned before slowly looking the large man from head to toe. His gaze slowly rose until his cold blue eyes stared into the lieutenant's deer-brown orbs. "I know who you are boy. Did you forget you already introduced yourself?" The Junior Alabama Senator, Jeffery Beauregard Suppressions waved his hand at the large black man as if he were shooing a fly. "Now get a got damn hose, bleach and some Lysol."

"Uhm, Senator, sir, we are under strict orders not to allow him," the officer pointed to Truth, "out of this box."

Supressions turned his back and left the cell. "Who in hell said anything about takin' the boy outta the cell. Get some bleach and some soap, spray the walls the floor the bed and spray that," he looked at Truth, "boy down real good."

"Sir, the water pressure per square inch that is released from our fire hose will peel some of the inmates' skin off."

"Don't worry 'bout the mule being blind boy, just load the damn wagon," he said.

"My name is Lieutenant Wolf Narcisse Quisling, not boy."

The Senator pointed a pale finger at the much larger Lieutenant. "Boy, you better watch the way you talk to a white man." He pointed to the Lieutenant's breast pocket. "Don't matter if the bars are little gold ones on your coat pocket or bars like those," he pointed to the bars on the small cell window. "They still cages that folks like me regulate. Now do like I say, and I don't mean get one of your lackies to clean this shit up. You do it boy." He turned his back and began walking away. "Come get me when this shit is thoroughly hosed down and disinfected."

****

Truth stood in the middle of the cell floor chanting. He'd travelled outside of his body into the reality that his mind created. Unaware what was going on back in the isolated underground death row chamber of the prison, Truth was in his own world.

It was pandemonium. Over fifty-thousand people were shouting, "Truth! Truth! Truth!"

At least another thirty-thousand shouted, "Testimony! Testimony! Testimony!"

Truth stood in the tunnel. Water was pouring off of him, and he wasn't even on stage yet. He felt like he was drowning while his skin was being ripped from his body. If the Georgia dome wasn't filled with so much love, he might have felt the pain but even if he did feel the hurt, the love was too overpowering for the hurt to be painful.

The noise was deafening, and his body was burning wet as he jogged out of the tunnel followed by his twelve riders.

Moments later all spotlights were on the dark coffee brother.

"It's your world squirrel," Zion said before stepping back. "Have no fear fam. Just do your thing."

The Urban Gele removed his hoodie, took a knee, and looked up.

The baseline dropped.

"Uncle Ogun give me strength, Momma Oshun give me wisdom, Father Shango order my words as I come awake. I know revenge is yours, but I don't know how much more I can take. It's so much more than my black life at stake. Forgive them all they know not what they do. Envy and greed got them blind to you. Allow me to be your spark, love them to life, and if they are too far gone, allow me to be the sword of justice to turn out their lights, Amen and Ase."

Truth stood up. Water was pouring off of him. His chest was tight, his legs were weak, but his spirit was strong.

****

"Why you shaking your head, boy?" Lieutenant Quisling asked as he backed out of the cell.

Truth stood in the middle of the cell, arms crossed, eyes sharp. Water dripped off of his naked and bloody body as he shook his head. "I feel sorry for you brotha," Truth said. "Truly, I do."

"Brotha," the lieutenant spat. "My brothers don't sell drugs, steal, or rob. Feel sorry for yourself. You the one stuck in this box."

"Brotha Quisling," Truth looked at the lieutenant. "It'll be much easier for me to get outta this box than it'll be for you to get out of the box," he tapped his forehead, "that you're a captive in."

"Sounds like something a person with no hope of ever being free would say," The big man said.

"Lieutenant, these walls can't confine me just like man's laws can't re or de-fine me. I'm free to be who and what I want to be. I control my thoughts, my dreams, even the way I choose to socialize this physical reality. That's freedom brotha.

On the other hand you have no dignity because you have forgotten the two million years of struggle that you have endured to get to this place in time."

"What the?" Officer Leach stood at the cell door carrying the dry towel, semi-clean underwear, and orange jumpsuit.

Quisling held the fire station issue hose as he turned to his best friend and subordinate officer. "Thirty-four years, and I don't know how many I done hosed down. None have ever stood up to the water pressure. Boy didn't blink an eye."

"I wouldn't have believed it if I ain't stood here and seen it myself, Quis." Officer Leach placed the towels and the clothes on the grey cement floor right inside the cell before giving his assessment. "Hell, look at his arms, chest, and legs. Looks like a runaway slave after the whip."

Dripping blood and water on the cement floor, Truth took a step forward.

Before his foot was down good, Quisling and Leach jumped behind the door where they slammed and locked it.

They stared through the six-inch cell door window.

"Frank, you see the boy's feet and hands?" The lieutenant asked as he rolled up the fire hose.

"Jesus Christ!" Leach said as Truth reached out revealing holes in his hands the same size as the ones in the middle of his feet.

Ten minutes later Quisling and Suppressions stood outside Truth's cell.

The Alabama politician turned to the lieutenant. "God dammit, what part of clean this shithole and that shit sitting on the bed, did you not understand Lieutenant?"

"I did. Hosed him and the cell down for a good twenty minutes, sir," Quisling pointed at Truth. "Look at the cuts all over his…" The guard took three hurried steps inside and grabbed Truth's left hand. "What happened to the." The lieutenant turned Truth's hand over before grabbing the other.

"I swear sir," the lieutenant shook his head from side to side. He pointed at Truth while looking at Suppressions. "The boy stood right here where we are now sir. I swear he was just now dripping blood and water. Cuts all over his body." The lieutenant shook his head. "This doesn't make sense."

The Junior Senator's face was an iron mask.

"Frank saw him." The lieutennant pointed a finger at Officer Leach, his best friend, "Frank!"

A moment later Officer Frank Leach was at the cell door.

The Alabama State Senator had his cell phone to his ear.

"Tell him Frank."

Frank's eyes roamed from Truth to the Senator and finally at the Lieutenant. "Tell him what?"

Quisling looked at his friend. The man he had worked with for over thirty years. The man his children called Uncle Frank.

"I brought the towels and clothes just like you instructed me to, Lieutenant Quisling sir."

Right as Suppressions removed the Blackberry from his ear, two guards appeared in the doorway. "Lieutenant Quisling, sir, please come with us."

"Frank, you just gon' stand there and not say anything," Quisling pounded his chest with an open palm. "This is me, Quis. Tell him about the cuts, welts and holes in the inmates hands and feet."

The Senator turned his head to Frank.

"Stress. The job." Leach turned to the Senator and shrugged his shoulders. "I had hoped he would have gotten treatment for his delusions."

Moments later, Truth, Suppressions and Leach were alone.

"Boy," he waved a sheath of papers in the air, "Have you ever played the game Monopoly?"

"My name is Truth sir, not boy."

"That's not what I asked," Suppressions said. "Monopoly, you ever played."

Can't say I have, but I play the game Life every day."

"These papers are your get out of jail FREE card. All you have to do is…

"That's not free, sir."

"If you let me finish."

"No need to," Truth said.

"All you have to do is…

"Forgive my interruption again sir," Truth said. "You said the word FREE and then you followed it with all you have to do. Now, is it a FREE get out of jail card or does my walking out of here depend on me doing something for you?"

The Senator smiled. "You are a smart one huh?"

"No sir. I am an intelligent child of Creation."

"Okay, intelligent child of whoever," Suppressions said. "I'm authorized to offer you the deal of a lifetime." The Senator pitched the stapled sheath of papers onto the bed. "Just sign on the back page, and you'll be released on January 20, 2017. In less than six-months, you can be a FREE man. Your life sentence vacated."

Truth flipped through all twelve pages.

"I did not see anything in these pages that makes me feel that you have the power to give me or anyone else freedom."

"Boy, you can't read then. It clearly states on line 27."

Truth interrupted, "Line 28 not 27. And that line just states that I will be released, and my record will be expunged," Truth said.

Suppressions laughed. "I'm just an ole country white man with a jurisprudence degree in Law among others. Last time I checked getting out of prison is freedom."

Truth nodded. "I'm just an ole intelligent African king with the knowledge and understanding of those who came before me and the last time I checked, you couldn't give me what you do not have."

"What?"

"Freedom." Truth smiled.

"Boy, you have no idea who you are talking too."

"I know absolutely unequivocally who I am talking to. A little sixty-nine year old boy that has never grown into manhood. A boy that hates the color of my skin almost as much as he hates the color of his own. That is pain brotha. You have no idea how much stress you're putting your mind and body through by hating yourself. Hate is hell, and I don't want know parts of it. Ain't nothing FREE about hate."

"Look you fucking retard," The Senator threw a pen onto the bed. "Sign the goddam' last page or I swear your black ass will never see the outside of this six by nine box."

Truth laughed. "There was a time not so long ago that I might have been scared. I doubt it but back then, I might have signed this garbage. That was before I remembered that you can't do anything to me that I don't allow you to." Truth smiled. "You can't even kill my body, brother. Your pale grey hate scientists will tell you that Black matter can not be created nor destroyed, it only changes forms."

"Look, I don't care if you found Muhammed, Buddha, whoever. I'm offering you freedom for just signing a got-damn statement."

"A statement accusing my dude of murder. You read the report brotha. Grey Forrest and Dusty White rushed into Zion's cell thrusting an ice pick and swinging loaded socks. Did you forget that Zion was in a coma for three days, and I had to have an appendectomy as a result of the attack?"

"I know what the damn thing says. Now I'm telling you what I'm saying." He paused. "It doesn't mean a hill of beans to me if you sign the damn thing or not."

Truth smiled. "What is a hill of beans worth these days?"

"Say again." Suppressions frowned.

"You said it doesn't mean a hill of beans if I sign. From the sale of a hill of beans, I imagine it wouldn't cover your flight from Montgomery, Alabama all the way up to Terre Haute, Indiana. It musta' took a lot of money or the potentiality to make a lot of money for a cracker such as yourself to come and beg me to assist you in hurting my people."

"I don't beg anyone for any damn thing," he sneered. "Especially from your kind. Whether you sign the damn thing or not, Zion Uhuru Jones will never get out of here. Do you here me? Never!"

"Never say never," Truth said.

"Never! Never! Fucking Never!" the Senator exploded.

"If you insist, I'll join in," Truth said. "I will never! Never betray Zion or myself again. Fucking never."

The Senator put the phone to his ear. Moments later he spoke into his Blackberry; "He won't cooperate."

The Senator removed the phone from his ear and placed it on speaker.

"Cowherd, Donald Chump here. Take the fucking deal or when I become president in three months, I'll make sure that you get the chair for not only Grey and White's murder, but Zion's murder also. Now I know your Christ is still breathing but believe this if you do not believe anything else. He won't be on January 21, 2017 unless you cooperate."

THELATHINI NA MBILI

Thirteen days later

3:36 PM

August 19, 2016
<u>Lithonia, Georgia</u>

Dummy, you just drove right past the church, Early thought.

Luke made a U turn.

"You just as dumb as I am. Just like I was, you were trying to figure out what January 21, 2017 meant and why Zion had carved that date in the brick wall of his cell before the Feds moved him and Truth from disciplinary segregation to Death Row a few weeks ago."

Luke pulled his tan F150 into the First Afrikan Church parking lot.

Park in the handicap parking right there at the end. To the left dummy, Early thought to Luke.

"We're not handicapped. I can't do that," Luke said.

Idiot, I'm handicapped as a... Well you know. I'm sharing your body, if that ain't handicapped, besides it's

156

Saturday afternoon. Just get outta the truck, put the hoodie over your head, and follow my lead.

"This is a church. I don't see why I have to hide. Don't you think I'll stand out wearing a grey hoodie in this ninety degree Georgia heat."

Not nearly as much as you will if a First Afrikan sees you.

"A church member?" Luke giggled.

A conscious First Afrikan church member.

"Why do black people always refer to themselves as Africans?" Luke asked. "There's fifty-three countries on the continent and ten times that many different cultures at least."

I'm not talking about any land dummy. Afrika is a consciousness.

"Okay, but you still didn't answer my question."

I did, but you didn't understand my thoughts, so I'll make it plain. If Muhammad, Reverend King, Carnell, Carlson, Hakeim, Robert, Daddy Cabral and a host of others got word that the man that killed me is on church grounds, we won't be breathing for long.

"I'm a cop. I mean I was a cop."

You could be the Queen of England, a First Afrikan could care less. If they think you killed one of theirs, it's a wrap. I'm not telling you what I think. I'm telling you what I know. Any one of them and a few sisters won't even flinch before taking us out.

He pulled the truck into the handicapped space next to a silver BMW motorcycle.

After putting the hoodie over his head, Luke got out the truck and took long strides around to the back of the church over the bridge and past the huge baobab tree into the cover of a nature trail. Up ahead, a dark brother in jeans and a black and green dashiki sat in a grey metal folding chair with his back to Luke.

"Doc?"

The charcoal-Jesus bronzed leader stood up, turned to Luke, and smiled.

"This racist cracka pulled me and Mira over for nothing, Doc. I told Mira to keep driving. She pulled over instead. Luke told me to shut up and then he called me boy. I asked if he ever heard of Black Lives Matter. He asked me if I ever heard of White man's Justice. Swear ta God Doc, dude just comes around the car, pulls me through the window and starts beating my ass, I mean my behind, Doc. Next thing I know I wakes up and Mira sayin' somethin'about a recording on her phone. Dude shoots Mira before he blasts me. BANG! BANG! BANG! Kills me, right. So like my spirit is rising out of my dead body, and Zion was right there. He told me not to worry, that everything was going as planned and then I met God, but we call the spirit ALL cause God is all and in all since God created all. But I don't know what happened to Mira. They say she's dead, but I know she's not. Oh, yeah Doc, I know I look like the white cop that shot me, but I ain't. I'm in his body. No, I mean..."

"Brotha," Dr. Logun put a hand on Luke's shoulder. "Breathe son," the Spiritual leader closed his eyes and took a deep breathe to demonstrate. "If you don't slow down you are gong to give me a heart attack, and brotha we gon' have a serious problem then. I've been searching for my queen for near half a century, and I've just recently found her," the sixty-year old leader's face lit up before turning serious, "Take me away from my sunshine, and you are really going to need a miracle to save you."

"Okay, Okay," Luke took a deep breath. *"I'll slow down,"* he breathed again.

A squirrel jumped right over Luke's foot and Early's thoughts were again regurgitated through Luke's vocal chords.

"So anyway, well, I just know we need you and the council of clerics for real now cause Zion asked us to set this thing up with these Aryan brotha hood crackas who were trying

to get at Zion in the Pen at Terre Haute, cause we worked there as a guard for a minute. Luke's racist police commissioner daddy had us transferred there, but that's another story altogether, but anyway, yeah, uhm where was I, oh yeah. So, me and Luke set it up, and Zion and Nap, I mean Truth ended Grey and Dusty, the two white dudes. So now Zion's spirit jumped into Nap and then Nap became Truth or no, Nap was Truth before Zion jumped in him." He paused to ponder. "*Doc, I done smoked up too many brain cells over the years, I done forgot if Truth was Truth before Zion or if Nap woke up and became Truth after Zion entered his body,*" he closed his eyes and tapped a finger to his head a few times as he thought. "*Let me back up a little, Doc. Okay, when I got to Terre Haute, Zion had me set it up so that Grey and White would have the opportunity to take out him and Nap, who is Truth now.*"

"That doesn't make sense, Early," Dr. Logun said.

"*I know, right.*" Luke said.

"Help me understand, son?"

"*Heck, I don't understand myself Doc,*" Luke said. "*Everything went so fast, we just did what was asked of us.*" *Heck, I can't even tell you how Zion knew that Nap's soldiers was gon' sell 'em out to Grey and White, but sure nuff, they did just like he said,*" he paused as he remembered, "*Yes, I do. I forget Zion is the Messiah or half of the Messiah, while Mira is the other half. Did I tell you I met ALL, Doc. He ain't nothing like you think. I know I'm all over the place but am I going too fast still?*"

Dr. Logun sat back down in the metal folding chair before placing his arms in the back of his head.

"*You think I'm insane, don't you Doc? You don't believe I'm still alive and living in this man's body?*"

The First Afrikan spiritual leader said, "Brotha, if we go by the Euro-socialization of the word and the idea of insanity then hell yes brotha, you are insane. If we use the Euro-measuring stick to quantify and or qualify insanity then I am insane for knowing that spirits exist, let alone knowing that your spirit has integrated with the host spirit in another's body."

"So, you believe me?"

"Son, I know who I am which is the equivalent of knowing who you are. Ubuntu, I am because we are, and we are because I am." The pastor stood up and looked up at the Afrikan sunshine in the American sky. "We are Afrikan hue by birth and rebirth seven thousand times over and every sound that has come from your mouth thus far, I see." He placed a hand on Early's back. "Spirit merging is nothing new son. Now slow down and take a seat," Dr. Logun held his hand toward the empty grey metal chair next to him.

Luke took a couple steps before pushing the chair down to make sure it was firmly planted in the dirt before he sat.

"This time organize your thoughts and continue with calm."

"Okay, Doc. I'm calm. Okay," Luke closed his eyes. *"Oh yeah,"* his eyes popped open. *"How about Chump, Doc? He ain't even president, and no way they gon' make him president, but Chump still pulled strings and got that old racist Alabama State Senator, Suppressions to come up to Terre Haute, Indiana outside of his jurisdiction and offer Zion, I mean Truth, a deal, a deal that Chump is involved in. Zion even knew this was going down."*

"That's it Dr. Logun sir.*"* Luke interrupted Early.

"I was wondering when you were going to enter the conversation Luke," Dr. Logun said.

"Zion told Truth to take the deal because it wouldn't actually be like he would be crossing Zion out because Zion's spirit merged with Truth's soul."

"Yeah, Luke but Truth turned down the deal."

"Dr. Logun, I know this sounds outlandish and it is. Furthermore sir, what I can't figure out is how an Alabama State Senator can offer immunity or any kind of deal to a federal inmate, and then how is Donald Chump even involved?"

"Money," Dr. Logun said. "Crackerization is spreading quickly in this country and if we aren't careful, the king cracker will worm his way into the presidency."

"Crackerization?"

"Money over hue-manity."

THELATHINI NA TATU

Seven Weeks Later

1:33 PM

Lithonia, Georgia
<u>October 16, 2016</u>

I can't blame no one but my self.

"What's that supposed to mean?" Luke asked as he bent the corner at Salem and Panola.

It means I have to have rocks for brains for listening to a white boy that got his education on Black life from the TV, and the school system.

Luke turned into the second entrance. "Everything's not black and white Early."

Maybe not, but everything is a shade of grey. Early thought. *Since you don't believe pig is pork, I'll have to suffer with your dumb ass. Maybe then...*

"The sun is shining. It's a beautiful Sunday afternoon," Luke said as he pulled into a parking space. "Look, there are still a couple of cars in the parking lot."

Shit!

"What?"

Daddy C, Toussant, and Brotha Malik. What are they doing in the garden? Toussant is the only one on the Creation Care Council, Early thought.

"Creation care?" Luke asked.

The grounds preservation team, Early thought. *Toussant is the only one out of the three that is supposed to be working in the church garden.*

"Calm down Early. You act like those three old men are gon' do something to us." Luke got out of the truck. "I should have came and explained what happened that night I shot you way before now. You forget I am a six foot three, two hundred thirty pound white man that deadlifts and bench presses more than all three of them old men weigh, and I was a Navy Seal."

Claude Cabral, known by most as Daddy C, stuck his pitchfork in the dirt before walking out of the church garden followed by the other two.

"Fellas, I'm Early. Early Morning," Luke said as the three men approached. "I know I look white, but I'm Early." Luke directed his attention to the church member that looked like a sixty something year old Malcolm X. "Daddy C, you know me. Now, I'm white. I ain't got no record anymore, so you can take me to the range now. We used to talk about you taking me shootin', remember? You always say never pull your gun unless you gon' use it."

Claude reached in his front pocket pulled out a small gun.

"POW! POW! POW!"

"I don't know how he knew, but the cracka was right," Claude said while putting the gun back in his pocket, "Cracka was right though, I always say never pull a gun unless you gon' use it."

"You had to shoot him here Claude on church grounds?" Toussant asked.

"After I pulled my pistol, I couldn't go back," Claude said, "Cracka killed my boy, Early and he gon' come up here smilin' at us. Hell, and we still ain't heard no word from Miracle."

"You didn't think that he might have information about what happened to her?" Brotha Malik asked.

"I did, but by then I had already pulled my gun." He shrugged his shoulders. "Had to follow through then."

"What are we going to do with him?" Toussant asked.

Brotha Malik looked down. "At least no one can see the body from the street."

The older Malcolm X looking Cabral looked to the church. "Maybe that's what people need to see. We oughta nail the cracka to the cross and put his ass right out front. Cracka killed one of ours and gon'come up to our house, sheee-iiiitttttt. Fuck em, and don't excuse my French because it's Sunday," Claude said. "Hell, I'll turn my self in."

Brotha Malik put one in the mind of Nat King Cole with short hair. When he spoke he even enunciated his words like Cole did in his era. "You'll be in jail, but Toussant and I will be just like that one," Brotha Malik said as they stood over Luke's body.

Claude looked at Brotha Malik and then at Toussant.

"Brotha Malik is right," Toussant agreed. "Lena would kill us both if we allowed the cops to take you."

"That's exactly why I'm calling Trane," Brotha Malik said as he scrolled through his contacts.

"That's my cat, ya dig," Claude smiled. "Youngblood got a lot of me in him."

Toussant laughed, "Claude, when did you escape from a maximum security federal prison. Hell, Claude when were you even in prison?"

"Up until thirty-six years ago, shit man, my life was a prison, ya dig?"

"Musta been the time you traded them streets for the church?" Toussant said.

"Nahhhhh," Claude shook his head, "That's when my baby came into my life."

Brotha Malik signaled for Claude and Toussant to focus their attention his way.

"Trane," Brotha Malik said into the phone.

"One sec," Coltrane replied. "Give the damn ball to Gore. Idiot. Why would you throw the ball three times when you are on the one yard line? Why Chuck? Luck, can you explain that to me cause I don't understand. Frank Gore has been the workhorse the whole game," Coltrane turned his attention back to the phone, "I'm sorry Brotha Malik, but my Colts are trying to give this game away."

"I understand."

"Finally," Coltrane shouted, "It's about time. I mean it's only fourth down. I been telling ya'll idiots to put Gore in the last three downs." Coltrane was on his feet. "They finally about to run it."

"Gimme that," Claude snatched the phone from Brotha Malik.

"Nooo!" Coltrane shouted. "Chuck, what the hell are you doing? You idiots deserve to lose. I can't believe they put Gore in on fourth and one and still threw the ball. Luck's unlucky dumb...

"Coltrane, this is Daddy C, get up right now and come to the church. We need you."

THELATHINI NA NNE

1:33 PM

October 16, 2016
Decatur, Georgia

Miracle's godmother, Assata Jackson, was on the phone when she pulled her red Dodge Charger into her apartment complex. She felt bad, having passed judgement on a sista' whom she never had taken the time to listen to until she gave the message at First Afrikan this morning. Her bestfriend Cherry wasn't making her feel any better.

"Girl, didn't Monrovia bring it this morning?" Assata got out of her car. "Let me take you off speaker girl." She put the cell phone to her ear."

"Oh, so Monrovia's no longer the hef...

"No need to bring up the past girl. I may have just possibly erred in judgment," the Angela Bassett look a like said while walking up the flight of stairs to her apartment.

"For three years you did not even come to church when Dr. Phoenix gave the message." Cherry said. "All because you assumed that Monrovia looked at you crazy while you were talking to her husband Denmark. I told you that she didn't have the spirit of jealousy in her."

"I know she don't now, but back then. Hmph," Assata grunted, "You didn't see the cross-eyed crazy look she gave me when I was just having a friendly conversation with Denmark."

"Well, what do you think about Dr. Monrovia Phoenix now?"

Assata placed the iPhone back on speaker phone before putting it in her bra so she could free both hands up to look through her purse.

"Okay, I misjudged her. Monrovia is the truth. The way she married Black feminism to faith, I have never heard anyone," she put her hand down the top of her dashiki dress to re-secure the rising iPhone in her bra, "I mean she had every woman in church glowing this morning. Cherry, let me get off this phone so I can find my damn keys," You know I can't walk and chew bubblegum at the same time."

"Bye girl."

As soon as the call disconnected, she reached in her bra pulled out the phone and pressed redial.

Cherry answered on the first ring. "Okay girl, you need a man.

"Tell me something I don't know," Assata said. "I don't know how we got sidetracked talking about the Phoenix family, but girl, I originally called to ask if you saw that clown on CNN last night bumping for Chump holding two American flags in his hand."

"I wish and I pray that he would just die. Literally. I can not believe that after all TJ Money had done that people are flocking to his ministry," Cherry said. "I don't care if he moved form Georgia to L.A., everyone knows what he did. The man was on death row a few years ago. I mean who rapes, robs, and murders, gets sentenced to death and five, six years later has a huge flock of followers, black and white that praise him as if he's the second Coming."

"That fake ass Bishop TJ Money," Assata said. "Correction. I meant The Hand."

"I ain't shaking it, and I ain't kissing it. Wouldn't wipe my behind with it," Cherry said. "I can't believe that fake-bootleg-made-in-Taiwan-knock-off-negro changed his name to The Hand."

"I still haven't gotten passed the fact that people are back following him," Assata said. "I have to admit though, his *Nobody's Perfect Ministry* is a pretty good gimmick."

"BAAAAAABYYYYYY?" Assata heard Cherry's man call out.

"It must be halftime," Cherry said.

"We gotta go back to the church," Coltrane said. "Daddy C needs us right now baby."

"Girl, let me run. You hear my lion roaring."

"Okay, give that king of yours a big kiss and tell him how proud we are of the work he's doing with our First Afrikan children."

As soon as Assata took a step inside her apartment door, the tiny hairs on her legs tingled. She felt a presence in the small two bedroom apartment. Slowly, she pulled out her gun and walked into the living room. When she was satisfied, she moved through the condo the way Treble had taught her when he shared her body.

"Auntie, is that you?" Miracle walked out of the bedroom that doubled as hers and a guest bedroom.

Assata put the .380 back in her purse. "Thank ALL," she raised her hands to the Heavens. Thank ALL," the glowing caramel sista put her hands over her mouth, eyes emitting eons of love at the young lady that stood in front of her, "My baby."

Godmother and daughter embraced. Tears of joy and relief washed down Assata's face while anger creeped its way into her heart. Anger because Miracle hadn't reached out to anyone since before Early's death back in April. Miracle hadn't even bothered to show up at Early's homegoing service. Assata reared back and slapped the young woman.

"Auntie!" Miracle grabbed her cheek.

"That's for scaring me to damn death. Six months ago you just haul off and disappear without telling no one. If I wasn't so happy and relieved to see you I'd do a lot worse than slap you girl, now where the hell you been and why didn't you call? I didn't know what to damn think."

"Treble didn't tell you?" Miracle asked.

"Hell nah. The night that Early was shot…"

Miracle's face contorted into a mask of pain and hurt before she slid down the wall to the hallway floor with her hands over her face.

"Baby," Assata got down on the floor and held Miracle as she cried.

"They killed him Auntie. They killed him and got away scott free."

"I know, baby. I know." Assata held the grieving young woman in her arms. "I didn't, but a lot of us thought the police had killed you too and disposed of your body."

"I was there when they killed him Auntie. Early didn't do anything. He told me to drive off, but I didn't. I didn't believe it. I believed in hue-manity. I didn't think the cop would harm him, let alone kill him," Miracle cried. "He was unarmed Auntie. They shot him down like he was a rabid animal."

Assata rubbed her goddaughters back, "I am so, so sorry baby. Hours earlier, the day before that crazy storm," she rocked Miracle in her arms as she explained, "I was on a morning run when Treble and I saw this Hispanic cop walk up to an Impala like the one you had before you got that Mercedes. Looked like a routine traffic shop, when next thing you know, a peach-pink arm reached outta the car and shot the cop before speeding off. I was only a few feet away, so we ran over to the dying brotha. I thought we were going to try and save the brotha when Treble took his hand and said, relax. I didn't know if he was speaking to the cop or to me until he told me that he had to do this."

"When I looked into the eyes of the cop, I knew what Treble had to do."

"His eyes?"

"The eyes of revolution. No fear. Determination. Love. And then I noticed that the cop looked exactly like the dead Argentinian doctor and military strategist Che Guevara."

"Do what Auntie? What did Treble have to do.

"A soul transfer. You know I don't believe in coincidences or accidents. Everything that happens, happens for a reason niece, and this cop being the spitting image of the great Che Guevara was the sign I needed to ease my mind about what was about to happen."

"I thought the body dies once the spirit transfers to another host." Miracle said.

"Me too, but Treble explained that, that's only the case when the host body was dying before the spirit merger."

"But, Auntie, you were dying in that prison hospital when Treble merged with you seven years ago."

"That's what I thought too, but I didn't have time to ask him. I heard police sirens and my run instincts kicked in and I got ghost real fast."

"Where is Treble now? I need to tell him about Zion. Maybe he can help me understand."

"Tell him what?" Assata asked. "Understand what?"

"Zion. Treble's son is dead."

"Don't say that Mira. Don't put that kind of energy in the atmosphere."

"What energy Auntie," Miracle's voice rose. "Zion is dead, I saw him in his cell. Early's dead. I know it sounds crazy, but the same cop that killed Early went to Indiana, became a prison guard and killed Zion in his cell."

"What are you doing?" Assata asked as Miracle rose up unballing and balling up her fist. Her eyes seemed to roll in the back of her head as the young woman went onto a trance.

****

Blue lights. White cop. Gun. Assata's friend. Bang! Bang!

****

Miracle's eyes popped open. The vision was clear as day. She saw the future as if it were happening now.

"I'm going to do what I should have done seven years ago when they took Zion."

"Okay, I'm not Zion or Treble I can't read minds, Mira."

"I'm'o make sure they hurt every time they unjustly hurt us. They gon' feel the wrath of the black woman."

Assata followed Miracle to the apartment front door. "Stop girl." She grabbed her goddaughter's arm. "If you don't start making sense right now Miracle Joy Brown."

"The last six months, I've been moving between two worlds Auntie, one we can see and one we can feel. A little over a month ago, I figured out what I had to do. Right then, I hitch hiked until I got to Vegas. The last truck driver that dropped me off gave me five dollars. A month later I had nine million. That's when I decided to come home and begin taking action against the system."

Assata looked at Miracle with a look that teetered between confusion and awe.

"Nine million?"

Miracle nodded yes, "I'm gon' need that and more to stay ahead of them."

"Okay, I'm a little lost. First who is *they* and who the hell is *them*?"

"Anything, Anyone that gets in the way of justice. In particular, *them* and *they* are the police and all who uphold racism, classism, and any ism that goes against the rhythm of righteousness."

"So, in essence, you gon' poke the pigs until they squealing for your blood?"

"Not yet. But trust Auntie," Mira nodded, "When I'm done pokin', they'll be doin' a lot more than squealing. Tired of them killin' our black males with no recourse. Let's see how their families feel when I start pokin'."

"Miracle, you can't go up against the most powerful system in the world and expect to defeat it."

"Why can't I? I'm...

"A black woman," Assata interrupted. "Niece, if I taught you nothin' else, I taught you that the white world has less respect for the black woman than they do these black males that they stompin' on. Only reason they ain't killin' us as fast as they are the men is because they don't see us as a threat."

Miracle nodded. "Oh, that's about to change."

"You tryin' to join Michael Brown and Sandra?" Assata asked. "Girl, you know the system is the power. You just a beautiful, black girl from Decatur."

"Auntie," Miracle smiled, "I am the most powerful system the world has ever and will ever know. And thank you for reminding me."

"Reminding you of what?"

"That I am a black woman. As a black woman, I am a Queen. The mother of all. And it's way past time that I teach the world why Black lives matter." She turned and walked to the door. "This is what Early woulda wanted. He always talked about fighting back, fighting for black," Miracle opened the apartment front door before turning around. "Auntie, I got this, I promise. I'll see you soon."

"No, the hell you won't. You'll see me now. I lost your mother. You've lost Early and Zion. Now more than ever we have to stick together. Hell, who else can we talk to about spirit transference and bringing our imaginations to life in an instant."

"If you really want to help Auntie, go talk to Treble," Miracle said as she walked out to the driveway.

Assata followed behind. "I ain't never said anything about wanting to help. I said I wasn't going to lose you. I've lost almost all my loves in my life, you are my last love and Popeye's a sissy if you think I'm gon' let any force other than Oludamare take you away from me."

"Okay, Auntie, but I really need you to get in touch with Treble. What was the Latino brotha's name Treble transferred into?"

"I don't know."

"You didn't read the name tag on the cops shirt."

"No I did not. All I was thinking about was getting the hell out of there and why Treble had jumped in the mans body in the first place."

"You have no idea why Treble...

"Dammit Miracle. Don't keep asking me the same damn questions. The answers are not going to change. I said I don't know why, or who, so stop askin'."

Miracle took Assata's hand and looked into her eyes, "Look into my eyes, Auntie. Relax your mind. Think happy thoughts."

"Look, Mira...

"Auntie, please, just humor me for a moment." Mira squeezed Assata's hand gently. "Concentrate Auntie. Look deep, deep into my eyes. Remember that day. That morning. April 3. You are running. Your breathing is in sync with each stride. The sound of gunfire disturbs your peace. You...

****

"Look up," Assata said as she traveled back in time through Miracles eyes.

Come on Babylove, that's my ride.

"What are you talking about crazy man? Them white boys that shot him pulled off, all I see is a dying cop." Assata said as they cut through the park and ran across the street where the cop was bleeding out.

She bent down. Treble whispered thoughts into the brown brother's mind. *Warrior, Latin King, I'm here. You've fought good son. The last ten years. All the Latino brotha's and sista's you've saved from the system. All the tampered and planted evidence that you took care of. All the fake smiles and false friendships you established and maintained with your blue bother enemies.*

The officer nodded.

It's time son. You've done well. Relax, allow me to enter your body, take away the pain. Allow me to fight, help finish your work. No more green cards for the original inhabitants of this Earth. Che. I need your body so I can finish what you began when you joined the force.

The sound of approaching sirens caused Assata to look up.

When her gaze returned to the dying Atlanta police officer the Latino cop opened his eyes before coughing up blood.

He placed a hand on Assata's shoulder. "The walls of Jericho have grown too strong to fall, hermano. No one man can bring them down."

I know hermano. That's why I'm here. That's why my sun and his queen are here. With your help Che, I can re-awaken my sun so he and the queen can rise up. May I come in? Treble asked.

"Oh Hell no you don't," Assata said. "I'm not dying for a cop," she said as she just realized, that Treble leaving her body would kill hers.

The Latino brotha smiled as Assata rose up.

****

Assata pulled away from her niece. "Mira, I don't need none of my neighbors in my business thinkin' I'm crazy. That spritual hypnosis stuff don't work on me, probably cause I done been to the other side, I don't know. Why you tryin' to make me remember something I never knew, we could be making tracks," Assata began walking around to the passenger's side while Miracle got into the drivers side and closed the door.

"Girl, open this damn door, now!" Assata said as she jerked on the passenger's door handle.

Miracles shook her head no. She tried to process what she'd just saw through Assata's eyes. Che Guevera, she thought before Assata's voice brought her mind back to the task at hand.

"Girl, don't make me fuck you up."

Miracle pressed the start button. Nothing happened. It was as if the battery was dead.

"You ain't leavin' here without me." Assata walked to the front of the car and sat on the hood.

Miracle kept pressing the start button, but nothing happened. She turned on the lights. They were fine but the car wouldn't even turn over. Finally Mira got out of the car and walked to the front.

"Came to your senses huh?" Assata asked, as Miracle stood in front of her.

Miracle held a hand out. "Auntie I need your keys. I have to get over to Panola road in fifteen minutes, and as you can see my car won't start."

Assata put a hand to her ear. "Say what?"

"I said, my car won't..."

"Shhh," Assata waved. "I heard you, now be still so you can hear ALL telling you that your car won't start because I'm supposed to take you, now bring your butt on."

******

Fifteen minutes later they were on Panola Road passing by the Publix grocery store plaza.

"The church. Is everything okay? Is that where we goin'?" Assata asked as they pulled up to a light.

As soon as the muscle car came to a complete stop, Miracle jumped out and ran with the iPhone that Oya Beyond-See gave her like it was a baton.

"Beep! Beep! Angry horns blew as oncoming traffic dodged and braked to avoid the sprinting young woman.

"Fuck it!" Assata hit the gas and took off before the light turned green.

Squealing brakes caused Miracle to turn around right as the nose of a dump truck hit Assata's Dodge Charger in the passenger rear.

The ruined car spent around like a coke bottle.

"Auntie," Miracle shouted as the grey muscle car came to a stop.

The driver's door sprang open and Assata jumped out. "Girl, you done lost you damn mind jumping out of my car in traffic. I'm done talkin'," the forty-seven year old woman kicked off her heels and took off running.

Miracle turned and took off.

"Don't run from me, girl," Assata shouted as she ran around the curb.

Both slowed at the site of the Dekalb County police cruiser up ahead across from the Food Depot plaza.

Assata came to a complete stop upon realizing that the cop had pulled over Cherry's red Lexus SUV.

THELATHINI NA TANO

1:53 PM

Lithonia, Georgia
October 16, 2016

Officer Darwin knocked on Cherry's driver's side window.

He was shouting before she even pressed the window switch.

"Lady, are you fucking blind?" The Dekalb County police officer pointed back to his cruiser. "Did you not see my flashing fucking blue lights?"

Coltrane leaned forward in the passenger's seat. "No, the queen is not blind, but you obviously are...

"I wasn't speaking to you."

"Well, I'm definitely speaking to you in regards to the language you are using in the space of the queen." Coltrane smiled before kissing Cherry on the cheek causing the cops pink face to darken.

"You two think this is a joke?"

Cherry gave the cop a fuck-you look before turning to her husband. Her pleading eyes and soft hands were her only tools to calm the silent storm that was sure to be brewing inside of him.

Coltrane's eyes eased Cherry's nerves just enough for her to turn her attention back to the raging Dekalb County cop.

Assata looked at the officer's neam tag, "Officer Darwin, why did you pull us over?"

"Give me your fucking license."

Cherry turned her head and looked at her husband. "I love you more than so much."

Darwin put his hand on his service weapon. "I said give me your fucking license."

Husband and wife ignored the hate that was threatening to ruin their Sunday afternoon. Coltrane couldn't help but smile whenever his gaze fell upon the face of everything he had ever wanted and needed. "My love is so much more than the so much that you love me more than," he said.

With one hand still on his service weapon, the Dekalb County officer reached inside the window and grabbed Cherry's shoulder.

Quicker than a thought, Coltrane's arms flew around his wife's body and his fingers locked onto the officer's peach-grey arm. "If you're not ready to die right now you will be wise to keep your hands off of the Queen."

Darwin broke eye contact and jerked his arm away, and took two steps back. He assumed a shooter's stance. "You!" He waved his service revolver at Coltrane. "Stay in the car smartass."

He pointed the gun at Cherry. "Let's see how calm you are when you're kissing the dirt bitch. Get the fuck out the car now."

Before the officer could breathe another breath, Coltrane was out of the Lexus and as soon as his head rose above the top of the SUV...

Officer Darwin fired his weapon. "Pow! Pow! Pow Pow!"

"Nooooo!" Cherry wailed as she climbed over the seat. She was about to open the passenger's door when she saw her husband's body posted up in an awkward sitting position with his back against the door. "Noooooo!" She rammed the front passenger's window with her shoulder so hard that the glass shattered and her small frame went through it. She landed on top of her man.

The officer paced in small circles tapping his gun against the side of his head. "Fuck. Fuck. Fuck."

"Ahhhhhhhhhhhhhhhh," Cherry screamed in agony as she rocked back and forth with Coltrane's bloody corpse in her arms.

The officer didn't see Miracle coming up behind him.

"You people don't listen." The young officer said to no one in particular. "I told him to stay in the fucking vehicle. I told him. Fuck."

"Ahhhhhhhhhhhhh," Cherry screamed.

Miracle held her iPhone out in front of her. "A million people on social media just heard and saw you shoot that black king."

Darwin turned his attention to Miracle and then to the Food Depot Plaza.

Officer Darwin turned to the tall dark woman that was walking his way with the phone in her outstretched arm.

"I tried reason." Miracle said, not breaking stride. "How long did you think I was going to allow you to assassinate ALL's suns?"

She was only a few steps away when the officer broke eye contact and looked at the smoking gun in his left hand.

"The world saw you kill that black king. I saw you kill that black king."

He assumed a shooter's position and aimed his weapon.

"You took my Early Morning," She balled up a fist. "My Zion," she drew her arm back and pitched it forward throwing an invisible ball of energy at the officer's neck.

Darwin's gun fell to the ground.

"Coltrane Jones is the last one." She squeezed her hands together.

His hands flew to his neck. "I can't breathe."

"Feel the pain of the black man." She squeezed tighter. "Feel it Satan! Feel Eric Garner!" Miracle shouted from seventy paces.

"I. I. I can't Bre—

Darwin's face started turning the color of his uniform. "I. I. Please." The officer fell to the ground next to the driver's door of the SUV.

She was only thirty paces away when she summoned the name of the murdering NYPD cop that choked Eric Garner to death. "Daniel Pantaleo, you did this."

The officer began losing consciousness.

"No the fuck you don't," Cherry shouted as she came across the hood of the SUV.

At the same time, Assata caught up to Miracle, and grabbed her arm. "Girl."

Miracle dropped her iPhone on the ground and turned to her godmother right as Cherry fell onto the gasping cop, knocking both of them to the street.

Although now, there was no visual the pink iPhone continued recording.

Cherry rolled over and picked up the officer's gun that had fallen to the curb.

Darwin was still having trouble breathing when Cherry rolled back over and straddled him. She rammed the warm barrel of the young white officers police issue nine millimeter into his mouth.

"POW!" The cops blood and brain matter splattered.

Assata and Miracle looked up just in time to see a Ford Mustang almost run into the back of the police cruiser.

Assata signaled for the man to take off, but instead he signaled for them to get in.

Cherry stood up. She saw a few folks looking and pointing before her attention turned to the strange reddish brown man waving for them to get in.

A moment later her attention returned to the cop she had just killed. She dropped the service weapon on the ground beside Officer Charles Darwin's dead body. "You shot the wrong Black woman's man," Cherry said. "Never again."

Miracle placed a comforting hand on Cherry's shoulder, "I promise you that."

THELATHINI NA SITA

3:00 PM

Greensboro, North Carolina
October 16, 2016

"Dumb fucking snuff chewing hillbillies," Chump looked out of the tinted rear window as his motorcade drove out of the Greensboro Colliseum parking lot past his enthusiastic supporters. Chump sat back on the leather seats of the customized black Suburban. He closed his eyes. "At least the blacks have a valid excuse. They're niggers, but these lazy dumb red necks have every opportunity."

The Republican nominee for president opened his eyes and leaned forward, "Son," he addressed the head of his secret service detail, "Your father was an idiot, but men like me and your grandfather understood our roles as white men. We knew this because we knew our history. When our forefathers needed money, they didn't ask for it, they took it." Chump put a finger in the air. "And when they did, they always had a plan to increase their take. Slave labor has always been the most efficient and quickest way to wealth. The slave is not a demeaning position in life, for without the slave men like me would not exist," Chump crossed his legs. "It's like chess, son,

182

the king has no value without pawns, knights, bishops, and the rooks, all are slaves some just oversee others. You follow me so far, Bobby?

"Yes sir, I believe I do," the heavily decorated war hero secret service agent said as the motorcade headed toward Greensboro North, Greensboro's private airport.

"Niggers, sand niggers, chili shitters, slant-eyes, none of them are Anglo white men. White men make up less than three percent of the world's population, yet we rule and have ruled the world since the beginning of time. The evidence is in black and white son. If everyone just played their roles in society like the animals do, then the world would be perfect." Chump pointed at the rear window. "Look at them skin head fuckers waving my *Make America Great Again* signs in the air. Stupid fucks don't even realize that they were indentured servants working right along with the darkies when America was Great. After I get the spics and the sand niggers out the country," Chump said, "We'll focus on building more prisons and keeping them filled with black, brown, and beige pawns."

"You're talking about reinstituting slavery?" The agent asked.

"Without there ever being a Civil War to do so," Chump said. "And if and when there ever is one, we'll have all the guns this time."

****

Fifteen minutes later the secret service agent opened the rear passengers door to the big SUV.

"Your Gulfstream G-880 Airbus is clear," the agent said. "You're welcome to board anytime sir."

Chump didn't move. "You know, Bobby, start addressing me as Mr. President and tell the others to do the same."

"Yes sir, Mr. Chu-uh, Mr. President sir."

"Bobby, I take it you've flown on Air Force One before?"

The forty something Dolph Lundgreen looking agent answered, "I have sir."

"And?" Chump asked.

"And what, sir?"

"Which one is…"

"Air Force One is prehistoric compared to your Gulfstream G-880 sir."

Sixteen minutes later Chump settled into the enclosed oxygen chamber on the plane's second level. He'd just sat down in the water massage recliner when he felt a hand on his throat.

His eyes popped open. "How did you get onto?"

"I specifically ordered you to do nothing." The chairman's veins pulsed in his arms as he increased the pressure around Chump's neck. "Nothing, you idiot. That does not mean for you to have one of your pitbulls go into one of my prisons and…

"I can't breathe."

"That seems to be going around these days."

Chump struggled.

The chairman loosened his grip just a little.

"I was just trying to get rid of Zion for good," Chump wheezed.

"Again, I told you to do nothing. I don't care if Zion had a gun to my head; If I said do nothing I fucking meant do nothing." He squeezed.

"I can't breathe."

"That's the fucking point."

"Please," Chump pleaded. Tears streamed down his face.

"I explain our plan to rig the election and you go out this afternoon and tell the fucking world that the media is rigging the election, that a fucking late night sitcom is plotting against your bid for presidency. Idiot, do you know how screwed we would be if anyone knew that we were in cahoots with the Russian government? Do you have any idea?"

Chump's body went limp.

The chairman immediately began mouth to mouth resuscitation.

Chump coughed.

Moments later, the chairman continued without his hands around the nominee's neck. "The producers at NBC are not plotting against you Chump, on the contraire, they love you. It's the scriptwriters that hate you, Chump. They have been out of work since you've been running. The producers are literally taking every word you say and repeating your idiotic musings."

"No, they are not."

Ignoring Chump, the chairman continued, "And since you are beyond out of control I have stepped in to save the day."

"What did you do?" Chump coughed.

"I just got into her head."

"Who's head?"

"Unbeknowst to her, Miracle Brown has become our greatest ally thanks to my prompting of course."

"How?"

"Let's just say, she is taking *'eye for an eye'* Old Testament action against people who are supposed to *'protect and serve'*" the chairman said. "That's the first step I took to save this election. The second and final one is I am bringing in someone else to advise and to ensure that you don't develop diarrhea of the mouth in public ever again."

"I don't need a babysitter."

"Reverend TJ Money…"

"The Hand," Chump interrupted.

"I don't refer to him as that," The chairman said.

A dumbfound look was on Chump's face. "A nigger?"

"I don't refer to him as that either."

"A fucking bible toting, shit colored, bush head nigger."

"I don't refer…"

"I know you don't refer to him as that," Chump bobbed his head sarcastically before pointing a finger at the chairman. "Well, let me tell you this and you can take this to the bank and cash it without I.D; the only thing a nigger can do for me is shovel my shit, give me his vote, and tell me what time dinner is being served. You can choke me, kill me…"

The chairman's hand struck like a viper. "As you wish."

Chump scratched and pulled at the chairman's pale arm. His grip was steel.

"I can't…"

"Breathe," The chairman said, "You know, I'm really getting tired of hearing those words."

THELATHINI NA SABA

10:36 PM

Buenos Aires, Argentina
<u>October 16, 2016</u>

The chairman and The Hand had arrived at the Argetinian naked beach less than an hour ago.

They were lying face down as the beautiful young aboriginal Charruas girls rubbed and kneaded their muscles by moonlight.

"Seven years ago, on this day you made the decision to push Chump out front despite my misgivings," the beige-brown man said as he stared at the tan-grey sand through the massage table's eye. "I told you that he was a disaster then and now he's blossomed into a full blown catastrophe."

The chairman smiled, "That's why you're going to help him."

"Help him?" TJ Money lifted his head from the table. "How do you stop a trainwreck?"

The chairman looked up from his massage table, "Change direction."

"Wouldn't need to if you had bet on Black."

"Bishop TJ Money..."

187

The founder and leader of the multi-million dollar *NOBODY'S PERFECT*: come as you are ministry lifted his palm, "The Hand."

"I told you, I will never call you that," the chairman turned and sat up from the table while removing his towel.

"Girl," the chairman gestured for the young woman who was massaging his back a second ago to come and drop to her knees. "Money, I know how you feel," the chairman looked up, "Pride, vindication for the way I vilified you seven years ago. You're secretly happy that Chump seems to be drowning, but if memory serves me correct and it always does, back then you suggested that I put you out front, a nigger preacher, the lowest form of man."

"But, Chump is an extraterrestrial idiot," the mega pastor said.

"After your miserably failed campaign to make Obama look the fool, I was supposed to push you up front, Money?" The chairman snickered. "A man who has lost his flock more than once, A man who was convicted of murder and sat on death row for seven years, A man who has turned against his own people on numerous occasions."

Money interrupted, "A man who convinced the world that he had been shot and killed and came back to life. A man who's conviction was overturned only days before the execution date. A man who had nothing but a bible and a golden tongue once released from prison and now has built an empire worth over a hundred million dollars."

"Terrell Joseph Money," Chairman Greenspan laughed. "You are a nigger," He pointed a finger at Money, "You will always be a nigger," the chairman yanked the girl bobbing her head back and forth between his legs by her ponytail.

"Owww!"

As she stumbled and fell away from the chairman, he stood up and began walking around the massage table that Money was being rubbed on.

"But you owe me, Constance."

"Owe you. I owe you?" the chairman snickered. "Did you forget that I provided the money that influenced everything you have ever done? Who do you think led the authorities and the parishoners away from you after you killed Bishop Percival Turner? Who do you think saved you from that crazy woman, Cherry and the One Free family?"

"I did...

"Nothing," the chairman scowled. "You did nothing but wait on me to save your sorry ass. I guess you do not recall that I sent Karen Parker to your rescue when you were on Death Row. The Innocence Project," Greenspan laughed, "Bullshit. I got your conviction overturned, and I provided the idea and the funding to help you get back to fleecing the flock." The chairman locked his fingers behind his back as he circled. "By my calculations you are..."

The chairman hawked and spit a glob of mucousy saliva on Money's neck.

"My bitch," the chairman removed the towel from his waist to wipe the remnants of spittle from his mouth. "But trust me Money, it is better to be the whore of a king than it is to be a nigger. You know, whore may be a little too strong. My Nehemiah, my cup bearer that's what you are Money. My cupbearer." The chairman turned his attention to the two aboriginal girls who were slowly backing away. "Don't you agree ladies?"

They froze.

Very few were on the naked beach this time of night. If it weren't for the moonlight, the two ladies would not have seen the chairman pitch the silvery grey money clip in the air.

"Si, senor, Si, Si," the ladies said as they pulled hundred dollar bills out of the sky.

Money started to rise.

"No, No," the chairman pressed his hand into the small of his back, pushing Money down onto the table before bending down to ear level, "Most whores would protest me spitting on them, but you didn't Money. Why? Because you realize that a glob of spit is not worth jeopardizing the lavish life that I provide, and for your loyalty I'm going to allow you to be the voice of Chump for the next three weeks."

"No! No! and hell no," Money looked up, "You have no idea how much respect I have lost since I got on TV with two American flags and endorsed him a couple months ago."

"I determine, act, and command, but never ask," The chairman sat back on the table and snapped his fingers for the girl to come back over. When she did he dropped his grey towel and signaled for her to assume the former position on her knees. "One million."

Money continued, "I've spent seven years building my flock. Black, white, yellow, brown, they all hate Chump. There is no way under any condition… "

"Ten million."

"Cash?"Money asked.

The chairman smiled. "When I win, I just might make you Chief of Staff, Money."

"You mean, when Chump doesn't win?" Money laughed. "I'm sorry Constance, there is no bigger threat to America than Chump, no way the voters will elect him."

"I didn't say anything about voters electing him," the chairman said. "Putin has found a way to count all of our votes twice. With Russia's help, we are going to steal the presidency again."

"That'll take a Miracle?"

"Exactly," he said before handing Money his android cell phone. "Press play."

THELATHINI NA NANE

3:33 PM

Harlem, New York
<u>October 17, 2016</u>

"Peace King," Jihad said as he and the young rap mogul embraced.

"Preciate you seeing me on such short notice JC."

The two grabbed a rear bench table inside the Harlem, New York mom & pop breakfast restaurant.

"Always love king," the fair skinned dreaded brother put a hand over his heart. "I appreciate you blessin' me and the universe with all the real in the thirteen bibles you penned."

"Like you said fam, it's all love," Jihad said as the two men sat down at the rickety back table. "I can't take credit, like yourself JC, love inspires me to move.

"Jermaine," The grandmotherly proprietor called out, "Boy, where you been?"

"Everywhere Momma June. I've been on tour."

"Uh-hmm," she said as she waved her slender wand like arm in the air. "Look at you. Gettin' all skinny making me look bad, like I ain't feeding you," she nodded. "That's okay cause you here now, Momma June got you." She turned and hollered out, "Earl, get this baby a stack of red velvet pancakes."

"Momma June, I ain't really all that...

"Shh, baby. I promised your folks back home that I was gon' make sure you ate good. Now I knows you married and Melissa is a fine woman but don't nobody burn like Momma June and Uncle Earl." She turned back to the kitchen, "Suga, we also gon' need a mess of scrambled cheese eggs, grits, turkey bacon, and fried apples."

"Momma June," Jihad said, "You don't love me no more old woman?"

The sixty-nine year old First Afrikan's smile lit up the small seven table breakfast spot. "Ah, sound like somebody needin' some lovin'," she opened her arms.

The author pushed the folded metal chair back from the table.

After they embraced, Momma June looked the author up and down, "Chile, somebody sho nuff feedin' you good."

"What you sayin' Momma?"

"I'm sayin' what I said now." She hmphed. "Baby, when you gon' put out the sequel to *World War Gangster*, now that was my book. Now I liked them *Preacherman* books you wrote, and that *Wild Cherry* girl, but that *World War Gangster*, that Bo Jack Jones uhm-uhm-uhm."

"June, let them be. Come on here woman I need you in the kitchen," Uncle Earl called out.

"Ah, I'm coming old man," she said before turning back to the two young men, her focus on Jihad, "I'm gon' have Uncle Earl whip you up the same thang as my godbaby here. Now Jihad, you know you was wrong for ending that book like that. That CIA girl know she need her behind whooped. Bo Jack done fell in love with Satan in a dress, and he don't even know it." The older woman pointed, "I don't know how many times I gotta tell young men to stop thinking with that brainless head in their pants. Now when is you gon' put that sequel out, Jihad?"

"June!"

"I'm comin, I'm comin," she shouted before turning back to the young men. " I'll be right back with some of Momma June's famous lemon apple tea."

"I'll just have a Sprite," Jihad said. "I don't really like tea."

"June!"

"You'll like my tea baby," she turned and hollered, "I'm comin' old man."

A moment later the two were alone.

"I think I know why you're here G," The anointed rap superstar lifted his iPhone. "The video. Facebook done crashed at least four times in the last twenty-four. The live recording done gone Anthrax. The freak tornado back in April. Most of us just knew she was dead. Then months later she just pops up on facebook live. I almost didn't recognize her, all that anger."

"I know. It's like she's a different woman. When that Flintstone took out Early, I bet that was the turning point," Jihad said.

"Every news station in the nation has Miracle's, Cherry's, and Assata's picture plastered across the screen," JC said.

"The First Afrikans are counting on you and the others to unite others through your music." Jihad said. "I need you to reach out to Common, Nas, Andre, Logic, Rakim, Krs, Kendrik, Talib, Mos, Ceelo, Erykah, and the Queen. We need all of you to call on everyone to stand up for the three Queens."

"Are you trying to start a war G?"

"I'm trying to prevent one, at least until Truth gets out."

"Truth?"

"Nap, he goes by the name Truth now."

"Nap got life, I thought."

"Not for long," Jihad beamed.

"Oh shit, don't tell me Nap, I mean Truth done got down with Zion?" the urban lyricist asked.

"Nap has become Zion, that's why he's Truth Testimony now," Jihad said.

"Oh snap. Game over now. Life, 'bout to get really real when Truth rise up," the lyricist said, "Whatever you need OG, consider it done."

Out of nowhere gunshots rang out.

"Pow...........! Pow! Pow! Pow!" Bullets flew everywhere.

"Get down, G" the conscious hip-hop artist said before he and Jihad took cover under the table.

Two minutes later smoke and dust were everywhere. JC coughed while rising from under the table. His attention was drawn to the CNN report that was coming over Jihad's iPhone.

"Tensions are high. America is an unstable keg of radioactive gunpowder. Random acts of violence against law enforcement have broken out across the nation over the last forty-eight hours.

"Moments ago, assailants wearing Donald Chump masks drove down Malcolm X Boulevard in Harlem, New York shooting automatic rifles from camouflaged military disguised Humvee's. The images, the carnage," the reporter seemed to be having trouble holding it together. "This is a sad day in America. A day that wouldn't be if Miracle Brown and Cheryl Sharell had not streamed the killing of Officer Charles Darwin on social media forty-eight hours ago. Their words, 'Never again, I promise you that,' have become a vigilante war cry. Has black America turned against the justice system?"

THELATHINI NA TISA

3:33 AM

October 18, 2016
<u>Oakland, California</u>

Blue lights lit up the Oakland California Autumn night as the Ford Interceptor SUV closed in on the stolen Chevy Impala. The stolen car's driver turned the wheel way too hard while the car was going way too fast. The car's axle sounded like a cannon as it broke in two. POP. The black car spun like a top before ramming into an electrical pole.

"He's running," the rookie jumped out of the passenger's seat and gave chase.

The officer in the driver's seat radioed in, "Suspect is now on foot. Black male, average height, average build, short hair wearing a black and white Oakland Raiders jacket."

This was crazy. Marion thought as he took the ten foot fence in three steps. All he could think about was how his NBA career would be over before it ever began if he got caught. All this to get into a fraternity. To become a Greek. It would seem that the car was easier to steal than the real thing from a zoo. The big bruhs said to bring back an Impala or his nine line brothers would run the five mile gauntlet naked.

Eugene Evans was curled up on a park bench under some newspapers scratching his arms when the six-four college hoops star startled him.

"My man," Marion held the three-hundred dollar Raider starter jacket in front of him, "you want this?"

Eugene snatched the jacket before the words were out of Marion's mouth good.

The hoops star was nowhere in sight when Eugene heard a voice a couple minutes later. "Hey you!"

The junkie looked up. Eugene was fully aware of his situation. *I'm a black man alone in a park and a white cop with gun in hand is calling me out.*

Eugene slowly rose from the park bench. He yawned before jumping up and hauling ass. The officer chased him for about eight blocks and for eight blocks Eugene screamed Help! Help! I didn't do it! I didn't do it until the cop caught up and dragged him down in front of a senior living apartment community.

Porch lights came on one after another.

"You made me run after you, I oughta kill you," the white officer's knees were bloody as he crouched over the bleeding and terrified middle-aged homeless brotha. The cop brandished his service issue flashlight above his head.

A brown hand grabbed the officer's wrist before the flashlight's steel handle crashed into the head of its intended target. "But you won't kill him now," the elderly black man who grabbed the cop's wrist said, "Never again, I promise you that." Before he got the words out of his mouth good, six elderly women reigned fists, bare feet, canes, a prosthetic leg, and orthopedic rubber soles down on the officer. The middle aged homeless brother suffered his share of blows before crawling from under the vicious ass whippin' the elderly were dishing out.

**** 3:33 PM ***

October 25, 2016
Newark, New Jersey

"Sir," the officer grabbed the man's arm. "Are you licensed to sell those DVD's?"

The man jerked away from the officer. "Don't put your hands on me cop," the older brother said. "Do you have a license to harass me?"

"Sir," the other officer said, "We are not harassing you. We just need to see your license. Do you even have a vendors license?"

"Man, ain't no body botherin' you. But you wanna bother me cause I'm Black."

"I'm black too," one of the officers said.

"Man, you quit being black when you put on that blue," the man shouted. "See, ya'll wanna Eric Garner me, but my people ain't gon' let that happen." A crowd of black and latino brothas and sistas began to form.

"Hey ya'll, they wanna know if I have a license to make a living. They wanna do me the way they did Eric Garner, Rakia Boyd, Little Nathaniel Heyward."

"Jose' Valdez," someone shouted.

"Mandel Jones," a sista shouted.

The names kept coming until someone in the crowd shouted, "Never again, I promise you that."

It was as if those words were a call to action as the crowd rushed the two officers and beat them mercilessly.

AROBAINI

3:33 AM

October 25, 2016
Lithonia, Georgia

"Where is he?" Assata asked. "Where is our gracious benefactor? I'm about to lose my mind down here in this big ass underground cave. He said nine days. We goin' into the tenth day, Miracle."

"He'll be here when it's safe Auntie. I don't like being down here in this four room tomb either, but at least it's comfortable, peaceful, and we have food, clothes, and a bathroom."

"How do we really know he won't turn us in?" Assata asked. "I'm sure the government has at least a six figure bounty on our heads. He doesn't even know us."

"Auntie, everyone ain't about money. All this spy stuff and these conspiracy theory books down here, Billy hates the *System* with the passion of the Christ, as he should. The hands of government have all but wiped his people off the map of hue-man history."

"Hating the *System* is one thing," Assata said, "harboring three black women involved with killing a white cop is another."

"Trust me Auntie, I didn't feel anything but good energy from him. Besides, Cherry ain't close to being ready to go anywhere, even if we could leave.

"You hear that," Assata pointed up at the low ceiling.

"Tehuti is exercising Maat," a masculine voice chimed from above, before tapping on the floor three times.

"That's' Billy," Miracle said.

A moment later the small man lifted up the ceiling door and walked down the toolshed stairs that led to the bomb shelter.

"Thank you, Billy. I don't know how we can ever repay you for your kindness," Miracle said.

"Well, I ain't so quick to be thanking no man that would do so much for strangers, folks he don't know."

"Auntie!"

"That's okay, Miracle." Billy smiled while fiddling with his ponytail. "My people don't believe in strangers. Like government is made up of a body of people and cultures, the Seminole Nation understand that all of hue-manity's cultures, brother's and sister's are part of one divine consciousness."

"Uhm-hm," Assata grunted with her arms crossed. "Funny how the owner of the Food Depot Plaza was just sitting in his car with a pair of binoculars. You gon' tell us you were just there, what people watching?"

"Watching people is way more interesting than reality television. I admit, *people watching* as you call it," he smiled at Assata, "probably saved your lives. When Mrs. Jones got pulled over, I was in the parking lot." Billy surveyed the huge cave like room. "Speaking of, where is she?"

"Cherry's probably sleep in the back bedroom. She's taking her husband's death pretty hard," Miracle said.

"Officer Darwin's coduct was inexcusable. Neither man had to die," he said before looking up at Assata. "I wasn't going to get involved until I heard the words of power that came out of Mrs. Jone's and Ms. Brown's mouth. It was a call for me to take action to make the words 'Never again, I promise you that' a reality. Right then I knew that if I did not heed the call then I would be aiding the same men and systems that are and have been killing our people since 1492. Never again, I promise you that," the indigenous man said. "I have resources to keep you safe. And I will. Give it a few more days, when Mrs. Jones is ready, I will take you to my people. My sister Hachi will help you find what you all seek."

AROBAINI NA MOJA

Thirteen days later

11:33 PM

Terre Haute, Indiana
November 7, 2016

Truth? Zion telepathically called out from his cell down at the other end of the grey mile, the term inmates and guards referred to Terre Haute Federal Penitientary's death row corridor.

Truth was on his bunk with his hands over his ears. He and Zion had been on the death row isolation wing of the prison for over four months now. He wished Zion would just stop trying. There was no way he was going to sell out to get out. "No."

Truth? Again, Zion telepathically called out.

Been bout that life near all my life Zee. Always was about me and if you didn't fit into my gaze of what you was supposed to be then you were food on my journey to my next destiny, Truth thought to Zion.

Truth. Zion called out.

I was a child for thirty-four years and didn't know. I'm grown now Zee. I will no longer poison myself by acting against the self-interest of my peeps, he continued shaking his head no while thinking, *I get it. Zee, you the Messiah. You done walked on water, parted the Red Sea, died a million deaths a million times all so I'd be. Nothin' you can say Zee. I will never sign my name to a lie to be free. Selling out you is selling out me.*

Truth. Zion called out.

"Nah, Zee," Truth voiced his thoughts out loud. "I know you in me Zee, but you also in you and yeah the world needs me out there but so do you, and I will not sacrifice you as you have done for the many. I'll die, Hell we all will before I sign on to Supressions, Chumps or anyone else's lies. You tell me I'm Truth. That's who you say I am Zee." He stood up from his bunk, balled up the thin sheet and the grey blanket before placing them at he head of the bed. "I ain't leaving you in here Zee. We in this together, baby."

Truth.

"We have to stay together Zee. United we stand. Ubuntu Zee, second Kings verses three to eleven."

Truth.

"What Zee? What?"

Be. Be the message, the tharozine the prison put Zion on after he took out Grey and White had him slurring his thoughts. *Be the first and the second king. Be the four lepers in three to eleven. With love and love only be Truth. Be.*

"I'm trying," Truth shouted while dropping to his knees in the middle of the cell. He still had his hands over his ears. He was trying to block out Zion's voice and at the same time he strained to hear the message through Zion's slurred words. "I'm tryin'.

Don't try. Be!

"I don't know how," Truth looked up. His arms shot up in the air. "I'm just a black kid from the hood. Who gon' listen to me, I mean for real. Only sway I got is with the hood. Ain't no suit black or white tryin' to hear nothin' from a kinky dread haired black kid without no formal education."

Zion hollered down the grey mile, slurring his words out loud for everyone to hear. "Remember King. Remember what you did. Remember Bethlehem. Remember Egypt, Herod, the people. Remember who you saved, how you saved, and why you saved. Remember you are the king. Be!"

"Be what? Huh?" he banged a fist across his chest. "You want me to be a sellout. You want me to be that nigga that would leave his man behind to die. I know what they doin' to you Zee. You don't know it, but they slow killing you with that Tharozine."

"Yo, pimpin'," another inmate from death row shouted down the grey mile, "Zion think you Jesus Christ, Nap. Damn! Them some good ass drugs."

"Nah, baby boy," Zion slurred his words. "Nothing good about drug. Truth is Christ. Truth rises above..."

"Yo Zion," another inmate called out, "I need some of that shit they got you on, but real talk ya'll need to chill, you know they listening to every word."

"I hope so," Zion said. "Maybe they will see the err in their ways once Truth decides to Be."

"Be what," another inmate called out, "all they want him to be. One man ain't got no win in Whitey's world."

"A teenage Afrikan shepherd boy named David did. An Afrikan boy who was said to have been born in a manger did. An Afrikan born in Carthage did. An Afrikan enslaved and held captive on the island of St. Dominique did," Zion slurred. "They all had one thing in common."

The sound of keys jangling interrupted the conversation. "Cowherd, let's go, you lucky S.O.B."

"Black Officer, Black officer see what happens why you try to put us in a coffin sir," the cons on death row chorused.

"At least I go home every day you sorry fucks," Officer Quisling said.

"Is that what you call that lonely place you go to every day to contemplate suicide?" Zion asked. "Is that the place you pay for with money from people and systems that have always and will always treat you like you treat us."

"Shut up, before I have your dosage increased."

"A couple months ago maybe when you were Lieutenant Quisling but now you are just Officer Wolf Quisling. You don't have the power black officer. You can't even put me in a coffin sir," Zion said.

"Yo' Zee, finish the story," an inmate called out from behind the grey steel cell door. "What they all had in common?"

Officer Quisling turned the key.

"Truth!" Zion said. "They chose to be, and they became."

"Became what?"

"Truth Testimony," Zion said.

"You might as well go on back to your perch, Quisling. I ain't sayin' shit, and I sure ain't signing shit." Truth said crouched in anticipation of the cell door opening.

"Stop talking crazy and come on here boy," the demoted officer said as he unlocked the steel door, "I don't care where you go, but you getting' the hell outta here."

Truth was ready. His legs were bent and ready to leap as he stood at the opposite end of the steel door. He was determined to do what he had to do. He came into prison seven years ago without any integrity and now he had enough to light a small nation and he was not leaving prison without his integrity. Before he'd snitch, he'd murder Quisling. Part of him did not want to hurt Quisling and another part of him wanted to annihilate the man with his bare hands for allowing himself to be a tool for Suppressions.

The cell door opened. Truth dove for Quisling. Somehow his foot got tangled up in the bed sheet that was nowhere near when he lunged. The impact of his head banging against the grey concrete floor was too much with everything else going on in his head.

"Got dammit, now I have to clean this damn blood up," Officer Quisling said as he kneeled down to where Truth was lying on prison cell floor.

AROBAINI NA MBILI

12:33 AM

Terre Haute, Indiana
November 8, 2016

      The two Terre Haute Regional Hospital orderlies walked into Truth's room.

"How you know dude ain't gon' wake up?"

"Come on T.O. dude been knocked out since our shift began. He 'on't look like he wakin' up anytime soon," Shaun said. "Besides, The Hand was on Bill O'Really earlier. They replayin' it now on FOX." Shaun picked up the remote and pressed the ON button.

"Dog, I just got this job."

"Here." Shaun pushed his mop at T.O. " If ole boy wake up or somebody walk in jus' ack like like you moppin', ole scary ass nicka'."

"Fuck you, white boy," T.O. shot back.

Shaun pointed to the thirty-two inch screen above.

206

****

"In less than eight hours, the polls will open to what is now a much closer race than anticipated. Experts suggest that the recent escalation in violence against the men and women who protect and keep America safe is a primary reason for Chumps surge in recent polls."

Bill O'Really pointed to the two hundred inch FOX studio screen before continuing, "Via satellite we have spiritual leader and one of Donald J. Chump's most trusted advisors, the Reverend Hand."

The African-American mega church leader wore a long all white daishiki, white linen pants, and white sandals.

He waved a long stick of incense in the air before correcting the host. "The Hand."

"So, Reverend Hand, what are your thoughts?"

The reverend was sitting on a white leather couch with his legs crossed. "First name is The capital T-H-E, last name Hand, capital H-A-N-D, Bill. No reverend. Just The Hand." Money smiled as he waved the long stick of incense in the air.

"Interesting the host said. So Mr. Hand..."

Money waved a finger in the air. "No. No. No, son. Not Mr. Just The Hand."

The Bill O'Really show's program director, Bob Head almost screamed into O'Really's ear. "For cryin' out loud Bill, will you just address him as the friggin' fuckin' Hand."

"The Hand," O'Really said, "tell our studio and viewing audience why you think the escalation of violence has resulted in Donald Chump's surge in popularity."

****

"Daaaaaaaaamn," T.O. said as he leaned on the hospital mop, "even his incense is white."

"Yep," Shaun agreed. "The Hand cleaner than the board of health on Easter Sunday." Shaun held his hand up in front of T.O. "The Hand, that name, is that not some gangster shit or what?"

"That's a thorough ass dude, Shaun. Playa made the white man call his ass The Hand."

"No, you mean the capital T-H-E capital H-A-N-D," Shaun mimicked.

"Shhhh," T.O. put a finger to his lips. "The Hand boutta' speak again."

****

"Bill. I'm going to speak to you and the world like I would my children if I had any," he waved the incense like he was conducting the words that were coming out of his mouth. "Solomon was the wisest man in the bible. David was the bravest man in the bible. Both of them were great kings. Ruled great God fearing nations. King Solomon had over a thousand women in his concubine. Hell, his daddy sent a man off to get killed in war so he could have the man's wife. Now you would be a damn fool as my momma would say if you'd elect King David, King Solomon, or Donald Chump as president of any feminist or womanist organization."

Almost thirty seconds passed before the studio audience laughter subsided.

"Let me tell you something Bill," he leaned forward. "Chump has built an empire that generates more money per year than some small and not so small nations. You ask what does this have to do with running a country? A country is a business. It's a huge business made up of smaller businesses that sustain society. Now I'd rather have a man at the helm of my business that has proven himself to be the Michael Jordan of the business world than a big mouthed woman who can't even keep government secrets secret. Is Chump perfect, hell no, and he will tell you that himself. He often does. Is he crass? Is he somewhat jaded? Yes, he is. Is he the greatest businessman on the planet, yes he is. Give him a chance, I guarantee with my and the rest of the administration's help, we will all pick this country back up and return it to the time when it was great. "

****

"When he talkin' bout'? This country ain't never been great for ya'll," Shaun said. "1491 was the last time this country was great for any man other than my ancestors."

"Shhh," T.O. gestured while pointing at the screen above the hospital bed.

****

"That other person running has fallen on her face. I won't call her by name because she will be a memory in a few hours, and I try not to focus on the negative energy once it is flushed from my system," The mega church pastor said.

"Just like the negative energy that rose up like a demon on a full moon. The bloody demon that crawled over the hood of that car and mercilessly attacked, beat, and finally murdered not just a peace officer, but the savage woman and her accomplices murdered a wife's husband and two children's father. They murdered a friend. Officer Charles Robert Darwin," He held his hand up in front of the camera, "a hand of the community."

Pictures of Officer Darwin, his wife, and children appeared on the screen.

"The violence all around America has compounded, accelerated, and exacerbated as other officers have been attacked and five of them murdered since Cheryl Sharell and Miracle Brown's savagery three weeks ago. They were right about one thing," the popular religionist held the stick of incense in the air, "Never again. Never again can we as a nation, as a people allow vigilantism. Never again," The Hand repeated. "I and the Chump administration promise you that."

Menacing looking pictures of Miracle, Cherry and Assata appeared on the screen.

****

"Damnnnnn," T.O. said, "Them bitches look meaner than a mu' fucka."

"Shhh," Shaun looked at his man. "You gon' watch The Hand or you gon' run your mouth big dog?"

****

"While America is busy watching *Saturday Night Live* make a fool of themselves ridiculing one of the greatest business men to ever oversee an empire, Ossama, I mean Obama, is busy pardoning murderers, drug dealers, thieves and the like. I'm a black man. I have suffered my fare share of police brutality. I have suffered my share of pain at the hands of the Man. I spent seven years in prison, five on death row. So, if anyone has a reason to hate the Man it is I. Some police are criminals, but all criminals are criminals and do we really want anyone from that last administration to keep running this country into the ground. Do we want a woman who lies about something as simple as an email to run this nation? Do you think she can protect you from terrorists abroad? Hell, she can't protect our young men and women hired to protect and serve here. I'll guarantee you this. Elect Chump in a few hours and all terrorism here and abroad will be eradicated expeditiously. This is real talk from a real brother of humanity."

****

"You can't be serious?" Truth said as he rose from the hospital bed.

The two orderlies bumped into each other before turning around. "I'm sorry, sir. We thought you were sleep."

"I thought the same about you two," Truth said. "Ya'll was really tuned all the way into that nut, huh?"

"Nut," Shaun looked at the bandaged patient, "The Hand is a G. Look what all he been through. And he still here and he done went from broke to ballin' to on Death row to broke to ballin' again. That's a real nicka' there."

"Truth looked at the bald brotha and then at the shaggy long haired white boy that almost came too close to using the N word. "Opey here is white, I halfway understand his hero worship," Truth looked at Shaun and then at T.O. "But you, I know you ain't down with that?"

"Aye man. My dude's name is Shaun, and you damn skippy I'm down," he slapped five with his boy. "You can hit your call button have us fired, but I ain't gon' sell out the truth. And playa," T.O. held his hand in front of his face, "The Hand is the truth."

AROBAINI NA TATU

5:33 AM

Covington, Georgia
November 8, 2016

"Crazier than a shithouse rat."

"Claude," Lena turned from the kitchen sink.

"I'm sorry baby," he bent down and kissed his wife on the back of her neck. "But, you have to be short-bus-slow to vote for a chump like Chump. How is a chump gon' protect somebody? Baby," he put his hands on his wife's shoulders.

Lena smiled. "Yes, Claude?"

Husband and wife gazed at the early morning moonlight shining on the forest outside through the cabin kitchen window. This was the third week that Claude, Lena, Luke and their youngest had been living in the safe house that Dr. Logun and the council of clerics arranged after explaining that Early and Luke were sharing the same body.

The patriarch of the Cabral clan had a look of concern etched on his face. "Baby," he shook his head, "I don't know. I just don't know."

212

Slight of build, mocha caramel complexion and a smile that brightened every room she had ever walked in, Lena Cabral's outward beauty was no match for her calm wisdom.

After rinsing off the glass and putting it in the dish rack she turned to her husband, "What don't you know Claude?"

"Early, Luke, hell, now I know the man is Black, but," Claude held a hand out toward the front room where Luke had been recovering the last few weeks, "I know he's one of us but he still in a cracker's body. I just don't know."

"Claude," Lena took her husband's hand, "Winnie is almost thirty. She is much stronger than you give her credit for."

"Baby, you talking to me about my baby girl. I'm talking about that white boy out there," he pointed.

She smiled. After thirty-six years of loving her king she knew him better than he knew himself. "You mean that First Afrikan in pink skin that your daughter is falling for?

"Ahhh, don't say that," he cringed.

Ignoring him Lena continued, "The First Afrikan that you tried to kill three weeks ago because you thought he had killed a First Afrikan."

"Yeah, baby, I was wrong. Dead wrong almost," he smiled, "But, I just want the best for my baby. If that maniac wins the election, then their relationship will become even more difficult, A First Afrikan and a white boy, Hell nah?"

"A First Afrikan and a First Afrikan you mean," she said. "Don't allow his skin to be your sin Claude Cabral." She gestured for Claude to come over to the kitchen entryway.

"Look at them," she said. "Look at your daughter, Claude."

He looked up. Luke was sound asleep. Winnie's lap was his pillow. She ran a finger through his blonde hair while watching CNN.

"Your daughter is happy Claude."

"Yeah, but for how long? How long before the white boy come outta him?"

"The white boy that you are referring to is in everyone," she jabbed him in the chest with her finger, "even you. Can't you see how much Luke, I mean Early is like you Claude."

"Like me?"

"Yes, Claude. Like you. He risked his life and almost lost it fighting aginst the system. He came to you knowing things might not go as peaceful as planned, but he came to you like a man, a black man, a First Afrikan." The queen of the Cabral clan looked through the doorway across the small dining room into the living room where her child was caring for the recovering First Afrikan.

She turned to her husband. "It's only been three weeks Claude, but you best get ready Claude Cabral because Winnie has that same look on her face that I had thirty-six years ago." She squeezed his hand before smiling.

"Early," Winnie prodded Luke awake.

Luke winced from the pain in his ribs as he slightly rose to turn his head toward the fifty-two inch outdated plasma television screen hanging on the log cabin wall.

"Mom! Daddy hurry!" Winnie called out.

****

"Just in. In a shocking development less than twenty-four hours before the polls open to elect the nation's forty-fifth president, President Obama has issued a full pardon to convicted drug and gang leader Owen Cowherd."

A dark menacing picture of Truth appeared on the screen.

"In 2009 before his arrest Cowherd released several songs that called for violence against law enforcement. Cowherd has also been linked to the same First Afrikan cult that is responsible for slain Officer Charles Darwin...

****

"Cult?" Claude said. "Bullshit," Claude waved off.

Luke struggled to rise.

"We oughtta sue," Claude turned to his wife. "See, baby, this is what I'm talking about. Cracka's done put a target on every First Afrikan's head with that fake news."

"In further developments, in preparation for his release, Cowherd fell and has been taken to an outside hospital," the reporter said, "as this story unfolds FOX news will…"

"Bullshit," the elder revolutionary's face wrinkled into a mask of disbelief, "He fell alright. Right into a crackas boot, fist, or flashlight. Nigga get a pardon and them crackas still wanna put shit in the game."

Pain was evident on Luke's face as he started to stand.

"What are you doing?" Winnie asked.

"Gotta go. Have to catch plane. Truth needs me," Luke said as he gently placed a hand over the bandages on his ribs and a hand on Winnie's shoulder."

"Daddy?" Winnie turned.

"Shit," Claude said, "You ain't gon' make it outta these woods, let alone to the airport," the fair skinned man said as he ambled towards the bedroom.

"Daddy, you can't let him leave."

"Claude, what are you doing?" Lena asked.

"Baby, I'm just getting a few knick knacks," he smiled, "Somebody gotta protect this fool from doing something foolish," Claude said. "I can't make it any plainer than what Miracle and Cherry said Never again will they take anotha black life without their blood being shed too, I promise you that. Now, let's go get Truth after I call in some reinforcement."

AROBAINI NA NNE

5:33 AM

November 8, 2016
Waycross, Georgia

Tensions were rising. All three women were on edge. Miracle, Assata, and Cherry were living in a treehouse in the middle of the largest blackwater swamp in North America.

"Shit!" Assata shouted. "If I see one more anything. I swear."

"It's only a baby," Miracle said as she sat the baby alligator down in the marsh.

"I guarantee you that the momma and daddy aren't too far behind," Cherry said.

"I'm done," Assata said. "Eight days in the wilderness. I will take my chances with the predators I know instead of the ones I don't."

"Auntie?" Miracle followed Assata back up the treehouse stairs.

"Snakes, Lizards, bugs, alligators, and creepy slimy shit I ain't ever heard of." Assata shuddered. "I must be out of my damn mind following you here."

"She's right," Cherry said as she climbed up into the tree cabin and closed the door. "We been in this swamp for eight days. Waiting for what? A fucking sign." Cherry waved an arm around the cabin that was really a large wooden tree house built into three trees with one ginormous root. "All these non hibernating ass reptiles are a sign that clearly reads if we don't get the hell out of here we'll eventually be food."

"In those eight days nothing has caused us harm."

"Speak for yourself niece," Assata said. "My Va-jayjay looks like something out of a free clinic VD brochure, all these damn mosquitoes and God knows what else is feasting on me while I'm sqatting over a hole in this damn," she threw her hands in the air, "Whatever the hell this is."

"Auntie, for real?" Miracle questioned. "There are over one hundred and ten different species of reptiles and amphibians, over forty species of mammal in these four hundred thirty eight thousand acres of swamp and marshland."

"Thanks a lot niece," Assata said. "Before your history lesson my primary concern were the squiggly's and the gators, now that you have shared that there are over a hundred creepy crawlers out here," she shook her head in confusion, "Fuck, Mira."

"I wasn't trying to scare you Auntie. I'm just showing you that if we were meant to be food, we would've already been eaten," Mira said. "Just think. We spent three days and nights trudging through the Okeefenokee with the Cypress Seminoles to get here and not only did we arrive unharmed, we didn't even see a snake or a gator until we got up here."

"I would have died dead right then and there if I would've walked up on one of them," Cherry shivered, "people eating snakes. I swear, you can rob me with a dead snake and get it all."

"I hear you," Assata said.

"I'm terrified of 'em too," Miracle said. "But after Billy's sister Hachi communicated to us that no harm would come to us if we stayed within the area she pointed out. I believed her and nothing has."

"Yet," Cherry said.

Ignoring Cherry, Miracle said, "Besides, if these swamps were so dangerous you think Chief Abiaka would send Hachi by herself every other day to bring us news and supplies." Miracle looked at her auntie, "Outside of the mosquito bites we're fine."

"Fine," Assata said. "Miracle, we have lived in a treehouse over a swamp for five muggy, damp, damn days.

"Auntie," Miracle looked at the woman who helped raise her, "you don't think I'm scared? How many times did I wake up in the projects screaming because I felt something crawling on me when I was little? Remember the whippin' I got because I was too scared to stomp on that spider when I was nine? You know better than anyone how terrified I am of bugs, reptiles…

Assata continued, "Dogs, cats, worms, squirrels, nearly every animal but man that's why I don't see why…

"We're here?" Miracle interrupted. "My fear of all this," she turned in a full circle on the wooden cabin floor, "can't compare to the fear of what will happen to our people, to hue-manity if I don't fight through my fears, our fears."

"Before you so rudely interrupted me," Assata said, "I was going to say I don't see why you just don't use your power."

"My power don't work just because I want something. Besides, I told you, I'm waiting on a sign."

"Whachu mean, a sign?" Cherry asked.

"The sign seems clear as day to me?" Assata said. "This wilderness is a sign for us city women to get back to civilization."

"We shoulda gone up to North Dakota with Billy, Osceola and the other tribesmen," Cherry said referring to the invitation that was extended to them eight days ago before the

Food Depot Plaza owner Billy Bolek turned the ladies over to his sister Hachi and his other Cypress Seminole brothers and sisters at the edge of the Okeefenokee on the southern end of Georgia.

"Why, so one of the folks in the two hundred tribes could turn us in in hopes that the American government would put a stop to the oil pipeline that's poisoning their water up in the Dakotas," Assata said.

"Auntie, did you forget that it was an indigenous man who didn't know us from Eve yet he risked his freedom and livelihood to hide us in the underground bomb shelter in his back yard after we killed that cop. Billy didn't ask questions. He nor the tribe has asked for anything," Miracle said. "To me that's a sign that we're where we are supposed to be. And if Billy, Hachi and the rest of the tribe risked their own lives and freedoms, do you really think that any one of them would turn us in?"

Miracle looked at both of them before continuing, "Cherry, I lost Zion and I lost my mom. She was murdered right in front of me. I know how it feels. You need to finish grieving, which under the circumstances is almost impossible but if you give me a little more time to figure this out...

"Both of you need to grieve," Assata said. "Speaking of, are you absolutely sure that Zion is dead Miracle?"

"I told you that I was there auntie. I saw him lying on that cell floor."

Assata crossed her arms, "Since you were little, you had dreams about Zion before you ever laid eyes on him. I've seen the boy's work. I believe He is all that and a gallon of kool-aid. And I know who you are niece. I've seen your work," she paused trying to find the words.

"Ohhh-kayyyyyy, so what Auntie?"

"So what?" Assata's arms fell to her sides as she relaxed. "You and Zion together are the ones sent by ALL to destroy evil. I can't see ALL allowing anyone to kill Zion before ya'll even have a chance to save the world."

"If Chump steals the presidency," Cherry quipped, "this world won't be worth saving.

"What I'm trying to understand niece is if God is ALL, which I know God is, then ALL don't lie," Assata said.

"Girl," Cherry said with a befuddled look on her face, "what are you talking about?"

"I'm saying that ALL re-awakened Isis with understanding, and she re-membered Ausar back together, and he was resurrected. ALL re-awakened the God conscious that was dormant in Moses before He re-membered Moses's body with understanding. So, how do you know that…

"Auntie, those are parables."

"Isn't everything a parable niece?"

"Hachi," Cherry greeted the youthful looking Seminole girl who was climbing through the cabin hatch.

Once inside, Hachi pulled an iPhone out of the leather pouch she wore around her waist.

"Hachi, you know reception is impossible out here."

The small woman pressed the playback button.

Cherry started climbing down the tree as soon as the Bill O'Really Show recording finished.

"Cherry, where are you going?" Assata called out. "Talking about becoming food, you won't make it a mile, hell you won't make it to the other end of this swamp before you become some animal's breakfast. It's dark so you won't even see it coming."

"I don't need to see "it" coming. You two can wait on your signs," Cherry looked up. "Mine just came in the form of a Satan that I failed to kill a long time ago. I promise I will be a gator, a snake, or a bear's worst nightmare if they or anything in this swamp fucks with me. Right now, man, animal, and or demon can get it."

"Cherry, you talkin' crazy," Assata said.

Assata, Miracle, and the young Seminole woman followed Cherry down the ladder into the early morning dusk.

"I should have stabbed him in his sleep when he was blackmailing me years ago. I should have shot him in the head before then," Cherry trudged through the marsh, "after he stole his bestfriend's congregation before killing him," Cherry said. "Now this fool done put a target on every First Afrikan's head with that bullshit. Hell, I killed that cop Miracle, not any First Afrikan."

"Dammit!" Miracle said while falling into a foot of swamp water.

"The tallest woman out here with two foot knee high rubber boots on and you fall into a foot of swamp water," Assata said as she and Hachi helped her up.

"You just gon' keep walkin'?" Miracle shouted, frustration evident in her tone.

Cherry kept on.

"I'm sorry about Coltrane, but no one asked you to shoot that damn cop," Miracle shouted. "I had everything under control."

Cherry turned and pointed, "Don't say my man's name. Don't ever let his name come out your mouth. You don't know shit about him Miracle." She balled up her fists. "Your country young ass playin' super hero while I'm living real life. Fuck all the theatrics. If you wanted the cop dead, you woulda handled that before I put that steel in his mouth. Miracle, you ain't had a damn thing under control."

Cherry walked into a clearing. "I'm tired of these crackas and these cracka niggas killing our black men, and we just march. Fuck that! My Kumbaya, Lift Every Voice and Sing days are over."

"I'm with you Cherry," Miracle said.

"Bitch, you ain't with me. You ain't never been with me. You know that cracka was gon' kill my man. You coulda had my girl call and warn us. But noooo," she waved a finger in

221

the early morning night, "Bitch, I swear if you weren't my girl's niece."

"My auntie and my momma raised me to respect my elders, so I'm going to let you have that one, Cherry, you're upset, understandably."

The sun began to peak through the forest as it began to rise.

"Bitch," Cherry said, "Don't do me no favors. Out of respect for my girl, I'm gon' give you a pass little girl for not warning me about that racist cop."

"That's the last bitch I'm gon' be. My name is Miracle Joy Brown, and you best remember that or I'll throw all respect to the wind."

Miracle and Cherry walked toward each other.

"And what? What the fuck you gon' do?"

"Both of you, chill!" Assata shouted as she hurried toward her niece and her best friend.

"Nah," Cherry said. "She wanna talk like a grown ass woman, let her walk like a grown ass woman."

While Assata hurried to the impending confrontation, she said, "After you two get it in, I'm gon' kick both ya'll ass's all over this damn swamp. We out here in the middle of...

"Yahaloo...! Yahalooooooo.....!" The little Semeinole woman rocked back and forth on the heels of her knee high boots while chanting. "Yahaloo....! Yahalooo!"

The three women turned. Their vocal chords were frozen, but their eyes were not. Six bulging and screaming eyes stared at the gators, panthers, and a few other carnivores that surrounded the three black women in the blackwater swamp clearing.

"Yahalooooo....! Yahalooo!" Hachi's long black hair stood up in the air. The brown leather tassels that hung from her leather top swayed to the rhythm of the morning Florida autumn wind as she held her arms out. It was as if she were hanging from an invisible cross. An angel in brown.

"Yahalooooooo......! Yahalooo....!" She walked forward. Panthers, wild boars, and gators parted like the Red Sea.

"Cherry, Assata, and Miracle watched on in stunned and terrified silence until the young Seminole woman was within whispering distance."

"You have disturbed the peace within. Your negative energy." She pointed to the snarling creatures around them. "My friends have allowed you into their home. They have protected and made sure to stay out of sight as much as possible as to not frighten you. Your anger and aggression towards each other is the very reason they are poised to attack. They sense uneasiness and discord; this throws off their natural balance, that is why they are poised to annihilate you three." Hachi words and gestures were slow, melodic, and relaxing.

"Before I loosen your tongues and allow you to speak I need you to look at my friends, our friends. Replace your fear with love," she paused. "Now slowly inhale all the air you can through your nose. Do not take your eyes and your love off of ALL's animated creations – animated crations that you three recognized as animals. Now, stand straight up, chest out and relax as you release the breath from your mouth. Nod if you understand."

The three women nodded.

Hachi continued, "Now, repeat after me."

"Yahalooo......! Yahaloo...!"

Panthers growled. Boars bared their fangs and tusks as they snorted and stomped. Some gators hissed, some made snapping sounds as they opened and closed their mouths.

"Yahalooo.....! Yahhaloo...!"

The animals charged.

AROBAINI NA TANO

9:33 AM

November 8, 2016
Manhattan, New York

Chump was in his campaign headquarters office suite sitting next to his key advisor.

"I do not care how or who does it, Hand. Just keep Owen Cowherd in the hospital until the results are in!" Chump said.

"No." he said.

"Excuse me?"

"I said no." The mega preacher repeated.

Chump tried to grab the white stick of incense out of the little man's hand.

He was too fast.

"Stop waving that fucking incense back and forth. And what do you mean no?" Chump scowled.

Money continued making smoke circles with the foot long incense. "Is it the "N" or the "O"?"

"What?" Chump asked.

"No?" Money said. "Which part of the word do you need clarification on? The Na or the ohh. Babysitting criminals is not part of my job description."

At five-six, TJ Money was not much wider than a coke bottle, but when he entered a room, his aura seemed to swallow up all the space. The way he exuded confidence, you would have thought the small black man was the billionaire property mogul and frontrunner in today's presidential election.

"I meant criminals other than you, of course," Money said. "I'm getting paid to make sure that you get the conservative black vote and that you don't do anything to prevent you from becoming number forty-five."

"You people think you're so smart," Chump said.

"Which people would those be?" Money placed one of his hands in front of his face to admire the manicure he'd received yesterday.

"You people. You know what I mean. I'm about to be the leader of the free world in a few hours, and you are refusing an order from me, Donald J. Chump."

"You're right. Mr. Soon-To-Be-President-Elect," Money said as he sunk deeper in the reclining office chair. "I'm on it now. Whatever you say Mr. Soon-To-Be President. I am so sorry. What was I thinking?"

"Okay, Okay," Chump smiled his genuine camera fake smile. "I accept your apology, now let's go, chop-chop." Chump clapped his hands together.

Money recrossed his legs and changed the direction of the swirling stick of incense.

"I need you to move now, boy."

Money smiled.

"Well?"

"Well what?" Money continued making wide smoke circles with the smell good stick.

"Are you going to handle it or not?"

"Before I address your current request, I need you to answer the question that I put to you."

"Dammit, Money I don't have time for...

"Just answer my question Mr. Soon-To-Be-President-Elect. It's called common courtesy," Money explained, " I asked first."

Chump threw his hands in the air. "What fucking question, Hand?"

"The "N" or the "O", which do you need help with?"

"God dammit," Chump stomped a foot on his penthouse office suite glass floor.

"That's right." Money waved the white stick in the air. "God damns, not man."

"Why must we always do this dance?" Chump asked.

"Because I don't like you." Money smiled.

"Why not?"

"We don't have that much time." Money stood up.

"Are you going to do what I asked or what?"

With his back to Chump, Money said, "You have my wiring information. In about two minutes I should receive a text from Cayman National verifying a wire for two hundred thousand dollars."

"Two-hundred thousand, are you doing drugs Money?" Chump exploded.

"Three-hundred thousand," Money opened the door, "Just say a word, any word Mr. Soon-To-Be-President-Elect, and we can make it four-hundred."

AROBAINI NA SITA

6:33 PM

November 8, 2016
Terre Haute, Indiana

"Ah. Ah. Daddy C, what are you doin'?" Luke was startled awake by the sudden rough ride. "My truck! Slow down!" he watched as Claude drove through snow and rugged terrain. "My rims! My ribs! Owww!" Luke winced."

"You can get another truck. Ain't nothin' but one Truth, ya dig," Claude said. "While you was sleep I got some intel on the hospital they got Truth in."

"Can we just stop for a second please?" Luke asked before closing his eyes and shaking his head. "I gotta pee."

"Boy, you piss more than me, and I'm nearly twice your age." Claude drove with a huge marked up colorful map over the steering wheel.

"Why we driving through the woods?" Luke looked over at Claude. "When did you become Dr. Charles Drew?" he asked looking at the nametag on the lab coat Claude was wearing.

"Right before we crossed the Kentucky State line into Indiana a couple hours ago."

Luke yawned, "I been sleep for...

"Not long enough." Claude tuned to Luke.

"No," Luke reached out. "Keep your eyes on the road. Tree!" he pointed

Claude whipped the big F150 to the left dodging one oak before whipping the wheel to the right barely dodging another while holding the gas station map in his free hand.

"You think we was just gon' march into the lobby and up to the information desk and ask what room Owen Cowherd's in?"

"That was the idea," Luke said.

They pulled to a stop near a stream.

Luke jumped to relieve himself.

Claude put the F150 in park. "Luke, your daddy fucked you up, but Early, you ain't got no excuse."

"Excuse for what."

"That dumb shit that just came out ya'll head. Hell, when you say or do stupid shit around me, I'm gon' tell you so you'll make it the last time you say or do the dumb shit again.

"Luke climbed back in the passengers seat.

"*That was the idea*," Claude's head bobbed as he mimicked Luke. "Did you think a Presidential pardon was enough to get Truth out the penitentiary? Think," he tapped Luke on the forehead. "Would the enslaver give the enslaved a key to freedom and end over two thousand years of rule over ALL's kingdom?" Claude asked while reaching in the back seat and unzipping a black duffle.

"President Obama...

"President Obama what? OJ was found not guilty, and they still got him. What you think a pardon gon' do, if the governemnt want him." Claude went back to the duffle. "Sheee-itttt."

"Daddy C, you do know that it's snow on the ground."

"Now that," Claude pulled out a pair of rubber boots and handed them to Luke, "is a prime example of dumb shit. I done drove all the way here ten hours, and you ask me if I know if there's snow on the ground?"

"Why do you always talk so low," Luke asked, "It ain't like anyone can hear you."

"Can you hear me?" Claude asked.

"Yeah. But…"

"Nothing," Claude said while fidgeting through the duffle.

"What's that," Luke stared at the contraption Claude was pulling over his head.

"Night goggles with a P77B infra red built in Nikon AF-S Nikkor 1200mm camera scope that can take a high definition picture of a black ant at midnight at three hundred yards."

"Where did you get that?" Luke pointed. "Is that thing even legal?"

"If I answer either, I might have to kill you," Claude said while he continued working. "You still wanna know?"

"Nah," Luke looked up as he pulled on the second rubber boot. "I'm good," he laughed.

"Same thing make you laugh make you cry," Claude said before he pulled the big duffle up front, "Come on," Claude hopped out of the truck.

Luke walked around the truck to Claude.

"So, how do you know for sure what hospital Truth is in?"

"Boy, you ask too many questions," Claude said.

"How do you know, Daddy C?"

"I know people."

"What's that supposed to mean?"

"If I tell you, I'll have to kill you. Now, put this on," Claude said while pulling out a camouflage snowsuit.

"Where's yours?" Luke asked.

"Boy, I done swam in swamps colder in this when I was your age," he reached into the duffle and pulled out a wide metal black briefcase."

"I bet you walked ten miles up hill to school both ways too."

"Backwards and barefoot in the snow, ya dig."

"You got jokes Daddy C, so what's the plan?" Luke asked, "It's obvious you have one."

"A man that fails to plan is a damn fool," Claude said while unsnapping the metal briefcase on the hood of the Pickup.

"I think the saying is a man that fails to plan, plans to fail," Luke smiled proud of his quick wit.

Claude turned and looked up at the much taller, wider, younger man. "Don't quote no shit nobody else say. An Afrikan creates where most imitate, ya dig?"

"Okay, don't you think it's time I knew the plan," Luke asked.

Claude pulled a Browning Nine Millimeter out of the briefcase. "Look if you gon' marry my baby you gon' have to get real Afrikan real fast."

"Whachu mean Daddy C?" Luke asked. "I am Afrikan and who said anything about getting married?"

"Son, if Afrikan was just a skin color than we'd all be free." Claude tapped a finger against his forehead. "Afrikan is an awareness of self to the degree that one acts in accordance to the good of all humanity."

"Yeah, I know that. You know sometimes it's easy to forget though," Luke said. "Hold up, who said anything about getting married Daddy C? I love. I mean me and Winnie done already...

"Hey, hey, choose your words very carefully son," Claude said while screwing a silencer onto the browning.

"Why do you have… Luke looked at the handgun. "We ain't killing no body," Luke said. "Where'd you get that Daddy C?"

"If I tell you I might have to kill you son. Besides, you don't know what we gon' do," He popped the clip into the gun. "Easiest way to clear a room," he held the silenced gun in front of him, "and an entire hospital if needed." Claude waved the gun toward Luke, "Now, as I was saying I know it's not my business but be honest boy, tell me how both ya'll feel about my daughter, don't hold back."

I swear ta ALL if you get me killed Early, Luke thought.

Chill Luke, I got this, Early thought. *Besides, I'm the one that loves Winnie.*

"You don't love nothing," Luke accidentally said out loud. "I love her, and she loves me."

"What the," Claude looked at Luke. "Oh, I get it," the older man nodded, "ya'll both love my baby," he waved the gun in the cold early night air. "Now that's some weird shit, but nothing about you two is normal. But I guess love don't dance to nobody's beat but the heart." He handed the gun over to Luke.

"What am I supposed to do with this?"

"Hold it until I say otherwise," Claude said.

"How did you know Daddy C? How did you know I, we were in love with Winnie?"

Claude started screwing the three aluminum pipes together that he removed from the briefcase. "Only reason I didn't slit your throat in your sleep back at the cabin was by the time the opportunity presented itself, my baby was already hooked."

"Why you was gon' kill me?" Early asked, "You know who I am Daddy C."

"Yeah, but it's just hard to trust that skin you in," he said lifting the contraption to his shoulder.

"A surface to air missile, hell to the double hell no. Daddy C, you done lost..."

"What?" Claude backed up before turning. The missile launcher was over his shoulder and pointed at Luke. "Didn't I tell you about talking so damn much," he turned and playfully slapped Luke upside the head with his free hand. "Shut up and put these goggles on."

"Whoaaa," Luke backed into the truck. "Everything is so big. The hospital," Luke reached out. "Whoaaa! Where did that come from?"

"A few hundred yards through the..."

"Trees." Luke said. "All the trees are gone. The hospital is right in front of my face.

"Claude tapped a button near Luke's left eye. The night vison's computer lens self-adjusted.

A few seconds later, Claude pulled the goggles off of Luke's head.

"Whoaaaa. The hospital was right here. I could touch it. No way," Luke said.

"Terre Haute Regional is three hundred and forty three yards away," Claude said while making some adjustments to the missile's site.

"We ain't blowin' up no hospital. You can be Ossama Bin Laden if you want, Daddy C," he turned, "I'll just be Ossama Ben leaving."

He'd taken seven steps before a bullet whizzed by his head.

"Motha fu- Daddy C," Luke grabbed his ear before turning around. *"You almost shot me?"*

Claude had a high tech missile launcher on one shoulder and the Browning in his free hand. "Calm down," I didn't almost shoot you. I shot past you. If I wanted to shoot you, you of all people should know that I would have. Besides *we* ain't blowin' up nothin. My baby, Lena would kill me.

Claude lifted the missile launcher over his head and placed it on Luke's shoulders "You gon' blow some shit up, Afrikan."

AROBAINI NA SABA

6:53 PM

Terre Haute, Indiana
November 8, 2016

Terre Haute Regional Hospital had served the Wabash Valley community of Terre Haute, Indiana for over one hundred and thirty years. At precisely 6:53 PM twelve nuns from the St. Francis Carmelite Monastery barricaded themselves at the East and West wing entrances.

"You have to move sisters," hospital security commanded.

The nuns sat arm in arm, grey candles on the ground in front of them.

"What do they want?" Renee Grant, the acting hospital administrator, asked her head of security.

Jim Bob Boone shrugged his pointy shoulders. "Don't quite rightly know ma'am. They just keep a hummin' that mumbo jumbo, 'hring shring' or somethin' or the other."

"Well, do something!" The fifty-year-old black woman demanded.

"What do you want me to do ma'am?"

"I don't know." She said, an exacerbated look shrouded her face. "This is your job."

He shrugged his shoulders. "I could radio the police."

"For some nuns?"

Security was so busy with the nuns, they didn't pay attention to the orange Reeses peanut butter wrapping that Claude glued to the outside wall of the uninhabited South wing that was under reconstruction.

Claude tapped his earpiece twice before asking, "Do you see your target?"

"Perfectly," Luke's voice came through the hearing aid like earpiece Claude wore.

****

Less than five minutes later Claude was a drooling, blind invalid being wheeled into the Emergency room entrance by an old friend.

"Arr, ar, arrrr," Claude mumbled

"Excuse me, Doctor," the nurse looked at the nametag of the man that wheeled Claude in, "Whitelove, haven't seen you before."

"Uhhh...

She waved. "We can make introductions later, right now some nuns got half the entrances blocked off. Short staffed. The election. We are swamped."

"Arh-Arhh-Arh-har," Claude grunted.

"Blind and def," Whitelove said. "Epileptic seizure."

Before doctor or patient could react, she grabbed the chart out of the doctor's hand. "We need you in maternity Dr. Whitelove, ASAP."

"But, I…"

Claude used his curled hand to wipe the drool from his salt and pepper goatee before tapping the transmitter in his ear. "Now."

The explosion n the South wing felt like an earthquake in the emergency room.

Instant pandemonium. People started screaming and scrambling for the exits while Dr. Whitelove wheeled Claude further into the hospital.

Moments later, Claude rose from the chair and picked up the labcoat he was sitting on.

Once the elevator closed both men in, the man disguised as Dr. Whitelove stuck out his fist and greeted, "Afrikan first."

Claude bumped fists with his, "First Afrikan."

The two men embraced.

"Lazarus Mcphee," Claude smiled before taking a good look at his college roommate, "the baddest white Afrikan that most can't see."

"The reason why after forty years you called on me," the priest said.

Claude hurriedly put on the lab coat, stethoscope and glasses and got up behind the wheelchair before the ancient elevator reached its destination.

"Is Denmark and Jebediah in position?" Claude asked.

"Backed up in the stolen ambulance as you requested."

"That's what I'm talkin' 'bout," he high fived the priest. "Only way to get shit done is to call on Afrikans who are ready to die for freedom," Claude said.

The two old friends were stepping off the elevator when they were approached by hospital staff. "Dr. Whitelove," the young man said, "We need you in IC," he pulled on Mcphee's labcoat, "Right now. She's hemorrhaging badly, the fourteen year old nor the baby have a chance without immediate attention."

"Charles," Mcphee put a hand on Claude's shoulders, "You go check on the patient in 514; I'll go with this young man."

Claude and Lazarus followed the young man although neither had an ounce of medical training.

"Say, brotha, you know where I can find uh, Truth, I mean Owen Cowherd?"

"They moved Mr. Cowherd a few hours ago?" The young man said.

"Where to?" Claude asked.

"I ain't supposed to know, but I sorta followed them to the city morgue."

Claude shook his head, "Damn."

"Nah, the Terre Haute Indiana City Morgue is in the basement while the renovations are being done to the old building connected to the South wing," the young man said.

Claude veered left while his friend and the young man went right.

Five minutes later, Claude found Truth.

Five minutes after finding Truth incapacitated, Claude climbed into the stolen ambulance parked outside the Emergency Room exit.

"Where's Truth, Baba?" the First Afrikan junior minister, Reverend King, asked.

Claude took a second to catch his breath before answering. "Jebediah, I need you."

"Baba, What's wrong?"

"Truth is in the hospital basement. Come on."

"What happened to Father McPhee?"

"We don't have time," Claude said with his hand on the door knob, "Come on Jebediah."

Denmark came up from the back of the Ambulance. "Whachu need me to do Daddy C?"

"Stay here keep your head down but stay alert and if shit goes sideways you get the hell outta here."

Claude turned to Jebediah. "Come on."

"Baba, no disrespect but my big ass can only move so fast. You know I just got my sugar back down."

"Jebediah," Claude interrupted, "They did something to Truth. He's out like a light, and I know they gon' kill him if Chump steals the election tonight."

"We just need to get outta here, Baba. The feds'll be here any moment," Jebediah pointed a finger at the people and cars that were racing through the snow to get as far away from the smoke and the explosion that nearly took out the uninhabited South wing.

"Nah, Baba I ain't never been to jail. I ain't 'bout to break my perfect record now."

"Fifty-two?" Claude said.

"What?"

"That test. Chemistry," Claude nodded. "Pat told you to pray."

"Ah, Momma told you that story," Jebediah closed his eyes and smiled. He could see his mother as clear as day. "Baba, I was in the ninth grade. I could never relate to them formulas, and all that. You know social studies was my thang."

"I know the story son. That's why I brought it up. Pat told you to pray about the test. You hadn't thought about that remember."

The big man nodded.

"Pat King prayed over everything and everyone, but when she told you to pray what did you do?"

"I prayed. I prayed hard Baba. I prayed with all my heart. I mean I prayed."

"What did you do after you prayed?"

"Shoot, I was tired. I had stressed over the test that whole evening?"

"How long did you know about this test?"

"I don't know? He shrugged. "A week or two I guess."

"I asked you what you did after you prayed Jeb?"

"I went to bed."

"Where you still stressed after you prayed?"

"Nah, Baba, I had let go and let ALL. Momma always said with prayer all things are possible. Oh, but a little stress did come back when momma made me get up and study. But, that too soon left my body. I stayed up a little longer. I looked at the study material but that was about it. I just knew ALL had me."

"So you went to school took the test, failed, and you felt let down. You were confused. Why, because you had tried to con ALL. You can't con the Lord son."

"I wasn't trying to…"

"Yes you were. You were trying to get the Lord to do all the work. That was selfish son. ALL can, but it's up to you to use that thing called will. I bet after that test, you prayed, and studied next time."

"Shoot, baba, the next few times," Jebediah said.

"James 2:14-26, faith without works," Claude said. "Did Nat Turner just pray or did he pray and fight for the reality he envisioned? Did Moses just sit up on the mountain and pray or did he come down and fight for the reality he envisioned? You are Afrikan first, First Afrikan, hued with the breath of life. No man can kill you son. You are the light."

The three hundred and sixty pound pastor jumped out of that ambulance driver's seat and was on his way inside the hospital before Claude opened his door.

"Shit," Claude said as he skip-jogged to catch up to the human steamroller that had no idea where he was going.

Claude caught up to the big man at the emergency room entrance.

"Come on," Reverend King said after noticing the elevator was either stuck or broke. The big man literally jumped down an entire flight of stairs twice.

"Sheee-itttt." Claude huffed while trying to catch his breath at the top of the stairs. "Fifth floor, I mean door, fifth door to the left," he said as Jebediah exited the stairwell into the hospital basement.

Claude's breathing had just returned to some semblance of normality when Jebediah kicked the stairwell door open a few minutes later.

The First Afrikan minister took the stairs two, three at a time.

"You just can't carry Truth outta here like that," Claude said looking at the minister who carried the six-foot, hundred ninety pound Truth over his shoulders.

He sidestepped Claude, "Watch me."

AROBAINI NA NANE

6:56 PM

Terre Haute, Indiana
November 8, 2016

Stonewall clapped. "Bravo! Bravo!"

"Shit!" Startled, the missile launcher fell from Luke's shoulders. He turned to face his father.

"Shit is right," Stonewall had his gloved hands behind his back. He stepped forward. "Let's go," Stonewall turned and started walking, "You can thank me later for saving you from that creek."

Luke picked up the Browning 9mm and pointed it at his father's head.

"Boy, one thing I always told you is don't ever pull your weapon unless you are going to use it."

He's right, just like Daddy C says, you done pulled the gun. Now, shoot him Luke.

"How do you know I'm pointing a gun at you?"

"Look down," Stonewall said with his back still turned. "If you don't look down now boy, you will never look up again."

The infra red dots began at his feet and went all the way up to his head. "Fuck!"

"Without condom nor lubricant," the elder Duke said.

Luke looked around the dark forest. "Where are your men?"

Stonewall pointed to the trees.

"Seriously!" Luke shook his head. "Camouflaged drones. Toy planes with guns."

"More like remote controlled flying guns. Each drone shoots .22 caliber shredders, and each has a twenty-five bullet capacity." The elder Duke was enjoying himself although the weather had dropped to twenty-nine degrees. "Once the infrared scope spots its target a little geek with glasses behind a computer miles away presses a button and the drone locks onto its target like a pit viper. Pinpoint accurate to within two millimeters of its target."

"How did you know I was here?"

"Boy, when you take a piss I know. You forgot who I am obviously. Now come on."

Luke crossed his arms but did not move. "Am I under arrest?"

"At the end of the day you are still my son, and the family has decided that your involvement with niggras could derail everything that the family is trying to do."

Luke twisted his face into a mask of hate. "Since you're not arresting me and your drones aren't going to shoot me then I'm not going anywhere with you."

"I was hoping you would say that." Stonewall pulled out a stun gun before shooting enough voltage in his son to put down a cow.

AROBAINI NA TISA

6:59 PM

Terre Haute, Indiana
November 8, 2016

Claude and Jebediah saw the flashing blue lights on the monitors behind the security and information desk before entering the Emergency Room area.

"Okay," Claude said, "Put Truth down and go out through the basement. I know it's a risk, but them Billy's are gon' shoot us dead if we walk out those doors, ya dig."

Jebediah kept walking.

"Dammit, Jebediah, you know how I hate dumb shit. And ain't nothing dumber than walking into a firing squad."

"No weapon formed against me will prosper!"

"Fool, that's what Nat Turner thought. You know how many Black men thought and said that before a cracka blew his brains out?" Claude pleaded.

The hospital emergency room sliding doors opened. "Not enough."

Claude took off his hat and threw it to the ground. "Shit."

To his left there were ten to twelve unmarked and marked local and state police cars. White and black men in uniform were pointing guns at Jebediah.

The First Afrikan minister looked to his right. The ambulance was maybe thirty, forty paces away.

"Stop right there, Jebediah King," a voice behind a bullhorn demanded.

"As I walk through the Valley, followed and shadowed by your weapons of death, I fear no evil. I have Truth in my arms and love as my guide."

****

"He is not going to surrender," the acting commander spoke into the earpiece.

"Shoot him," Stonewall Duke said.

"Commissioner Duke, he's unarmed. We just can't. I cannot make that call."

****

"This has to be the dumbest shit I have ever done. Damn," Claude said as he followed.

Jebediah continued, "I have the freedom to act. My freedom to choose is the essence of my divinity. I will. Therefore. I am free. I created everything you see. The created is ill equipped to kill the creator, you just have to believe."

****

The commissioner patched Chump in after the Terre Haute Indiana police lieutennant sent the live video feed.

"The polls are closing in twenty minutes, as you have just saw and heard. I am destroying the bitch. Now, it's up to you lieutenant, you can open fire on the fucking black terrorists or in a couple months after I am sworn in I will make you, your family, and you friends pay dearly for your insubordination. Now on the other hand, after you take the monster and the gorilla carrying him down you will be a national hero, and I will have no choice but to offer you a high ranking post in my cabinet."

****

Jebediah was maybe ten paces from the ambulance when the eleven officers fired.

****

"I am hue. The breath is in me. The breath moves me. No man can extinguish the breath. I am the breath that breathes life." He chanted as he brought Truth closer to the vehicle. "I am ALL."

The smoke from the hail of gunpowder and pulverized hospital wall behind Jebediah provided cover as Denmark opened the rear Ambulance doors.

Claude dove inside. "Them some sorry shootin' cats."

Jebediah ran and got behind the wheel while Denmark and Claude secured Truth in the back.

Moments later the Ambulance drove through a two car barricade. Bullets riddled the Ambulance.

"Anybody hurt," Jebediah asked as he bent the curb out of the hospital complex.

"Nah, Jeb," Claude replied. "We good."

"Damn right we good," The big man said as he sped down the road. "We got ALL. We are gods. You see how them crackas looked when they bullets missed me. Hell yeah. Hell yeah. I told 'em. You heard me D," the big man said to the bright skinned young First Afrikan who dropped everything on

245

a moments notice. Left Sapporah and Kaena, his two babies and his wife, Monrovia back in Georgia to come help save Truth.

Jebediah slowed the big ambulance down to fifty-five.

"Why we slowing down brotha?" Denmark asked.

"No need to rush. I got us. I already proved that. Them crackas ain't even following us.

Jebediah never saw the Drones or the infrared lights that beamed down on the stolen ambulance.

****

Watching the entire scene on his iPad from the back seat of the black Suburban, The Hand smiled before engaging the guns on the two drones. It only took a moment for the drones to lock onto the target.

The overpass was coming up soon.

The ambulance slowed down before coming to the curving road ahead.

Money pressed ENTER on the iPad and a moment later a hail of bullets blew out lights, the front windshield and finally the driver side front tire sending the vehicle in a tailspin knocking over the twenty-five mile per hour speed limit sign before flipping over the guardrail.

****

"Please ALL." Jebediah prayed as they started a death tumble toward the awaiting freezing dark body of water that made up the Wabash River.

HAMSINI

Thirty-three days later

3:33 AM

Atlanta, Georgia
<u>December 3, 2016</u>

At President-elect Chump's prodding, General Lesure hired the "Patriot Act" to discreetly take out the head of First Afrikan. According to a de-classified NSA report, the group of elite mercenaries for hire did not exist. Just another conspiracy theory the report had concluded.

William Sherman VI, the chief strategist for the band of 'killers for hire' blinked four times in rapid succession triggering the camera inside his night vision goggles.

"Any idea what could be producing that much smoke," the group's chief strategist asked as the night vision cameras zoomed in on Dr. Logun's home.

"Hell if I know son, I'm not a…" The smoke cloud coming from Dr. Logun's chimney made the head of the NSA lose his train of thought.

"Not a what, sir?"

"A got damn psychic. Hell, you men are the best trained killers in the friggin' world. Just get in there and extinguish the target."

"My body heat sensors read two live bodies on the main level."

"The target and his wife," the General said.

"I know sir," Sherman said, "Their heart palpitations indicate that they're asleep. I'm not concerned about them. It's the immense heat coming from the basement that calls for concern. There could be others. We just can not ascertain the probability for casualties on our side if we do not know what that heat source is."

"They have that Family and Friends day thing later, or rather their church is supposed to. You know how much they like to celebrate. Hell, they probably cooking up a mess of food, I don't know."

"I don't like it sir. We should do some further reconnaissance and come back once we…"

"Got damn your time. I fuckin' saved yours and all your men from the needle eight years ago when I gave you the list of who was on that committee. We've paid you over ten million over the last few years to eliminate certain undesirables in and outside of the American government."

"I understand that sir," the leader said, "Me and my men are truly grateful, but…"

"But nothing son, You are a friggin' Seal, a friggin' patriot like the name we came up with when my predessesor put this team together ten years ago. For Christ sake, just get in there and do your damn job son. Have a little faith."

"Respectfully sir," Sherman said, "Faith has nothing to do with it. Planning does. I just can not with a clean conscious send my men in without…

"Clean conscious," the head of the NSA said. "Boy, you wouldn't know what a clean conscious was if it kissed you in the mouth. All the men, women, and children you have killed for us and God knows who else. Now you can go and do your friggin' job now and get paid an extra hundred thou or you can pre-order forty-two tombstones for the wives, children, and parents of your men."

"I don't respond well to threats, sir."

"A boy makes threats," the NSA chief said. "A man does what he says."

The eleven cameras in the night vision goggles gave the head of the NSA a front row seat to the action. He could have had the house blown up or he could have done a number of things to make it look like an accident, but the President-Elect wanted to send a message to the group that The Hand labeled, a terrorist cell.

General Lesure sipped on his Grand Marnier while watching the trained American killers close in on the ranch home in the middle class predominantly African-American suburban community.

Lesure was daydreaming about being appointed Secretary of State after Chump was confirmed next month. Moments later, he tuned back into the sixty-inch computer monitor.

As of late, Will Sherman, the team's chief strategist began to question whether he himself was really a patriot or just a hired mercenary. He knew too well that second guessing self led to uncontrollable consequences. After losing Antwon, his thirteen year old son, at the hands of a reckless police officer last year, it was hard for him not to question what a patriot really was.

Sherman figured that the second-year patrolman must have been scared. Antwon and the two boys had been playing cops and robbers with plastic guns when the patrol car pulled up to the park. His two friends ran, but Antwon did not. The officer's loud and threatening tone must have terrified the thirteen year old into not dropping the plastic gun when the officers commanded. As soon as Antwon turned to face his accusers, they shot him down like he was an unarmed blackman pulled over by the police.

While Sherman was reflecting, Strom the team leader gave the signal and the team threw tear gas threw the windows before going in guns blazing.

HAMSINI NA MOJA

3:43 AM

Atlanta, Georgia
December 3, 2016

Heat. Intense heat is what the Patriot Act's chief strategist and second in command felt before he even opened his eyes. His team were the first thing that came to mind as the scent of cordite and rusted metal rushed the assassin's senses. Will Sherman slowly opened his eyes.

At first nothing. He blinked several times... Blurred images. Like his vision, everything was foggy.

He wanted to wipe the sweat that was trickling down his eyelids. He dared not move before he could assess the situation. He'd already ascertained that the gray walled and floored warehouse like room he awoke in was lined with thick plastic.

Sherman heard pain and heartache in what sounded like a black man wailing in grief. He turned. It was the target...

"I don't know what else to do. I love you. I love the ALL in you. We all came from ALL. I'm so sorry. I'm so sorry I failed you. I'm sorry that I don't know how to heal your pain.

I'm so sorry brotha. I love the ALL in you, the First Afrikan in you my Afrikan hue." Logun cried.

It looked like Dr. Logun was rising, no floating up. Like... Like a butterfly... The image was blurry, but his voice couldn't be clearer.

"I failed in seeing your pain. I failed in exorcising the demons that would make you take another life for money. Money! An object that we hue-mankind creates. An object that we together give value to... Lord please forgive me and have mercy on me as I return this soul to you."

Will Sherman blinked several times in quick succession. His eyes cleared right as the Reverend Doctor Logun rose up and brought the gun to team leader Major Strom Thurmond's head.

"Pshhk," The blood and brain splatter made more noise than the silenced bullet that extinguished the life out of the paramilitary mercenary gang leader.

Lost and hardened blue orbs stared off into space as Strom Thurmond IV's body crumbled unceremoniously to the grey plastic lined concrete floor.

After a long moment of silence someone clapped, and the area was illuminated.

Thirty-four year old Will Sherman had no words as he covered his eyes from the instant influx of light.

"Excuse me Mr. Sherman," Dr. Logun said. "I'm... I'm having a hard time," the spiritual father and leader of First Afrikan bent over and would have fallen over from grief if it weren't for Louis Muhammad, the eighty-three year old leader of the Nation of Islam. This is only the second time that the honorable Minister Muhammad, Dr. Logun and the other ten spiritual leaders charged with helping to raise and re-awaken Zion and Miracle were together.

Minister Muhammad, one of the council of clerics prayed, "Allah be with you young Will, Allah be with all of us in our time of peril, sorrow, and loss..."

"Peril, sorrow, loss" The mercenary spoke up knowing his next words could be his last. "You just shot a man dead," he pointed a gloved finger at the Minister, "You and that Muslim..." Disdain and disgust were in his eyes and voice as the strategist for the team of mercenaries pointed and spoke. "Why are you all crying?"

Now that his focus wasn't so blurry, Will surveyed the basement with his eyes. He should have been terrified by the bodies. The men he had fought and killed with for almost a decade. He should have been more terrified at the creamatorium on the other side of the basement. Now he knew why so much smoke was being emitted from the chimneystacks on the roof.

"You killed them. All of them even the black guys. Animals! You talk so much about race and you kill your own as if they... as if they were rabid dogs," the thirty-four year old mercenary rose to his feet.

Dr. Logun was in too much grief to respond.

Seventy-five year old Reverend Jeremiah White stepped up. "You and," the controversial Chicago truth teacher pointed to the body of the slain leader, "Strom did this. Chump did this. Your ancestors did this. Our ancestors did this. What you see is a response to the call of action that the system of division and hate began when Queen Isabella and King Ferdinand went to Pope Alexander in 1493, and he issued the *'Doctrine of Discovery'*, the document to facilitate a moral reasoning that allowed for the rape, murder, abuse, and Chattel enslavement of our brown brotha's and sista's of the world. We are men, hue-men...

"Hued men don't kill police officers. Humans don't..." Sherman looked at his fallen brothers, "Humans do not..." images of police officers kicking, beating and spitting on an unarmed black man flashed through his mind. "Humans do not..." before he could complete his thought for the second time images played in his mind. Images of two white police officers pulling up to a park gazebo and jumping out of a squad car. A frightened thirteen-year old child frozen. Terrified. Drop the gun they said. The child looked down at the plastic gun in his hand. Before he could look up. POW! POW! POW! POW! Dead before the toy gun hit the pavement. "Humans don't... shoot and kill innocent... men," a quandary of emotions flooded Will Sherman's spirit. His eyes watered. "I am no better than," he shook his head in hopes of clearing the visions he was having, "I mean you are no better than Hitler, Genghis Khan..."

Minister Muhammad spoke up, "Pilate, Mann, Crow, Mbuto, and we can not forget George Washington, hell all fifty three slaveholders, rapists, murders, and thieves that drafted the most divisive document that has facilitated the legal rape and murder of human beings since Pope Alexander's 1493 'Doctrine of Discovery.'

Dr. Hakim Fast, the orthodox Muslim leader and council of cleric member, stepped in. "Young William, the men mentioned had dark souls, their Afrikan light was buried so deep that they had to be washed from this world in hopes that they would be delivered from evil in the next. So, you are absolutely correct. Hued men don't kill police officers. Hued men fight for peace. Peace is freedom," the half indigenous, half black Afrikan Islamic cleric tapped a finger against his temple, "Freeing the dome of anything that interferes with loving humanity is the walk of an Afrikan, young William," Dr. Fast smiled.

The powerful and well spoken leader of the Nation of Islam chimed back in, "It's no secret William, even your scientists and fellow Europeans finally came to accept that the first woman and man was an Afrikan. You're the strategist young William," The Minister said, "If hue-manity began in Afrika, than we are all essentially what?"

William replied, "You say this, but your people... Your leaders in Africa. Jacob Zuma, South Africa's successor to

Mandela, Nigeria, Sudan, they all have Afrikan leaders, and they are just as bad or worse than…"

"Worse than what, any Euro-peon?" Dr. Logun spoke for the first time since shooting the ten men in the head. "Worst than General William Sherman, your ancestor. Worst than Donald Chump, your current boss. Worse than the men in uniform who murder Black children, black women and men at random. Worse than you Will."

"According to my intel your…"

"Will Sherman, your intel is about as worthless as the ten bodies that are about to go into that oven," Reverend White pointed to the crematorium at the far end of the basement. "Since my eighteen year old son Michael Brown was cut down by your bullets two years ago, you've murdered my thireen year old son Tamir, my fourteen year old son Cameron, my eighteen year old son VonDerrit, My seventeen year old son Laquan," The Chicago pastor shook with grief.

Archbishop George Rawlings came from behind the huge oven and continued, "You killed my baby, my eighteen year old princess Carey, my eighteen year old son Qusean, my nineteen year old son Miguel, My son… Oh my son," he shook his head, "Dillon."

Ousted Afrikan Joel Naison put a consoling arm around the Catholic Archbishop. Joel looked at the mercenary that shared his same skin tone, "You fuckers killed my son Levi. He was only eighteen. My nineteen year old daughter Karen, Sergio, my eighteen year old son. Roshad, my nineteen year old son and ohhhh, ohhhhh," he wailed, "My love. My baby girl, nineteen year old Diana, she didn't know. She didn't," the famous author lecturer, wailed, "none of my children deserved…. No parent should ever outlive their children."

Sherman pointed, "You are all…"

"Afrikans?" Dr. Logun said.

Sherman shook his head no, "Murderers."

"Dr. Logun spoke up, "Killers of darkness so light can shine in the hearts and minds of all.""

"Murder all the same!" Sherman spat.

"It's not all the same young William." Dr. Fast explained, "We murder anything that obstructs the love of bringing humanity back to the time when love ruled all decisions. The time when the love of humanity ruled over our lower selves instead of greed and envy. Before the Euro-peon consciousness arrived on these shores our people took life to give life, it was never for greed and envy because these emotions did not exist in the tribal conscious. The tribe is one unit with many hands."

Will stood at attention. "Why are you explaining anything to me? Why don't I have a bullet in my head like the others?" he asked as his eyes wandered to were the men had fallen.

"Because we don't murder Afrikans," Dr. Logun said.

"What does that have to do with me?" The Alabama blonde haired native asked.

Dr. Logun smiled. "A few minutes ago when you first came to, you asked why? Why was I grieving and for who was I grieving?" The sixty-year old pastor let his words marinate in the mind of the young fearless white man he stood in front of. "I was, we were all in pain. I had to take the life of men, men no worse, no better than me, men that I could not, we could not heal. Men who were in so much pain and couldn't figure out any way to mask that pain other than killing off Afrikan and black life. I grieved for the good in," Dr. Logun turned to the ten dead bodies, "them that the physical world will never know. If we could have just killed the evil spirits that held the good in them down. We would not of had to…"

The ousted and disgraced Dallas pastor Joel Naison emerged from the sea of brown faces. "The reason we are not grieving over you now is because you are more Afrikan than Euro-peon."

Will Sherman was more confused than ever. *Had this guy lost his mind? Before the scandal broke in I think '09, Naison was one of if not the most popular man of God in the country.* "But... But..." Will pointed, "How can you? A white...

"Afrikan," Joel interrupted. "I think of myself as more of an olive brown, maybe even pale peach brown, but not white." The Texas pastor shook his head, "Definitely not white." I am Afrikan son. You're smart so they say. Take the number five, multiply it by five. What do you get?"

"You're a disgrace. A white man," The young man looked the older pastor up and down. "I don't have time for this. If you are going to shoot me just do it."

Reverend Naison looked back at Dr. Logun. "You guys keep saying this one is smart. No information we have suggests he or any of them were colorblind. Yet he doesn't know simple colors. And he is seriously thinking about lunging and choking the life out of me," the pastor said with his back still to the angry muscle budging ex-Navy Seal.

"I pray he doesn't do that Joel, that will be a big mistake," Bishop Rawlings said before sliding one of the dead government assassins onto the metal conveyor belt that pulled the bodies into the crematorium's fire. "They say being burned alive is the most excruciating pain a man could suffer."

The Dallas, Texas pastor turned back to the young man. "Now, you really don't wanna die. I'm so sorry about what happened to Antwon last year, but Anthony still needs you. You know what it means to lose a child at the hands of ignorance and fear. Stop hiding behind the mask. You're not one of THEM William Sherman. You share their skin tone, but you got way too much love in you too hate. Save your other black child. Anthony is still here."

The soldier's eyes widened.

"Same way you have been watching us," Reverend Naison smiled, "We've been watching you and all the governments alphabet boys and girls. How do you think we knew you were coming?"

Dr. Logun tapped Naison on the shoulder, "May I?"

"By all means," Naison stepped aside.

"Two-thousand and three," Dr. Logun tapped a finger against his temple for a moment, "Oh yeah," he pointed the finger in the air "You were stateside for a brief period William. Carla Weber, you met her at 'Pin Ups', an adult entertainment club. You and her went to the parking lot and got into your truck. That was the last time you saw or probably even thought about her until almost a year later, when in Afghanistan you received a letter and some pictures from Carla. Before you even read the letter you knew those boys were yours. Not only did they look like you, but you felt them. You loved them immediately.

You wrote Carla back reassuring her that you would take care of her and the children. And for thirteen years you have. Antwon has never seen you, but he was your son. He stood his ground like you would have. But he didn't have a chance. Antwon did exactly what you would have told him to do when the officers ordered him to stop."

Trained to endure any torture that the enemy could dish out, William was unprepared for the emotions that were possessing his body. At first a stream of tears.

Naison picked up where Dr. Logun left off. "You wrote to them boys every week and you still do a year after Antwon's death. Thirteen hundred and fifty-seven sealed, stamped and unmailed letters. You even paid over twenty thousand dollars to help get Carla off of drugs. And," Reverend Naison placed a finger in the air. "Carla Weber is not only drug free, but she is a registered nurse today because you paid for her education."

Reverend White jumped in, "Now what I wanna know is how in the Hell can somebody with so much love for humanity practice so much hate. Boy, you have to be absolutely miserable or you're a pain freak."

The women, the pills, the money, the kills, William thought, *He's right. I hate my life. I hate me. Nothing is enough. Nothing will ever satisfy me. I will never be good enough.*

Reverend Logun walked up and put his arms around the man that planned and tried to kill him and his wife a few hours ago.

"Get your fucking hands off me." Every muscle in Will's body bulged as he tried to shake the hundred-seventy pound, sixty-year old Afrikan off of him. Dr. Logun was barely hanging on before Joel and the other clerics joined forces and hugged and held Will for hours.

HAMSINI NA MBILI

Forty-five days later

3:33 AM

Terre Haute, Indiana
January 20, 2017

"Just do it, damn." Claude looked up from his bottom bunk.

The sixty-year old First Afrikan pittled with his goatee while pondering if he'd given the young man up top sound advice.

Claude Cabral had been in the Terre Haute, Indiana County Jail with Daniel and Denmark since election night. No charge, no bond, no court appearance. Outside of the First Afrikan community, no one seemed to care, but the three men knew better. The focus was on freeing Luke and Truth. The three First Afrikans in the county jail knew that without Truth no one could ever be free.

No one had seen Truth since the feds took him when they pulled the four men up from the Wabash River embankment the night of the arrest two and half months ago. 'Just do it', Claude thought back to the advice he'd just administered. If he hadn't 'just did it,' none of them would be in jail. It would be different if they had saved Truth, but they had not.

"I am pops, soon as I rise up outta here, " the young man whispered from his top bunk, careful not to wake the other inmates.

"Say what?" Claude asked, sorry my mind was somehere else.

"You said 'just do it'. I said I am, as soon as I declare myself a soverign citizen and rise up outta here, real talk."

The older First Afrikan put down the *USA Today* he'd been reading. "Real talk is that I'm so tired of folks talkin' 'bout what they gon' do. If I had one penny," Claude pointed a finger in the air, "just one for every hard leg that done told me what they was gon' do."

"I ain't every hard leg, pops. Nahhhhhh. Real talk, I ain't ever comin' back here, pops. This the last time onetime gon' put this black ass in a cage. Real talk pops, soon as a nigga rise up out these walls, yo, pshhh, I'm gon' get my paper up. Then I'm gon' get out the game and open a car wash." The skinny young man waved a hand in the air, "*The Jerome Frazier.*"

"So, you sayin'," Claude took off his glasses and sat up on his bottom bunk, "when you get released you are going back to selling that shit, the same shit that got you in here."

Jerome shook his head. "Naaaaaahhhhhhhhh pops."

"Oh, so you're not going to go back to sellin' that crack."

"Pops, it's 2017, not 1997. Heroine is where the real money is now. And I'm just gon' grind for a quick minute, jus' until I get my paper up."

"I know, I heard that part several times already," Claude said. "So, you are going to get out, get you some dope, I mean if you have to hit a brotha in the head and take their dope, you are gon' get you some Horse, so you can get that paper...

"So, I can open up the *The Jerome Frazier*," he interrupted.

"Where did you go to school Jerome Frazier?"

"Huh?" the young man said.

"Where did you get your B.S.?"

The skinny twenty-two year old waved an arm in the air. "You 'on't need no B.S. degree to open up no car wash pops. My boy Junie big brother own two car washes. Sometimes he might detail a whip, but for the most part all he do is sit back and stack. That's what I'mo' do, pops, sit back and stack, yeah pops," he nodded, "sit back and stack."

Claude stood up from his bottom bunk. "Look at me, son."

The young man did as he was told. "I want you to see every facial tick that appears on my face. I want you to feel and hear every letter of every word that comes outta my mouth. Is that clear?"

"Ah pops."

"Is that clear. Yes or no."

"Yes," Jerome nodded.

"Bull S-H-I-T," Claude said. "If it walks like bullshit, talks like bullshit, and stinks like bullshit, then it's sho' nuff bullshit. Bullshit with a capital stink.

"Ah pops you too old school...

"Stop callin' me pops dammit. My girls don't call me Pops. You know what," he pointed a finger at the young man. "Next time you address me as pops, I'm gon' ball up one of these old school fists, and I'm gon' swing my old school arm and pop you in yo' young ass mouth. Everybody in this pod call me Daddy C, Claude, or Mr. Cabral."

"Damn, Po- I mean Daddy C, you hard on a nigga."

"I'm real on a brotha. That shit you talkin' is bullshit. You expect the sun to shine on you when you shittin' on your people. For what... a thing. An object that don't beathe, that don't love. You gon' sell poison to the motha fuckas who the reason you in this world," Claude shook his head in frustration, "for some thin processed pieces of a tree with green ink and pictures of motha fuckas who hated you before you were even born. And, dig this young'n, if you do come up as you say and open a car wash, sheee-iiiiiiiit... Let me find out... Uhm hmm," Claude nodded. "I'm comin' up in there and I'm takin' everything that looks like its worth a dollar.

"Come on Pops, you trip...."

"POP!"

"What the?" the young man rose from his lying position on the top bunk. Once he realized his mouth was bleeding he said, "I'm gon' fuck...."

Claude grabbed the young man's county jail orange jump suit at the neck and pulled him off the top bunk. The noise that Jerome's body made upon hitting the concrete floor, woke the brother up that was sleeping in the bunk a few beds away.

"Oh snap!" the brother said. "You done killed...

"Shhh," Claude held a finger to his lips in hopes that no one else would wake up. "I didn't do shit but try to get out the way. He fell on his own, understand me young'n?"

"Yeah, Daddy C, he fell."

Claude stepped over Jerome and hurried to the steel cell door.

"Man down!" Claude banged on the door, "Man down," he shouted. "I don't think he's breathing!"

Jiggling keys and the pitty pat of hard toe shoes was Claude's indication that someone was on their way.

"What's the problem inmate?"

"Look officer, a man is down. I don't think he's breathing."

"What happened?"

"I don't know? I guess the brotha fell."

"You say the inmate is your brother?"

"Got damn. Does it make a motha fuckin' difference. A man might be dying or dead now and instead of callin' for help…" Claude bent down and hollered through the food slot vent… "We Afrikans will kill this white boy in…"

The steel door flew open. The middle-aged superior officer burst through followed by four other county jail officers. They searched both sides of the pod By now everyone inmate on both sides of the pod were wide awake.

"Okay, you guys think you're real smart." The commanding officer remarked. "Since you guys wanna play games, no phone for a week."

"Playing games," Claude stepped forward. "That boy is still out cold and you motha fuckin crackas talkin' about games, Hell, if I wouldn'ta' screamed bloody white boy murder, Jerome Frazier mighta been a corpse by now."

"You can't play the race card with me inmate. I'm Black," he laughed while turning back to the four white officers that he was in charge of.

"You didn't ask one question when you thought a white boy was in trouble. Your cracka black ass ran up in here like I threatened your own child," Claude looked the guard up and down, "If that boy does live it's because I made you think he was white." Claude squinted to see the name on the black and white plastic nametag. "Sergeant Arnold, don't ever say you black. What you are is something no one wants, a burnt cracker."

The much darker and much bigger officer took a couple steps forward until he was kiss close to the older First Afrikan. In a lower menacing tone Sergeant Arnold said, "Old man think he's somebody special, Fulton County said. Old man has a shotgun-in-the-courthouse-Black panther-mentality they said. Separate him from the inmate population, they said. I told them that a piece of dried dog shit stuck to the bottom of my shoe would never take me off course. But when that piece of dog shit begins to stink up my jail then," the big man took his cuffs out, "you know what I do with stinking shit at the bottom of my shoe inmate?"

HAMSINI NA TATU

3:33 AM

Guantanamo Bay, Cuba
January 20, 2017

The United States first seized the forty-five square mile area of land at the southeastern end of Cuba in 1898 during the Spanish-American War. In 1901 after America defeated the Spanish, America bullied Cuba into signing a treaty that would allow the use of Guantanamo Bay forever.

In 1934, the treaty was amended and instead of America paying 2,000.00 per year for the land, America agreed to increase it to 4,085.00 per year and in over one hundred and sixteen years since, the Cuban government has only cashed one check and that was by mistake.

Before the Naval base became a huge torture chamber and dungeon in 2002, it was used as a refugee camp for HIV infected people and Haitian refugees among other things.

No captive has ever escaped. One hundred and ninety-nine have tried. One hundred ninety-nine have died.

Thanks to one of Daddy C's many connections, the five men sat in back of the highly armored multi-million dollar command station that was built to look like a UPS truck.

"Rev, you really should keep your old ass here where it's safe," Malice joked with the retired Chicago pastor.

There was a time not so long ago when you wuldn't have even gotten a smile, let alone a joke out of the reformed gang member and enforcer for the Atlanta drug kingpin Black Escobar. Eight years ago, Malice salivated at the idea of taking out Zion and Early, that was before Zion touched the big man and made him remember how his mother had sacrificed her life for him to be here.

"Don't let the clergy collar fool you young buck," the middle-aged revolutionary said. "Make another joke about my age, and I'm'a run through you like caster oil boy," the retired Chicago pastor turned his attention to Will. "Wonder bread," I need you to teach this boy some manners when we get back stateside." Reverend White swiveled back around to face Malice. "White boy whip that tail, I'll have somethin' to laugh about for the rest of your life big boy."

"Will, don't want none of me," Malice said, "He know I done walked on water and parted the Red Sea. Now, what you think Will can do to me?"

Will replied, "You think you the only one that walked on water and parted the Red Sea, that's your problem, for two thousand years you've been underestimating me."

"Ahhh," Ammon and Isiah laughed.

"Wonderbread one, Malice, zero," Reverend White said as he high fived Will.

The First Afrikans sat around Will while he ran a systems check making sure all fifty drones were operable and on the same radio frequency.

The munitions expert and war strategist tapped the forty-two inch monitor. "Right there is the Naval station," he moved his finger to another section while the other First Afikans watched from their sitting positions in the back of the truck. "Two point two three kilometers to the left is JTF, the Joint Task Force section," The others watched Will's gloved finger move a couple inches, "Right here is where Uncle Sam keeps the people they fear most."

"Uh, that's underground," Ammon, one of the First Afrikan soldiers, remarked. "You said Luke and Truth were above ground."

"They are," Will said.

"I don't care where they are. Early and Truth are the keys to my Uncle Jebs freedom," Isiah said, "I'm bringing them home."

Will put a hand on the Howard University honor student's shoulder. "We... are bringing them home. I wish we could free so many more." Will said, a far off look in his eyes. "Most of the prisoners are here because they fought against the people that were terrorizing them and trying to rape them of their land and natural resources."

"America's gon' get enough of fuckin' with other nations," Reverend White said. "I just hope I ain't around when the China man get with the Japanese brotha and the Japanese brotha get with Kenyan brotha and the Kenyan brother gets with the Indian brotha and the Indian brotha gets with the Nigerian brotha. I can see it now." The retired Chicago pastor waved a hand in the air, "Big conference like the Bandung in '55, when the world's brothers of color got together in Indonesia to form economic coalitions and promote decolonization. Back then, the oppressor was spread out. You had the USSR, Italy, Great Britain, and some other little punk ass Euro-peon nations that had their foot on brown folk necks. Now, all them other countries," the pastor shook his head, "weak as puppy piss. The head, the body, and the ass end of the snake is in one place now."

He pointed a finger in the air. "This time the brothas and sistas gon' get together and compare notes about how much chaos and calamity America and the Euro-peon nations have done to their countries and their countrie's people," Reverend White paused to ponder.

"Nah, I changed my mind. I hope I'm at that conference." He nodded, "Yeah, I'm gon' be that signifyng monkey way down in the jungle deep. Gon' talk about how that lion done stepped on everybody's feet. Instead of that lion kickin' my butt thru the jungle town, we gon' all get together and beat him til he black and brown."

"Pops, you bout a hundred years too late to be a rapper. Stick to rhymin' in the crapper." Malice said.

"I done told yo' death threat ugly butt 'bout muckin' with me," Reverend White looked at Malice. "Ugly motha trucka can't even get a date off the calendar. How many onions have you made cry Malice?"

"Dang, Rev," Ammon said, "Yo goin' in on Mally Mal real hard."

"Fellas come on, we have less than ten minutes before showtime," the former Patriot Act mercenary said. "As I was saying," Will pointed at a spot on the computer screen. "According to our intel, Luke and Truth are being held here."

"That's the Naval section of the base," Isiah said.

"Stonewall may be a sadistic evil son of a bitch," Will said, "But Luke is still... well, he thinks Luke is still his son, I think."

"That cracka don't care about nothin' but power," Reverend White said, "They got that boy isolated from the rest of the inmate population because they don't know what he'll say or do if they put him with hard core freedom fighters."

Ammon interjected, "You mean Daddy Duke wouldn't be able to live with himself if anyone other than a white man or natural causes killed his seed."

Ten minutes later Malice, Will, Ammon, and Isiah changed clothes before jumping out of the UPS truck and jogging across the old airport hangar to the laundry truck that Raul Castro and freedom fighter Assata Shakur secured before they arrived last night.

Fifteen minutes later the men pulled to the base's main security gate.

****

Seven miles away inside the airport hangar at Leeward Point Airfield, Reverend White watched from the UPS truck command station.

Reverend White held the control key down while pressing F7.

On the smaller thirty-two inch monitor, fifty drones armed with guns and cameras rose up.

"Nineteen, eighteen…" The pastor counted down.

****

The Afrikans pulled the truck around to the base's laundry depot.

"Three minutes. That's all the time we have to grab them and get out. Anything, anyone gets in the way or tries to stop us shoot them three times," Will pointed, "Heart, head, neck."

The four men touched fists. "Afrikan first, First Afrikan they said right before the drones descended onto the JTF side of the base where the detainees were being held.

The base's whirring alarms were almost drowned out by drone gunfire.

Smoke clouded the entire base, both sides.

Soldiers and civilians scrambled for cover while the four men now dressed like MP's ran into the Navy base police station right past the two checkpoints. It was mass hysteria. No one seemed to be following protocol.

The staff and the MP's who were not making a mad dash to the JTF side where all the commotion was coming from seemed to not pay attention to the three black soldiers running behind the white man with the lieutenant bars on his shoulders and breast.

Will came to an abrupt halt upon reaching a huge stainless steel windowless door.

Isiah pulled a tape like substance from his pocket and ran a line from the bottom of the doors edge all the way around to the steel doors other edge. Will followed behind Isiah with a playdoh like substance. Ammon stuck seven firecracker leads in the playdoh.

Malice attached a metal clip to one of the leads and rolled out a twelve-foot spool of wire before they all huddled up at the far end of the hallway. Malice touched the two wires together.

"BOOM!"

The two hundred pound steel prison door falling to the concrete floor made more noise than the explosion had.

"Put these on," Will said after pitching the military fatigues, ID and disguises to Truth and Luke."

Luke pointed at Will, "That's the cracka that...."

"Move! I'll explain later," Isiah said hoping to quell the confused looks that Luke and Truth had on their faces, "For right now, all you need to know is that Will realizes and has embraced his Afrikan manhood."

They ran through the first security checkpoint before slowing down and walking out of the Guantanamo Bay Naval base military police station.

****

Back at command center UPS, Reverend White was on the satellite phone with Omega, his eleven year old niece.

"Uncle J," the little girl said, "First, you have to calm down. You panicking will only make us both nervous."

"Okay, sweetie," he closed his eyes.

"Now breathe in and breathe out slowly Uncle J," she said.

"Okay," the spiritual leader for presidents, bishops, and other world leaders followed the little girl's orders without question.

"That's better," the sixth grader said. "Now, lets get you a visual even if we can't restore audio. First, Uncle J, I need your IP address."

"We just have to find the radio frequency," Omega said as she typed. "There."

The reverend listened to his niece's little fingers tapping away on the keys.

"Okay, it's done. You have eyes everywhere that they do. And you can use your computer's north, south, east, and west buttons to move around the base."

"I see them," he pointed.

"Is that all?" Uncle J, cause I have to finish getting ready for school."

****

The six Afrikans were greeted with a cloud of grey smoke that served as a barrier for the twelve MP's that pointed twelve rifles directly at them.

Ammon slowed and turned to Isiah. "Guess they figured out the drones were shooting smoke bombs instead of bullets."

"Hands up," A slithery voice behind the smoke barked. "On your knees. Now!"

The others slowed. Isiah was the only Afrikan that did not break stride.

Ammon reached out. "You see them AK's, Isiah?"

Isiah walked to the front of the line. "I done walked on water."

Will took Isiah's hand before chiming in, "Done parted the Red Sea."

Malice grabbed Will's hand and took his place beside them. "Burned water."

Luke took Malice's hand, "Killed concrete…"

"Last warning!" the opposing faction shouted as the line of First Afrikans grew.

Ammon and Truth caught up to Luke before locking hands. They all asked, "So whachu' think you or your weapons gon' do to us."

HAMSINI NA NNE

3:36 AM

Terre Haute, Indiana
January 20, 2017

"Nah, what do you do with it," Reverend Jebediah King asked as he stepped up next to Claude.

"Matter fact," Denmark asked as he stepped forward, "What do you do with shoe shit? I'd like to know also."

Forty-three of the fifty-two men who were being housed inside the overcrowded county jail pod asked, "Yeah, what do you do with shoe shit?"

The sergeant took a step back, put his cuffs back in the belt holder, and turned to the cell door, "I don't have time for this. Men, let's go." As soon as the cell door lock clanked shut, the sergeant shouted from the other side of the steel door. "I should take you all and put you so far in a hole that daylight wouldn't find nare nunna' you. Ever!" he shouted. "When I was in there, I shoulda'."

"You should have done just what you did, shit your pants and got the hell outta here quick, faster than a hurry."

"You threatening me inmate. Is that a threat?" Sergeant Arnold barked, "Are you threatening me inmate?"

"Give a motha fucka a chance to answer, damn," Claude said. "Now Sergeant, I know they didn't teach you this in police school, but a threat is an expressed intention to do bodily harm or injury. Have I done that? No. But, you did. And when you found that you were up against real men, you stuck your tail between your legs and ran. Understandable. Any coward would have reacted the same way."

"Coward?" the sergeant was nearly screaming, "you talking behind a steel door where I can not identify the voice."

"Now Sergeant," Claude spoke in a soothing tone, "before you go to asking yourself and me another dumb ass question, what I am about to say is just an example of what a threat is. Just an example now, so don't get your panties in a tiff."

"Who do you think you're talking to inmate?" the sergeant's tone was almost at the point of screaming.

In his usually measured calm, quiet tone Claude continued, "Now, If we would have stomped you and your boys into a Terre Haute Indiana County jail cop smoothie," He shook his head no, "Bad example, that would actually be assault or worse. I'm sorry Sergeant, a better example of what a threat is if I would have said if you come in here again and get in my face, I will end you. Now that's a threat."

"Let's see how big and bad you are after the inauguration," the sergeant said.

Sergeant Arnold peeked through the small square window in the steel cell door. He could only see the common area where food was served, games were played, television was watched, and the phone was talked on.

"Three African voodoo cultists been here for one night and you losers following them like sheep," Sergeant Arnold said.

Reverend King said, "History verifies to us what happens when the sheep follow the shepherd as it shows us the outcome when they follow the wolf, so it seems that our

Afrikan voodoo is much more desirable than the hate that you do."

"Black officer," the men sang, "why you wanna put us in a coffin sir?" Right before breakfast the guards brought Jerome back from the infirmary.

"Dog, you look like Alibaba with all that gauze wrapped around your head," a young brotha said before slapping a domino down on the stainless steel cafeteria table in the day room.

Jerome had his head down when he bent the corner to the area where he slept with twenty-five others.

"Jerome Frazier, come here," Claude sat up and patted his bunk. "Have a seat son."

The young man looked up at the man responsible for the bandages around his head.

Jerome looked around the cramped area where sixteen prison bunk beds were lined up on both walls.

Wanting to save face after noticing a young man waiting to see how he was going to respond to the man responsible for his injuries, Jerome pretended that he wasn't scared and walked over and stood in front of Claude.

"Son…"

"Dude, I mean Mr. Cabral, you had no right man. I'm tellin' you my plans when I rise up and you sneak me. That's some coward bull."

"I didn't sneak you son. I told you what I was going to do if you addressed me as Pops again." He patted his bunk, "Now sit down. I know you in your feelings. But, you don't wanna keep that aggressive stance with me; others may come in and you may feel like you have to do something to save face and that," he pointed a finger in the air, "would be a big mistake. One of us will end up being carried out of here and that would make them crackas who got us in this cage tickled pink."

Reluctant, Jerome sat down anyway.

"Now son, listen and learn, alright?"

The young man nodded.

"In this world, in this life a man ain't got nothin' but his 'word'. A nigga, a cracka, no one can take it. You have to give your 'word' away son. Your word is your integrity and your level of integrity determines your level of hue-manity. Understand?"

The young man shrugged indifference.

"How did you feel when ya momma promised you that thing when you was little and you believed her. You believed her because she was the woman that brought you in this world. She was the woman that made you feel loved when no one else did. She fed you, housed you, and fought for you, maybe not when you wanted or most needed but she did fight. You loved that black woman despite her battles with the bottle. I mean you loved that black woman so much."

The young man put his arm over his face... *Man up bitch ass nigga. You in jail. Don't let that old man's words make you cry.* Jerome thought to himself. *Wipe that damn tear from your eye fuck boy.*

Claude put his hand on the young man's back before whispering, "How did you feel when she didn't deliver on her promise. Hurt, didn't it?"

The Jerome nodded holding his arm in an awkward position over his face.

"Think back son. Think back to when she didn't do what she had promised she would. You asked her. You begged over and over. She promised over and over."

The young man was fighting a losing battle with his emotions as he remembered.

"How did you feel? The initial impact... Hurt like Hell, right?"

Jerome nodded yes.

"You 'on't want no body to ever feel that pain ever, do you son?"

"Yes," he shook his head. "I mean no, I don't wish that pain on nobody. To this day I just don't understand Pops. Momma know how I felt. Kids always callin' me dumb and stupid and then the adults treated me like I was dumb." The young man looked up. "Pops, I started studying for the six grade spelling bee when I was a fourth grader in special ed. Every day after school and on most weekends all I did was read the dictionary. In them two years I can't tell you how many whippins' I got for reading the dictionary upside down. Momma said I'd never be anything if I couldn't read right side up."

"You won that spelling bee didn't you Jerome?"

Jerome nodded his head yes. "Nobody was there. I felt like I didn't exist, like I was nothing. Momma got mad when I asked why she wasn't there. She told me that I was the man of the house and that sometimes shit just happens, and I had to just accept it. Those were her exact words. I'll never forget.

"Pops, I could have won the state spelling bee and went on to the Nationals in DC when the kid from Ivy prep left the second 'C' out of the word convalesce."

Claude thought out loud, "A second C?"

Jerome continued, "Everybody know that convalesce is c-o-n-v-a-l-e-s-c-e and not c-o-n-v-a-l-e-s-e."

"Now everybody does, "Claude said. "So you went on and did it, didn't you."

"I had to. I spelled Convalesce with two k's and misspelled the next word on purpose. I saw all the cameras and all the families there and momma wasn't there, ain't no way I was gon' let the world see that nobody loved me Pops."

"A hell, that was the third or fourth "Pops" that done come out your mouth in the last five minutes," Claude smiled before pointing a finger at the young man, "You are the only one. You hear somebody else callin' me 'Pops', you handle it. I shouldn't have put my hands on you son. I was wrong, but I wasn't wrong for the love that led to me laying hands on you

Jerome. Again I'm sorry," Claude said. When you get outta here, well when I get out you movin' to Atlanta and you gon' work for me. I'm'o help you open up that car wash."

"For real, you gon' give me a loan?"

Claude frowned, "You done lost your mind for even thinkin' some dumb shit like that."

"I need money."

"What part of you-gon'-work-for-me don't you understand. Now don't pull that special ed shit on me. You are better and way smarter than anyone who done told you otherwise. Don't worry about a place to stay. I got you."

"So you gon' pay me?"

"I just said you was smart and you go and ask some dumb shit like that." Claude shook his head. "Now son, how the hell you gon' eatna dpay room and board if I don't pay you? Better yet don't answer that."

"How much and what will I be doing?"

"I'm gon' pay you by the job. And you'll be doing whatever I think will prepare you for running our car wash.

"Well, you gon' pay me by the day, week. How many hours?"

"Look, you want this car wash, do what I say, and we'll have it up and running in no time, ya dig?"

"We?"

"All the work it's gon' take to get you right and the money it's going to cost us to do this right."

"I promise, if you do this you ain't ever gotta worry about me selling any drug harder than sugar, Pops."

"I know that," Claude said. "Wouldn't have hired you if I thought otherwise."

"So why you lookin' out for me?"

"This is some bull shit!" Reverend King shouted from the dayroom. "Hell nah!"

Claude and Jerome ran into the dayroom.

"Jebediah?" Claude shouted at the big angry Afrikan.

"Man, look at this bull shit, Baba," he pointed up at the TV screen, "We ain't even got seventeen hundred active members at First Afrikan. Donald Chump is the Anti-Christ for real."

"What ever it is we can fix it Jeb," Claude said.

"Baba, you don't even know what's goin' on."

"Look man, I been fightin' for freedom and been kickin' cracka and nigga ass for over two thousand years. Get closer to freedom with every life I live, so whatever you 'bout to say Jebediah, swallow the words and hold the thought if you ain't gon' put no "do" behind the talk."

"What you talkin' 'bout Baba. I 'do' everyday, at least I try. From teachin' to fixin' HVAC to…"

"That's all?" Claude frowned up.

"That's all?" Jebediah roared. "On Sundays, both services."

"Is that all?" Claude shouted over the reverend. "I know this brotha, partna of mine, ya dig. Had it hard ever since his momma gave birth to him in a manger with straw and shit. You know it was funky and cold in that barn. Anyway this cat, he fixed stuff, handy man like you Jebediah. He was a carpenter, and a teacher, like yourself Jeb. Brotha knew his Afrikan history. My man had the gift of gab, good story teller like you Jebediah. You could be Caesar and if you was hurtin' the people, this cat took his good talk and followed it up with a better walk. Now they strung his ass up on a cross, ya dig."

"Baba?"

"Hold on Jeb, let me finish," Claude said. "I was sayin', since I know how 'they' do, we ain't gon' let 'them' shoot, hang, crucify, do a damn thing to us. Motha fuckas ain't even got a name. 'They.' 'Them.' Fuck 'Them' and the horse They rode in on. "Claude pointed up at the television screen. "Now Jebediah are you gon' to tell me what hate is coming out of number forty-five's mouth this time?"

"Yes sir," the big man said.

"You know Jebediah, we are, all of us right here in this dull grey common area, are going to do something about what ever you are about to put in the air. I don't wanna hear shit about no job, no, I have to take care of so and so, nothing. Whatever you say Jebediah... is a call, and we gon' answer that call with action. Not, some this is what we need to do or if I had this I would do that. We," Claude waved an arm around the dayroom cell, "are going to put a foot in the ass of the problem."

"Or die trying?" Denmark said.

"Die my ass," Claude turned to the much younger Deacon. "Ain't nobody dyin' on my watch unless we doin' the killin'."

HAMSINI NA TANO

6:36 AM

Waycross, Georgia
January 20, 2017

The sixteen-foot serpent massaged its belly with soil, shrubbery, twigs, weeds, everything it slithered over. It's diamond back brown skin camouflaged it from prey and predator. Fortunately for the Burmese python, it had no natural predator. Everything with a heartbeat was its prey. The only reasons a Burmese would awake from its winter slumber like now was if its habitat was disturbed or it hadn't eaten its fill for the winter. A sufficient meal for a Burmese the size of the one slithering into the clearing was any one or two of the four meditating women.

A few feet away in the clearing the sun peaked through the clouds and seeped through the trees. Naural light illuminated the area where the four women sat in a circle holding hands while a small fire burned in the middle. The fire's smoke waved its way through the clouds with the same rhythm the python moved to.

The morning sunlight and the condensation in the air made her breath visible as the little Seminole medicine woman chanted, "Tehuti, my ability to know is unlimited. I understand that what seems as my not knowing is merely the momentary inability of my knowledge to take verbal form in my mind.

I understand that ALL manifests its divine plan in the world of Man by incarnating in the soul of men and women – the elevated consciousness realizes their unlimited ability in the form of action that most would deem improbable if not impossible.

Before there was me ALL so loved the World. Every creature, every plant, every man, woman and every ant is why ALL gave its only begotten Light." Hachi raised her thin arms before hugging the sunlight that beamed down from space and through the forest.

The huge serpent massaged its belly as it crawled onto Miracle's lap.

"Miracle, you are the begotten Sun," Hachi explained.

The sixteen-foot serpent was quiet as death in a lifeless desert. Its long forked tongue skirted out as it slithered its way onto Cherry's lap.

The First Afrikan women's heads swayed from side to side to the intonation of the little indigenous woman's voice. They seemed oblivious to the serpent's presence.

"Cherry, you are the begotten Sun."

The serpent was moving on to Assata.

"Assata, you are the begotten Sun."

The snake moved on to Hachi. Before slithering up and around her body, the python opened its mouth and bit down on the apple that had fallen out of Hachi's knapsack. Apple in mouth, the serpent slithered around the young girl's back before coming around to eye level with the Seminole spiritual healer.

Hachi smiled but never opened her eyes as she took a bite from the apple that was protruding from the serpent's mouth.

The snake crawled over to Miracle and slithered up and around her back before coming eye level with the young black woman, Miracle took a bite of the apple without opening her eyes.

The snake coiled around Cherry and when it came eye level, Cherry's eyes popped open. "Sweety, I ain't got nothing against you anymore, but if you don't uncoil your long ass from around me and get that nasty ass apple out my face," she stared into the serpent's beedy black eyes. "Don't give me that look Cora," Cherry said to the snake. "Nothin' against your slithery ass, but I don't get this close to no female, and I definitely don't eat nothin' after no other female done tasted it first."

The snake uncoiled itself and disappeared into the grassy moss.

"You are a selfish something," Miracle said. "She's supposed to be sleep for at least another couple months, but she woke up to share in the love of knowing." Miracle shook her head. "You just had to hurt her feelings."

Cherry threw her arms in the air. "I forgot. Hell, a few months ago we were all terrified of snakes, hell worms and all the beautiful creations that ALL breathed Life into. I'll go apologize," Cherry said before unfolding her legs and placing her feet on the moist Earth beneath them.

The others were still suspended a few inches above the ground. Although Cherry broke their circle, they quickly closed it with the three of them holding hands.

"I never thought I would ever be sleeping with snakes, hanging out with alligators and spending nights in deep thought with owls," Miracle said. "We see it in movies but who would have ever thought that animals had feelings. It makes so much sense now," Miracle said. "Man thinks he is all wise, but it's the simplest living creations that live in harmony that are wise."

Assata chimed in. "It took us confronting some of our greatest fears, these animals, to understand what love is and what love does. It makes sense. You don't need words to feel love. Love is in your spirit, and it is realized when the word moves from a thought to selfless action."

Hachi explained, "This is how the Seminole Nation has survived, lived, and thrived. The colorless one's suffering must end. It's been seven hundred eighty three thousand moons, incarnate after incarnate. Generation after generation, hate reproducing the hate of the father. The most oppressed is the oppressor, the lowliest slave is the enslaver," the indigenous woman squeezed Miracle's hand. "Be, Miracle re-awakening. Be, the mother. Be, Afrikan. Be, love. Don't question. Do. Don't watch. Do. Don't wait. Do." Hachi shook her head in defiance, "ALL is not outside of you." She smiled. "ALL is in you." She squeezed Miracle's hand. "Be all you can imagine. Go outside of your emotions. Go beyond the possibilities of impossibility. Go beyond the conceivable. Everything, every answer, every question, every thought begins and ends with you Miracle Joy Brown. Be compassion. Be reason. Just Be. And you will see and achieve."

HAMSINI NA SITA

9:39 AM

Waycross, Georgia
January 20, 2017

Cherry was napping next to Cora, the python and Edgar, the seven foot alligator. Edgar hadn't left Cherry's side since the day the animals charged at them like lost children finding their parents.

For the last three months the four Afrikan women, mothered nature and its animated creations.

Hachi frowned, "Doves."

Moments later the sunlight dimmed as a nation of white doves flew over the Okeefenokee black water swamp.

"Little late to be flying South for the winter," Assata stated.

"Doves don't migrate." Hachi put a finger to her lips. "Shhh!"

The four women sat cross-legged arm length apart in a circle.

Behind the sound of soaring birds an ever so faint harmonic vibration could be felt.

"Crying," Hachi flapped her arms as if she were flying with the schools of birds.

Miracle opened her eyes. "This is what it sounds like when doves cry," Miracle remembered out loud.

Hachi, Cherry, and Assata cried with the doves. The gators, the snakes, the panthers, wolves, and even the beetles cried in tune with the doves overhead.

"Momma," Miracle slipped into trance. "Momma Oya Beyond See how can you leave me standing in a world so cold. Maybe I'm just too demanding. Maybe I'm like my mother too bold.

The doves cried louder.

"You've abandoned me... Left me out in the cold... unlike the days of old... before racism, when this country was great. love for animal, nature, all women and men... but that's history... a time when there was peace and harmony... every creation was community... the reason for this journey... we'll never stop searching from the deepest below to the highest above... We'll fly to eternity to reunite with you love."

Purple tears rained down on the women. The sky opened up, and the Afrikan storm and wind goddess Oya Beyond-See descended to Earth. She held a purple machete to her lips and sang into it as if it were a microphone, "Dream if you can, a society filled with love, oceans of violets in bloom. Animals strike curious poses." Her purple knee high boots landed seven inches above the moist ground.

Assata, Cherry, Hachi, Edgar, Cora, every thing breathing that heard the whispering cries responded by crying in harmony with the sea of white birds that were still flying over the blackwater swamp.

It was like the trees, the leaves, the birds, the gators, the women everything living was a great big family swaying and chanting the same tune.

"Daughter-sun," a purple tear ran down the godesses's face before she gently touched Miracle's dreads with a long purple and burgundy fingernail. "Destiny's child. Flawless, formation, forward, freedom."

"I don't understand?"

"Tomorrow," the Afrikan warrior godess ran a loving finger down her little sister's face. "Tomorrow you will take the information, put it in formation to truth. You will flawlessly move the world forward until freedom for all is attained. You are Destiny's child," Oya Beyond-See smiled, "Flawless! Formation! Forward! To freedom!

"Why are the doves crying?"

"They cry for the forgotten, for the loveless. They cry because they are leaving the place they call home."

"Why?" Miracle asked.

"In many indigenous cultures the dove is a symbol of love. When they have a massive migration like the one you are witnessing, it's because the love has depleted to levels too low for them to survive. In a few hours the level of hate and chaos in this land will be at catastrophic levels."

"What's happening in a few hours?"

"Evil's child will be sworn in as the forty-fifth president of this land."

Miracle's eyes were saucers. "Donald Chump? Impossible." She shook her head. "No way the people would elect him. I mean he makes Hitler look like a saint. Not his actions yet, but his words. I mean Chump is 'Mein Kampf' in action. What happened?"

"You happened, Daughter-sun."

"I happened?"

The golden brown goddess smiled.

"Me?" Miracle pointed to herself.

"Anger, disgust, rage was the fire that inspired what you did to Offcier Darwin. No love, no compassion, your selfish sin. Streamed it live on Social media. Is that the way you really want the world to see you?"

"He shot…"

"You knew Darwin was sick. Poisoned his entire life. Never asked for this plight. Never asked to be taught to hate. Never asked to live a life where the love seemed to always come too late. Without love and compassion, doomed to a godless fate. You are supposed to fill that hole, pull Heaven from hate. The world is lost and down. Be the Miracle that brings joy to all brown."

"Momma Beyond-See, please do not take this the wrong way, but this is war. You said it yourself. Good and evil. I had to send a message."

"I know, and your message has that carrot topped crooked tooth chairman spinning around drunk with glee. Daughter Sun, don't you see, you can not defeat hate with hate or any of its seeds. love is the only weapon you need to succeed."

"I love our people so much that I decided to allow Coltrane's soul to be returned to your world Momma Beyond-See. Me sending Officer Darwin's soul back to you was supposed to be an example of the lessons that you three taught me."

"Okay, let's see," Oya Beyond-See tapped a purple heel in the air before putting her hands on her hips. "Five black lives where lost, you streamed it live."

"No, ma'am," Miracles black dreadlocks waved as she shook her head. "Only one black life."

"Daughter-Sun," Beyond-See touched one of Miracles long dreads, "We are all black life."

"I know that, Momma Beyond-See, bu..."

"No buts, just Be, the reality that you want others to see. Be free from the ignorance that hate trained you to see. Scared to have a conversation, fearful of any interaction or personal relation with all of the Lord's animated creations. Four months ago, if you would have stumbled across a baby snake."

"I would have died dead."

"Now think of some of the happiest times in your life, Daughter-Sun, things you did, things you said."

"These last few months. My new friends. Cora, Edgar, Charlie, Stumpy, Big Jaws, Baby. Like everything else, they just need love. I'd always thought that snakes were this evil, creepy, slimy, creature of death. What we, humanity have done to the environment and to them in the name of a dollar is irreprehensible. We are the monsters, not these beautiful animated creations."

"Think daughter-sun, who saved your life when you and the others where surrounded by seventy seven angry alligators, panthers, wild boars, wolves, cotton mouths, and pythons?"

"Love," Miracle said. "Love turned the animal charge of death to them charging to love." She nodded. "Now, I see, Momma Beyond See. I went after that man with anger. I put so much anger and hate in the air, it was real easy for Cherry to absorb my negative energy, so easy for her to kill...." She put a hand over her mouth and looked into the eyes of Oya Beyond-See, "the man and not the problem. Hate was to blame, not the human."

"Darwin has already been incarnated and will have to experience this life cycle again as his spirit has for going on seventeen-hundred years. You can't even begin to imagine born into a world were hate, anger, and rage raise love to be like them, generation after generation. No one has ever loved his spirit to this life or the next." Oya Beyond-See took a step back and held her purple machete toward the sun, "Love is life and life is love. There is no other religion, Daughter-Sun," She smiled, "Justice ain't just us."

Miracle dropped her head, "I didn't use reason before I acted. Undeserving officers have been killed as a result of the anger I displayed that day?"

"Yes, daughter-Sun."

"Chump was elected because of me?"

289

"Yes, daughter-Sun."

"I have to fix this. I have to love humanity back to freedom."

"Yes, daughter-sun."

FirstAfrikanTruth.com

HAMSINI NA SABA

11:39 PM

Washington, DC
January 20, 2017

President Chump ordered secret service to escort Chairman Greenspan to the White House Situation Room.

The door to the Situation Room flew open and almost came off it's hinges as the chairman entered. "Come in Con, join the party pal," the president slurred.

"Are you insane?" Greenspan roared. He looked at every face in the room. "Are all of you in-friggin'-sane? Strippers in the White House Situation Room."

"No place safer. And what better situation can we have than this, them," Chump pointed to the two strippers getting it on, on top of the two hundred and twenty-eight year old black oak conference table.

The chairman directed his anger at the man who was enjoying the stripper that knelt between his legs. "And you Money."

The reverend raised his hand in the air. "The Hand."

291

Ignoring Money, the chairman continued, "Get out! Everyone with a hole instead of a pole between their legs, get the Hell out! Now!" he shouted.

Six minutes later, twelve nervous men sat around the table that forty-four previous presidents commandeered and planned the future of the world from. Eleven black suits were captivated by the only white suit in the room.

"Mr. Chairman sir," Doctor Ben Dover, the man slated to head HUD, Housing and Urban Development, raised his hand. "Shouldn't President Chump be sitting or standing where you are?"

The chairman of the U.S. Federal Reserve Bank braced both hands on the shiny dark table before looking into all twenty two eyes of fear in the rom before boring into the doe eyes of America's most beloved retired neurosurgeon, Dr. Benjamin Solomon Dover.

"Ben Dover. Dr. Ben Dover," The chairman frowned. "Get up, take the envelope in front of you and get out."

"Respectfully sir," I am a part of this cabinet like yourself. I serve at the pleasure of the President as well as answer only to the President," he looked over at President Chump who seemed to be engrossed in something on his cell phone.

Dr. Dover's chair tipped over backwards. All eyes were on his rising figure and the eyes followed as the sixty-five year old surgeon, author, politician and 2008 Medal of Freedom honoree was thrown head first against the White House wall with so much force that his entire torso was embedded in the sheet rock. The former Republican candidate for president's pants came undone. His black suit pants and boxers fell to his knees.

"No, you are whatever I say you are," the chairman said. "Right now you are an ass. A brown pimpled ass. You are not white and will never be white; therefore, you will never be a part of this men's club. But, there is a place for you in this administration. Brown shit like yourself needs a toilet. You will use the toilet we give you to stir shit up and keep up enough stink to keep the blacks, spics, desert dirt, fish eyes and skirts fighting each other. But for now, since you are so adamant and vehement about staying while I allow the president to lay out the plan for the next four years, you will be doing so from your ass out position."

The chairman averted his attention over to Money. "Take the envelope and get out."

The Hand opened the envelope. He counted six zero's behind the one before reading the words. He smiled, rose from his chair, and left the room.

"Now, see. That's the type of darkie I can stomach. Someone who will do what I say when I say for a piece of paper with a dollar sign followed by a number."

The nine men at the table laughed.

The chairman waited with his arms crossed. After his angry silence drowned out the noise, he uncrossed his arms and braced them on the antique oak conference table.

"My soliloquy was not designed to illicit laughter. It was the truth."

HAMSINI NA NANE

11:42 PM

Terre Haute, Indiana
January 20, 2017

Dr. Mao Tzu laid in bed playing the '*what if*' game in his mind. What if Zion is not the truth? What if he doesn't get out? Will President Chump be the downfall of man? What if the prison finds out what I've been doing? He looked over at his wife. Should I tell Nirvana the truth?

He'd always told her the truth. Always. Never in fourteen years, seven years of courting and seven years of marriage had they kept anything from each other. He knew he was coming close to Nirodha, the Buddhist term for unconditional Peace. That is the only explanation he could come up with, why someone so beautiful, so perfect could love or even want to love him.

He often watched as he did now to the sheet rising and falling to the rhythm of her breathing. He could have had the absolute worst day a man could have, but once he left the Terre Haute Federal Penitentiary, drove home, and walked into their home a feeling of peace overcame his spirit as his wife's smile greeted him. No television. No lights. No computer.

Nirvana's mind, body, and spirit were enough but the soulful sounds of Earth, Wind, and Fire never sounded more peaceful as they did when Nirvana's naked body became one with the vibrations emitted from the seventy thousand dollar Bang & Olufsen stereo that piped music through sound vents in every room of the small six room home.

Mao reached over to his nightstand and fiddled around until his fingers came upon the lighter. After lighting the candle he sat up in bed. "Nirvana."

She giggled at the soft touch of her husband's feathery fingers on the back of her neck.

"What bad monsters are keeping my husband from sleeping and worst letting me sleep," the East Indian woman asked her Chinese husband as she sat up in bed.

He shook his head no while exhaling.

She put a hand over his. "The prison."

He nodded yes.

"You swallow the pain of so many."

"I didn't swallow this pain."

"How do you mean?" She ran a finger down her husband's hairy arm.

He took a deep breath.

"Zion," she asked, "the young man you've taken a particular interest in?"

He nodded his head yes while releasing the breath from his lungs.

"Are you ashamed of whatever you did?"

"No," he shook his head.

"Did you allow your heart to be your guide?"

Yes, he nodded.

"Did you ask the Uni-verse, to guide your thoughts, words and actions?"

He nodded his head yes.

She looked up into his eyes. "Mao Tzu, I am your rose, but do not forget I have thorns, and I will use them to protect you if called upon." She took his hand and kissed it.

"I substituted Zion's Tharozine cocktail with placebos. In a few days he will be at full memory."

"That is good?"

"Yes. It is," he said. "But, it will be only a matter of time before *'they'* figure it out."

"When *'they'* do, Zion will be free, and we will be ready for *'them'*. Remember, the words of your great ancestor, Sun Tzu.

"All warfare is based on deception. Hence, when we are able to attack, we must seem unable; when using our forces, we must appear inactive; when we are near, we must make the enemy believe we are far away; when far away, we must make him believe we are near."

HAMSINI NA TISA

11:45 PM

Washington, DC
January 20, 2017

"Fear is our most important and effective weapon," President Chump said to the world's richest and most ruthless men alive. "I've always said that we must appear weak when we are strong and strong when we are weak. Victorious warriors win first and then go to war, while defeated warriors go to war first and then seek to win."

"Sun Tzu, The Art of War," Rooster Murdoch remarked.

The president turned his attention to the media mogul.

"What you said about war came from Sun Tzu's book," The WOLF network media mogul said.

"Rooster," Chump replied, "I quit worrying about people who steal my sayings a long time ago."

"But…"

The chairman stood up. "Gentlemen, I called this meeting so President Chump and I can show you all how we are going to turn the hands of time back a couple hundred years," The chairman pointed a finger in the air, "to the time when

America was truly great. Within the next four years the world will be ours." The chairman looked over to CIA director Bush and NSA Chief General Lesure, the two men that helped him devise and carry out 911.

"Nine-eleven was a friggin' test run compared to what we are going to orchestrate, an extremely successful test run I might add but a test run all the same," Greenspan paused. He searched for weakness in the eyes of every man in the room. Satisfied that every single man in the room was scared and weak, he continued, "When fear is created and heightened in a community, the people panic and only think in terms of self-survival. Just look at how we switched blame from Bin Laden to Hussein overnight and the sheep followed. Why," the chairman banged a fist onto the table, "because of the fear we created."

Chump stood up. "Look at me, hell, I have never hidden who I am. I have never disguised my views on women, niggers, foreigners, or anyone else, and they still elected me. They voted for me because I planted trees of fear in their consciousness. Fear of the sand nigger strapping bombs on their backs and screaming Allah Hu Akbar before blowing everybody and everything to Kingdom Come. Other peoples's fear allows me to do whatever I want with minimal to no recourse."

The president removed his gold framed reading glasses from the inside of his suit jacket. He looked around the room at each of the four billionaires before turning to the heads of the FBI, NSA, and CIA. Next his eyes rested on his chosen few. "Jeff Suppressions and Stonewall Duke, men who understood how to use hate as inspiration. His attention returned to the six-page document that he and the chairman had prepared. He placed the gold-rimmed glasses onto his face before clearing his throat.

SITINI

11:48 PM

FOUR YEAR PRESIDENTIAL AGENDA

"The complete and total annihilation of Zion Uhuru and every First Afrikan on U.S. soil is priority number one. Tomorrow at oh seven hundred hours we will release the carnage that the drones left behind."

"You really think that's a good idea Mr. President," John J. Walmart asked. "We killed those men and women. We replaced the blanks on six drones with bullets. The attack on Guatanamo could potentially be like a call for every bleeding heart that wants to hurt America."

The chairman rose from his seat. "Fear!" He raised an arm and used the energy in the room to pull the retired Black neurosurgeon from the White House wall.

Without a word the black politician got to his feet and scrambled out of the room with his pants and boxers around his knees.

"Now, that's fear," the chairman said. "The same way we convinced the Afrikans that they are Niggers and the

Christian that he is a Christian, we will do to all of America and the world. We will make them believe that they are powerless, just like old Ben Dover."

Now as Chump was saying," the chairman smiled, "in a few hours we will release real and doctored footage of the attack on Guantanamo."

"William Sherman, what about him?" CIA Director Bush asked. "He is probably the top military strategist in the world. We trained him and the other members of the Patriot Act team."

"We trained, Hussein, Bin Laden, and the got damn Taliban," The NSA chief interrupted. "Look at them now Gerald."

"Asshole," The CIA director mumbled while the General continued.

"Decorated United States veteran and military assassin siding with a bunch of...."

"Niggers! Embrace the word men. It's just us in here," Jeff Supressions, the man slated to be the next U.S. Attorney General, joined the conversation. "Even if there were niggers in here, you shouldn't be afraid to call a nigger a nigger. The coons have never given us a licensing fee for an exclusive on the word we created. I have called many a nigger and to their faces, and none of the cowards have ever lifted a finger to stop me from doing it again. Fuckers will march and wave signs in the air and boycott a gas station for a day and if they get really upset, they riot and trash their own communities."

"Dumbest thing I ever heard," the President said. "If I have a problem with something or someone. I'm going after it and them."

"Back to the agenda at hand," the chairman called the room to order. "Tomorrow we release the video. Tomorrow we indict and arrest the seventeen hundred members and First Afrikan collaborators, beginning with their leader Logun, his wife, and all the males he's sired. Every last one will be charged and convicted of high treason and murder. All seventeen hundred will be tried and put to death. Zion Uhuru will be the last of the seventeen hundred to be executed. While they are being charged and rounded up we will execute an order to send as many legal and illegal immigrants back to their countries."

"Mr. Chairman," Haliburton Rockefeller, the oil magnate, raised a hand in the air. "Illegals make up over fifty percent of my work force. I pay them a third of what I pay my lowest paid black worker, and I work them twice as long."

The other moguls nodded understanding.

"How am I," he waved an arm at his billionaire cronies, "How are we going to…"

"Prisons," The chairman said. "In less than two years you'll all have all the slave labor you need. No minimum wage, the slaves, I mean the inmates who decide to work for our universal-core group will be housed in cells with air conditioning and heating. They will have television access and more freedom of movement while the ones who refuse will be housed in cramped quarters with no A/C or heat. Instead of being paid up to 1.20 and hour we will force the non-complying inmates to work in prison upkeep or the kitchen for maintenance pay, which as you all know is 5.25 a month," the chairman said, "Trick I learned from Rosy back in the '30's. Old Teddy or Frank, I get 'em mixed up, anyway one of them did a study with rats living in close quarters with very little food and meager living conditions."

Chump interrupted, "The rats fought and killed the weaker rats for the crumbs of food they were given. Whole lotta trouble just to prove that niggers will kill each other over crumbs we give 'em, hell all you have to do is pick up a book. Nigger savagery has been documented throughout history."

"Thank you for that unsolicited and unwanted commentary, Mr. President," the chairman looked to his left where the president sat. "Before I was so rudely interrupted, I was saying, while we are kicking the undesirables out of the country we will also spearhead the building of more prisons that we will own and take public. Every American with a dollar can invest. When they begin to see the spoils of our labor they will vote for any law and amendment that I, I mean the president, brings forth."

"And if they do not?" Vanderbuilt Carnegie, the steel and shipping mogul asked.

"We push it through anyway," the chairman said. "In two years the American people will be making so much money that they won't care what we do; they may even vote to make Chump America's first king, but if they don't we'll make him King ourselves. We do not need a Congress, Senate or a House to decide what must be done to bring the world under our New World Order."

Chump beamed at the idea of having total control.

By then the wall will be built. No nigger, black or white will be able to escape from Texas and New Mexico."

Everyone but the chairman wore a confused look.

The chairman further explained, "We are consolidating our efforts and making Texas and New Mexico America's first prison states. The temperature is conducive for year round slave labor."

"Sounds like we have finally found a way to return America to a time when it was great," Rooster Murdoch, the WOLF network media mogul remarked.

"Before that idiot Lincoln was forced to abolish slavery this country was on its way. With the Prison Industrial States plan, we will lose in sports and music sales will suffer, but we will be thrice as wealthy in four years, and seventy to eighty percent of the colored male population will be in slavery. I mean prison," Chump said.

UHURU

11:51 PM

Terre Haute, Indiana
January 20, 2017

David Scott and his second in command Associate Warden Che Zapata sat across from each other in the warden's office.

"I'm not gon' lie. I didn't want you here and you wouldn't be if you had not gotten shot by Chumps drunken teenage nephew back in Atlanta last year. You kept your mouth closed then. Now I know Chump payed you off," he nodded, "but you still kept quiet. That white boy that shot you deserves to be locked up like the rest of the criminals wrecking havoc on our streets, and he will one day. His family will not always be able to buy him out of trouble."

"I agree," Zapata said.

"I know ole Stonewall told you that coming to Terre Haute to be my A.W. was a promotion, probably told you that you were being primed to take over for me when I'm promoted to director of the Bureau of Prisons. All of that is true, but my time is nearing and you have to be ready. This is a concrete jungle with the most dangerous and deadly predator known to woman or man bursting from its confines." He held a long finger to his forehead. "The criminal mind. The only way to control it is by instilling extreme fear into it. To do this you have to commit acts against it that's more atrocious than anything the criminal ever imagined. Some criminals will die, but those deaths will keep the other beasts in line," Warden Scott looked at the tatted up Argentinian to see if he could detect any signs of weakness. Satisfied when did not, the warden continued, "What's it been now, six, seven months since you transferred in?"

"Going on seven months sir," Zapata casually removed some household rubber gloves from his pocket.

"When you got here, I asked one thing from you Zapata, do you remember?" The tall, rugged looking, middle aged cowboy hat wearing black warden asked.

"Loyalty," the Argentinian A.W. said.

"Correct." Warden Scott stood up from behind his desk and nodded in Zapata's direction. "I can stomach a liar, thief, even a murderer but I can not and will not tolerate disloyalty." Warden Scott crossed his arms while looking down at his young A.W.

Zapata waited for the warden to continue. After a couple minutes Zapata asked, "What's the real reason you called this late night meeting Warden, sir?"

Scott pointed a finger. "I've been watching you these last few months Zapata and you haven't given me any reason to distrust you. Like I said you proved that you can do the job and keep your mouth closed when needed. I think you are a man of honor, loyal to a fault. Are you?"

The Warden bent down and opened a drawer and

took out a box of heavily salted crackers and a bag of flaming hot Cheetos and put them on top of the desk.

"I am." Zapata nodded.

"I'm going to trust that you will follow my orders down to the letter, amigo."

"Yes, sir."

"I'm tasking you with making sure that inmate 46932-019 gets three crackers and three Cheetos in the morning and that's it for the day."

"For how long, sir."

The warden smiled. "Ten days."

"You expect him to live off a couple crackers and water for ten days?"

"Who said anything about water. I cut that off two days ago."

"When do we turn his water back on?"

"February one. Don't worry, I ran the idea by President Chump a few weeks ago. He loved it so much that he asked me to implement this as a disciplinary action the day he takes the oath."

"That not just torture, it's murder," the Latino A.W. said. "Man can't survive without water for a week."

"The boy is a cop killer. He deserves much worst. Did you forget why he's in here Zapata?"

"Not for one moment." The A.W. crossed his legs.

Warden Scott took long determined strides around the desk until he was standing directly in front of the A.W.

"He killed two NSA agents," Scott barked.

"You've killed far more people than Zion has and for much less." Zapata yawned while speaking. "I don't understand why anyone hasn't killed you way before now?"

"Who in the Hell do you think you are speaking to?" The warden huffed.

"Really," Zapata looked up at the huge growling man that stood over him. "You have so little time to live and you ask who am I speaking to when it's just me in you in this office."

"I'm trying to be patient with you Zapata, but you are making it difficult. Tell me now, are you siding with that godless monster?"

"Definitely not Warden. I've watched how you run this prison, how you inhumanely treat these men, I would never side with you."

"Men," the warden said. "Men don't run drugs, steal and murder. And I'm not the monster."

"Then, what are you then Warden? You use experimental drugs on hue-man beings. Tharozine on hue-man beings just because they have a self-determining influence on others. Twelve inmates have died in the six months since I've been here, eleven of 'em killed by you and your staff. Tortured, beaten." He squeezed his eyes shut before shaking his head in attempts to block out the images of a seventy-five year old sickly blind inmate being beaten with flashlights because he wouldn't walk faster. "You do not deserve to share air with the lowliest worm in this world."

"I could break your little ass in two like a twig…

"You can try."

"You're right," Scott took a step back. "You're not worth it. I thought you were ready for the next level, but I was wrong. I'll make sure you get paid for the rest of the month. Turn over your badge and ID. You clock out now. I'll take care of inmate 46932-019 personally." He smiled.

"No you won't," Zapata said while unbuttoning his shirt. "I've been taking care of Zion my entire life and I'll continue as long as I have a breath in my spirit."

"What kind of nonsense you regurgitatin' boy?"

Well, Warden sir, I'm trying to give you a little closure as to why it's about to go down in the next few minutes." Zapata Smiled.

"What's about to go down?" The warden took a step toward his A.W. while cracking his knuckles. "I said what's about to go down? Speak up boy." The warden bent down and grabbed the arm rests on each side of Zapata's chair. "My father use to say don't write no checks your ass can't cash, and I think you was just about to write one before I said something."

Zapata held his arms out in a praying posture. "First, I'm going to pray that every spirit that you, David Columbus Clarke have ever had a hand in hurting jumps into my body so they can feel me as I cause you immense pain until your body shuts down and dies. I pray that your demons are exorcised from your spirit in the afterlife."

Scott laughed, "I should snatch you outta that chair for even voicing those thoughts."

Zapata leaned forward in his seat so he could remove his work shirt. "Don't wanna get your blood on the shirt I'm wearing out of here."

"What?" The warden shouted. "My blood?"

Zapata held a hand in the air as he slid on the second rubber glove, "Next, I'm going to tell you that you are the sorriest excuse for a black man that I have ever known or read about."

Scott reached out and grabbed Zapata by the collar and lifted him from his seat. "You took your shirt off, and put on some kitchen gloves, now what you gon' do?"

"This." Zapata elbowed Scott in the nose.

"Sum' bitch," the warden dropped the much smaller man to tend to his broken nose.

Zapata fell to the thick carpeted office floor where he kicked the warden in the groin, before getting to his feet and throwing an uppercut that sent the big man flying into and across his desk.

"I could kill you in an instant, but you and those like you have been trying to kill my boy since birth." Zapata walked around the desk to where the warden was regaining his footing.

Scott tried to catch Zapata off guard swinging a huge meathook fist while spinning around. The A.W. ducked under the swing, which sent Scotts off balance body lurching forward while Zapata came up with a spinning round house windmill kick that burst Scotts left eardrum.

"Ahhhhhhhhhhhhh!!!!!" the warden's baritone voice became a high soprano.

"Shhhh," Don't scream now. This is nothing compared to all the hell you've put others through. Did you not think that one day you would hurt or kill the wrong black mans child." He hit the warden in the mouth, knocking five teeth down his throat.

"That young man that you refer to as a number is my child." Zapata slapped his chest. "Zion Uhuru has a black father, well a black father in a Cuban brotha's skin, that ain't afraid to die and sure ain't afraid to kill for him."

"No more! No more!" the warden pleaded.

"Did you show Tee Thomas mercy when you cut his water off and he died after seven days from dehydration?" Zapata hit him in the chest, puncturing a lung.

"I'm going to show you more mercy than you showed Mr. Thomas though, I don't have seven days to watch you die." Zapata hit him in the chest so hard that the wardens heart gave out."

Zapata removed his blood splattered T-shirt and used

it to wipe the wardens blood from his face and arms before putting his uniform shirt back on. He looked back at the body. "You should have listened to your father about that bad check writing thing. My dad use to say you reap what you sow."

Che Zapata turned to the door. "Sun, if you can feel the vibrations of my soul and the meditations of my heart, know that I'm on my way. I'm so sorry about the water, I didn't know." After closing the office door, he reached inside his uniform shirt pocket and removed a metal object shaped like a silver sun with pointy rays all around it.

"Never again, Never again, will the godless arm of government string you up on a cross, sun." He threw the object. It took out the first camera, before boomeranging back and dropping sideways into Zapata's open palm. "I promise you that. The powers that be asked for trouble, I'm going to give them more Treble Uhuru Frazier than they can handle. Mess with my sun…"

NEVER AGAIN

I promise you that

BE:

The RE-Memebered

THE FINAL CHAPTER

OF THE **BE** SERIES

8-18-18

Rael Talk ... This is for you

King, Queen. It's ALL love.